Finch Books by Lanne Garrett

Single Books

The Cinder City Embers: Singularity

A Cursed Crow

The Seven Year Crow

The Court of Less

The Song of Blood and Bones

A Court of One

A Curse So Dark and Twisted

A Reign of R

A Cursed Crow

A REIGN OF RUIN

LANNE GARRETT

A Reign of Ruin
ISBN # 978-1-80250-596-2

Interior text design by Claire Siemaszkiewicz
Finch Books

Published in 2024 by Finch Books, United Kingdom.

Finch Books is an imprint of Totally Entwined Group Limited.

A REIGN OF RUIN

Dedication

To that one neighbor. Without you, I wouldn't have been awake to write this.
And for Dave, for always being excited for me.

Then stormy waves rush on to drown,
Or raging flames come scorching round,
Fierce dragons hover in the air,
And serpents crawl along the ground.

—excerpt from *Queen Mab* by Thomas Hood

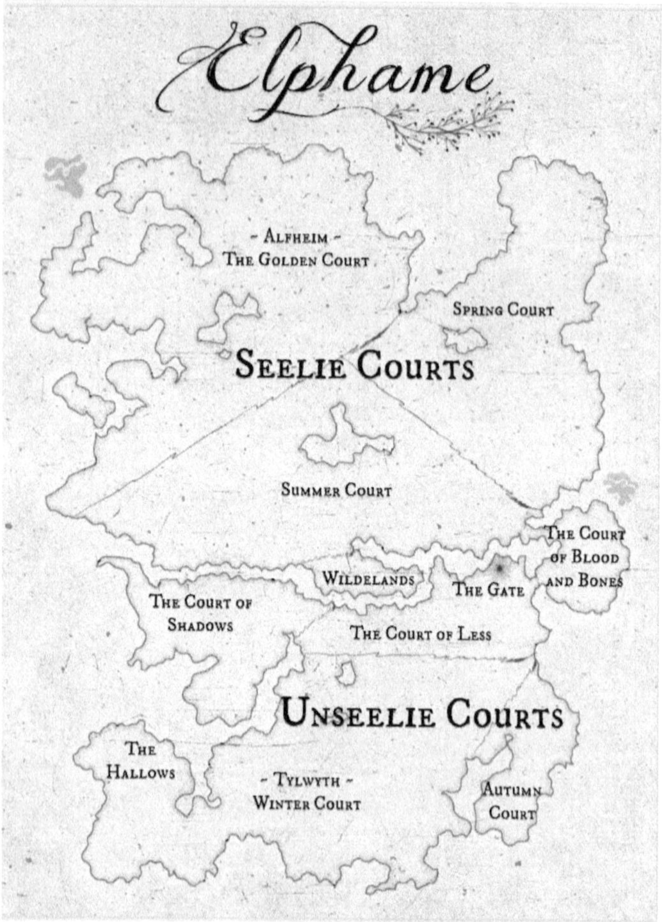

Elphame

- Alfheim -
The Golden Court

Spring Court

Seelie Courts

Summer Court

The Court of Blood and Bones

Wildelands

The Gate

The Court of Shadows

The Court of Less

Unseelie Courts

The Hallows

- Tylwyth -
Winter Court

Autumn Court

Chapter One

Time moves differently when you're wounded. Agony has this way of stilling a clock and allowing you to feel every passing minute. Down to the second, I felt the moments limp by like a hurt animal, scared and alone. While the pain of life crawled by unbearably slow, my days bled away like lightning bolts flashing across the sky. That was the ebb and flow of Elphame. If we weren't on the verge of destruction, we weren't living. If we weren't running from the monsters, we *were* the monsters. Although I was born for this, to suffer in Elphame, my feathers plucked and my will drained, each day since leaving the mortal realm I was reminded of how close to my grave I'd gotten. But after being cast off the island, leaving my family behind, I looked into that hole in the ground and felt no fear. I was too angry to be scared. It's hard to dread the only thing in this realm that stops the suffering.

Putting one foot in front of the other wasn't as easy as others made it seem. But whether it was easy or not, I pushed forward, each step more deliberate than the last. The very lives of my family depended on my drive and ruthlessness.

Anything that took my attention away from finding my way back onto the island drove my Malice to the surface. My heart was torn in too many directions, and my soul screamed whenever I was pushed to do anything other than find my missing family. My mind may have grown used to war and fighting for every inch, but my heart and soul weren't made for horror. I was homesick for my loved ones, and every hour that passed felt like an eternity in hell. Those who had given everything to ensure my survival were still lost to me, and it ate away at my calm.

It had been days since I had stormed Satyr Island and rescued our people, those taken as a warning I hadn't heard. Given a choice to save Solas or our people, I'd left Solas behind, chained to a wall beside Zephyr and Nix on an island I could no longer reach—and I had tried many times. My guilt for leaving my family behind had tugged on my soul. Although it had been the right decision, there wasn't a moment when I didn't think I could have done something different and saved them all. But I couldn't protect everyone and chose to save those who had depended on the throne to help them. And what a prickly throne it had become. It felt like sitting on shards of glass.

I didn't wear a crown, and we didn't own a throne. But damn it, if it didn't feel like both were pressing down on me with the weight of the entire realm. Balancing the safety of the Dark Courts, smoking out traitors and enemies and trying to rescue my family while keeping the mortal realm at bay felt like torture. I finally understood why Elphame had so many mad kings throughout history. Each day felt heavier than the last. But that was the reality of Elphame, and I had not been spared any of those lessons.

Since coming to this vile place, I had learned many brutal truths the hard way while living an existence most would consider cursed. Misery spared no one—and neither did fate. We all suffered, regardless of birthrights, which court we belonged to, what blood pumped our hearts or which God we prayed to. Nothing was free, and no place was safe. It was the way of the world. It didn't matter on which side of the Gate you stood. When the suffering came with your name on it, it arrived with more hurt and hate than the soul could handle. It had no mercy or kindness. And we shared that anguish like a drowning man, almost desperate to unload the weight onto someone else. Fae rose and fell on the backs of others. We crawled and limped our way from one day to the next, stepping over each other if needed. Truth be told, the mortal world was no different. No realm was unique in how it tormented its people. We all suffered equally.

But no lesson learned had prepared me for who I would willingly become to survive this realm, to protect what was mine, to keep my head above water. No truths had readied me for the incessant conflict that would become my daily routine. From Crow to crown, I wasn't spared any more than anyone else. But this was the way of Elphame, the very pulse of this realm. And I had learned this brutal reality on my knees, like so many had before me.

I shouldn't have been surprised. Before the Gate was cursed to be a one-way ticket, Crows had returned from Elphame with enough horrors to fill dozens of Darkmore journals. Since I'd committed them all to memory, I believed every word of what it meant to become a Crow. It was hell and horror with no room for anything more. There would be no days in Elphame without a fight for another sunrise. That was what it meant to be a Crow—to suffer, to feel life in its rawest and most gutting forms. This was also the path of a Soul-Eater. From birth, I had been cursed to look death in the eyes and dare him to try me, and every day, he took his best shot. That was the hardest truth to swallow. This would never end until the day my heart finally stopped beating. I had been warned, and I still picked this path. Even knowing what I knew now, I'd still choose it.

Until me, no Crow who had survived remembered their truths with clarity. But horror has this way of stealing from your mind, clouding your memories and turning them into something grotesque. For the lucky ones, they simply were too damaged to recount what caused their brokenness. Most stories were from fragmented minds and long-shattered resolve, destroyed souls who remembered nothing more than unanswered prayers. But what remained true was that each Crow recalled their first day as if it had only just happened. Every detail was crystal clear. No one ever forgot their Taking. Many couldn't remember the parts in the middle, the parts their minds refused to hold on to. I wasn't that lucky. I hadn't forgotten. Not a single detail was out of place. And it was in those memories where I was tormented, day in and day out. But that was the thing about misery… It would remind you daily of your suffering. It taunted you with promises that would never come true. But it wouldn't be Elphame if it didn't hurt. I wouldn't be Fae if I didn't have to look over my shoulder. And Whitwick reminded me of how very Fae I was each time I stepped through the Gate. That I was dragging around a wounded soul reminded me of how mortal parts of me still were.

My entire existence surrounded the Gate, from birth to my first death, and today was no different. It didn't matter that my world felt like it was burning down around me. The world still turned. Wars were still pending. And I still stood yards from the doorway between realms, willing myself to step forward. But my feet were firmly planted. I didn't want to go into Whitwick to deal with their problems. I had enough of them of my own. Saving those who protested against the presence of Fae was not high on my list of problems to solve. I had tried to convince the Seers to deal with the issues, but mortals were *my* people, not theirs, I was told. But they weren't. Not really. Not anymore. Mortals stopped being my people when they started seeing me as the enemy.

I stood on the now-trampled grounds of the Court of Less. The creatures and beasts of the Dark Courts had lifted every rock in search of our enemies, taking up chunks of earth in the process. They'd get no complaints from me. I was one more useless comment away from setting a fire and watching it all burn to the ground in hopes of smoking out the conspirators. And if they weren't here, I'd willingly go to Whitwick and start a fire on that side of the Gate. I was on the dregs of my patience and pitied those who called on my attention.

Aeden, my Royal Guard, stood at my side. When I arrived, he kept a noticeable distance between us. He had said he could feel my temper and Malice rolling just under my skin, and it reminded him of standing too close to Solas and Zephyr during war. I took it as a compliment.

"I don't know why Lily couldn't have dealt with this? It's not like I'm not busy." My voice was bitter and heated.

"I'm sorry, Perdi," he replied. He sounded sad for me. "But court matters do not stop because there is a different issue on the table. The wheels don't stop turning, even when you want them to."

"Are you telling me that even in battle, Solas still deals with this crap?" I asked.

"First, you're not at war—close, but not quite. But, to answer your question, yes, unfortunately, Solas would still be dealing with this. The only time he was not at work was during his mealtimes with you. His voice in the court literally stopped for you both to have dinner. Zephyr dealt with matters for those few hours Solas was with you. With both of them gone, you're the only one left."

"This never ends," I replied. A groan that sounded more like a growl escaped my lips. Whitwick had turned from a problem into a smoldering fire, and I didn't think I would help the situation.

"It will end, Perdi, if you want it to. You just won't like the choices you'll need to make for that to happen," Aeden replied, and I couldn't argue his point. I put myself in the middle. No one but me had expected me to remain there.

We stepped through the Gate together to find eight Seers standing shoulder to shoulder, blocking the Gate. On the other side, there were arguments, screaming and cursing the Fae. Lily turned to the Gate and opened a pocket for me to step through. Her eyes went back to the crowd. The Seers had been rotating between Whitwick and the island. They didn't trust either place—and neither did I.

"What's going on?" I asked her.

She didn't take her eyes off the few dozen men in front of us. "They say they would like us off their land. We can leave willingly, or we can leave through some force they speak of. I believe they mean to say *they* will force us." She huffed a laugh at the threat. She was amused. I was not.

I stepped forward, Aeden a foot behind me. "What is the meaning of this?"

My father made his way through the crowd. "Perdi, there are some men who wish for the Fae to leave."

I nodded and glanced around. I walked from one end of the group to the other and back to my father. "I see no men here."

"These men." My father motioned to those who stood behind him.

"Again, the only man I see is you," I answered.

Mr. Nicholas, a grocery shop owner, drinker of whatever didn't kill him and smoker of what soon would, stepped forward. The moment he was close enough for me to smell, I knew he'd die of sickness within a couple of years, tops. He smelled like death was already writing his name on a list. Both his eyes were bruised, and I fought not to smile.

"I want them gone," he said, while pointing to Lily and her people.

"Mark, it is lovely to see you. However did you get two black eyes?" I asked.

"That is not your concern." He spat his words but glared at Lily. I knew exactly why he wanted Lily gone.

"Where is your lovely wife Helen?" I asked, with a smile that was forced and as friendly as I could muster. "It has been a long time since I've paid her my respects. Where can I find her, Mark?"

"At home, where she belongs. This is no place for her."

"Lily, please go get Mrs. Nicholas for me," I asked without taking my eyes off Mark. Lily was gone with a wind that forced me to step forward from the push of power that bested most Fae. Her unrivaled strength was why she sat at the table of Blood and Bones.

Although Blood and Bones now belonged to Solas, by birthright, he was shaping the court back into what it had once been. It had never been meant to be a place of threat or war. They had been forced into that position during a revolt and kept there by Solene. Initially, it had been a place of peace—a place to train their people, give solace to those who needed it and heal those who found life was too much to bear. To return to the ways of peace, Solas needed a Seer to help him, and Lily was a wise choice. In these last months, she had formed a council, a small group of trusted Seers whose primary purpose was to heal Elphame. Lily was fair, reasonable and held no hate for anyone. To see Mark with bruises on his face could only mean one thing. What he had done to earn them would make me want to wring the life from his neck. I did not have the calm resolve of a Seer. I had the temper of a Soul-Eater.

"You have no right to meddle in my business." Mark stepped forward and brought my thoughts back from Elphame and the hope for peace.

Aeden stepped to my side, not to scare Mark. No. He was giving me room for whatever choices I would make, and being behind me would limit my movements. Mark took another step forward. I stretched out my back and neck and let my arms fall to my side. I could feel the tension vibrating off him. If he were going to swing, I'd be ready. "Is there something I can do for you, Mark?" I asked, but he didn't answer. I glanced at the distance he had closed between us. "Is there a reason you've stepped into my personal space?"

He clenched and unclenched his fists. I looked back up from his hands and met his eyes. I raised my eyebrows as if to invite him to do what he so desperately wanted to do. I watched him struggle between decisions. Before Mark could do something stupid, Lily returned with Helen. I didn't have to look too closely to know she was covered in bruises, some old and some as fresh as hours before. She couldn't have come, even if she'd wanted to. I looked into her eyes and felt my rage boil. I turned back to Mark and could see him shrink. It's one thing for everyone to know he beat his wife but another to have it put on display where it couldn't be ignored.

"Here is how this night will go, and this will be your *only* warning from me, since you clearly haven't listened to Lily or her people," I started, but Mark decided to step around me toward his wife. "Whatever it is you plan to do, Mark, I really wouldn't do it. I'm warning you."

"She is *my* wife. You may be the whore of Elphame, but you're not *my* whore, and I don't have to listen to a damn word you—"

The moment he pointed his finger in my face, Aeden was gone from my side. One moment he was there. The next, he'd grabbed Mark and had him pinned on the ground before I could warn the man again. The heat that poured off Aeden was enough for me to step back. My stomach knotted with unease. I didn't know if Mark would die for what he had done, but I wasn't going to protect him from Aeden, either way. Aeden twisted Mark's pointed finger until it crunched under the force, then leaned into his face.

"If you touch her, if you even *think* of touching your wife again, I will return, and I will fucking end you. I will do it for your wife and children and to send a message to the rest of your realm. The weak have the protection of the Fae. I will oath myself to every man, woman and child in this entire goddamn land, just so I know every move you make and every thought you have. Do I make myself clear?"

Mark opened and closed his mouth, finally nodding.

Aeden shook him against the ground. "And it goes without saying, but allow me to make it clear as possible. If you want to keep your tongue, you will not speak to my queen in such a way. If you lift another finger to her, you will lose both hands. I believe in warnings, but only one will ever fall from my lips. You are very much beneath my warnings. You will stand, apologize, go home, pack one bag of clothing, leave all valuables behind and wait for your wife to forgive you or call me back to kill you. No oaths between our realms protect you from me, not for this. If you harass her, hunt her, harm her or scare her, you will be found and skinned alive. You'd best wish it is me who finds you, not the ladies who guard this Gate. They will do things to you that I haven't the stomach to even think of. You may live in the mortal realm, but you best hope they don't drag you back to ours."

Aeden stepped back and lifted Mark to his feet. Mark scurried from Aeden and apologized as he ran from the crowd. I couldn't help but smile. I had been waiting for the day someone would protect the weakest members of Whitwick. I had spent my life watching it happen and not being strong enough to help.

"My lady." Aeden stood back at my side. "I apologize for the interruption. Please, continue."

"As I was saying..." I smiled and readdressed the group, "the only ones I see here are those struggling to live decent lives. You harm yourselves and your families and are a bleed on Whitwick. You leave chaos and misery in your wake. You drink too much and fall into drunk madness. Rage, I understand. I, too, struggle with mine. But you allow that anger to rule you, and with fists, you take it out on those you love. So, it appears the only ones who want the Fae to leave are those who are scared of the Fae paying them a visit."

"You can't kill all of us." A voice from the crowd.

"Yes, I can," I answered matter-of-factly. "I will. I will do exactly that to protect the peace and your families. Since you won't protect them, I have no problem doing it for you."

"There will be war," he called out again.

I shook my head. "No, you fool, there won't be. War requires two sides to battle each other. There will be nothing more than death between both realms—and death isn't war. A fight between Fae and mankind is nothing more than a well-planned funeral for you all. Do not sentence all Whitwick to death simply because you can't hit your wives anymore. How many people will charge into Elphame, a certain death for you all, just so you can keep drinking and abusing? From where I'm standing, only a couple of dozen, and I can deal with that without needing anyone to help me."

"Fae doesn't rule here, and neither do you. You are *not* the law."

"You're wrong!" I screamed. "There are laws here that protect others from partner violence. No one follows them. There are laws that do not allow you to use physical violence to solve your problems. You just don't follow them. Many laws govern Whitwick, but no one cares enough about their neighbor to follow them. If you will not protect your people, I will, and that is final. If that means I have to come back here every bloody day to check on your family, I will. We will go door to door, checking on your wives and children. If it means we patrol your streets, we will. And if it means we have to drag every one of you into the town square and hang you for your crimes, I will weave the rope myself—not because I am now Fae, but because I grew up watching you do it, listening to it, seeing your children at school with scabbed lips. I watched as each of your wives limped home from the grocery store with barely enough strength to keep their hearts pumping but too terrified not to keep moving forward. I was once powerless to stop it, but not anymore. There will *never* be another day where that will be allowed."

My father sighed and turned to the group. "The Guardians will not turn their eyes from this any longer. We have spoken of it many times. Those who disregard the law will be arrested and jailed. We were going to address new laws and enforcements at our next town hall, but now is as good of a time as any. It is unfortunate it took the Fae to show us that we, too, can be monsters."

I stepped back to Lily and spoke loud enough for the others to hear. "Take Helen home. Make sure Mark doesn't come back. If this happens again, alert the Guardians, but do everything you can to protect them until they arrive."

"And if the Guardians can't or won't stop them?" she asked. She searched for the freedom to act, to defend. Now that the Seers weren't locked away, their very duty was to protect. Without that, she wasn't entirely herself, who she was meant to be—and I could relate.

I swallowed a rock in the back of my throat. "Then you act in any way you must to protect those who are too weak to save themselves. This..." I scrunched my face, fighting between tears and vomit. "This cannot happen again. And if the prisons of Whitwick can't stop them, the prisons of Elphame certainly will. If they survive stepping through the Gate, justice will be swift, but it will come."

The crowd silenced at that threat. It was one I didn't want to make. The Fae had been the nightmare of Whitwick for as long as they could remember, and I used the Fae again to control them. I didn't feel guilty this time. I wouldn't let them beat their wives, and if I had to drag the Sluagh through the Gate to keep the men in line, I would.

"Perdi," Lily leaned into my ear, "things are getting a lot worse here. I fear you'll be returning and soon."

I nodded. "I know. I can feel it. Something has changed."

"We'll do what we can for as long as possible, to buy you the time you need. But I don't think it'll be enough."

"Unfortunately, I agree. Blood will spill, and by then, it will be too late to stop what's coming," I replied. Aeden followed me back to Elphame and waited for me as the wave of nausea subsided.

"I do not like going there," Aeden finally said.

"You have quite the temper, Aeden," I said as we moved through the Court of Less. I rubbed my arms, feeling dirty from my trip through the Gate. The dread I had experienced, hanging in the air in Whitwick, still clung to me like sweat.

"I could say the same about you," he answered without even a hint of judgment. "My father was a strict man, but he had honor. He had one hell of a temper but never once lifted a finger against my mother. Only once did his anger make my mother step back. He begged forgiveness and cowered from his shame, as he should have. He would have killed anyone who touched her. He valued her and her love above all else. It was something he made sure I had learned before I left for the Aos Si. I am made for battle and death and doling out punishment like candy. But that? Harming your family? It's something I can't stomach and will not tolerate. I could never harm my partner like that. The very thought of someone doing that to those I love…? Rage doesn't describe how that man made me feel."

"Disgust, embarrassed for her, ashamed for him, angry at everyone else for letting it happen, regret that I didn't kill him to prove a point and take her nightmare away… That's what I felt," I told him.

"That sums up what I'm feeling."

"When we go back, Aeden, we have to work to fix the relations and not beat them all. We can't fix violence with violence."

"Yes, we can," he countered. "But I see your point. If we want peace, we must offer peace…until that is no longer the option."

"Exactly," I replied. "But all peace comes with a price."

"And we'll all pay for it." He sighed and rubbed the creases starting between his eyes. "Do you think there will ever be peace between both realms?"

"I want to say yes, but no. I don't believe so. I think, eventually, it'll come to a head, and many will die before there's silence, not peace. We'll exist together, but I doubt there will be more than that."

"A bleak future," he said.

"Bleaker for those of us who have to live with it for centuries," I replied. "I'll meet you back at the manor later."

Aeden nodded. He would be meeting with the Aos Si for updates on the island and their progress in finding a Mage. "Perdi, remember. If you kill Finn tonight, you won't be able to hunt him tomorrow."

"Good night, Aeden," I replied. I couldn't comment on his remark without lying to his face.

I was uncomfortable with the secrecy I was now living, but trust was something I couldn't afford—not when traitors were alive and well and had my name at the top of their lists. I was hunting, but it wasn't Finn I was tracking. I was pursuing my traitors in secret, and at my side, an unlikely ally, Finn. Together, we followed the trail of those seeking my death, the traitors of the Dark Courts. The roots of hate had spread far and wide, leaving me and Finn no choice but to play dark and dangerous games, unable to trust a soul. When we returned from the island, someone close to the crown began hunting us both. The energy of our dark traitor was the same we had found on the island, in Elphame and even as far as Whitwick. His magick was both familiar and unplaceable. Whoever was following us would be the key to getting my family back.

I'd had two choices when I'd returned from Satyr Island. I could swallow what had happened and work together with Finn or I could die alone, never having saved my family. Teetering between truth and lies, right and wrong, absolution and revenge kept me looking over my shoulder. I spent my days trying to keep Whitwick from boiling over and invading, only to die on Elphame soil, and the nights with a mask on and stalking my enemies across the entire realm. I didn't know what was worse, hunting them or living with the horror of the aftermath once I'd finally caught them. But one way or another, vengeance would be swift. Those who did this to my people and my family would pay dearly…because nothing was free in Elphame. I would hunt them to the ends of the earth for what they did. No one takes from a Soul-Eater and survives. I was pretty sure that rule was written somewhere.

Chapter Two

My dreams no longer brought me comfort. Each time I closed my eyes, I ventured into a dark and bitter world where I struggled to wake up. The harder I tried to find Solas while I slept, the worse my nights became. My thoughts were twisted, and my mind spat out cruelty and memories I'd rather not relive. I dreamed of stepping through the Gate, of Elphame, of spells and curses. The fog chased me through the streets of Whitwick. Each time I tried to scream, I choked on my fear. There was something familiar in the flavor. It tasted of mortals, magick and hate. It tasted like a place I'd once called home. It rolled across my tongue and reminded me of the dread coating the hills of Whitwick.

Tonight, I dreamed of Finn. When Zephyr had used Finn to pull me from the island, my Malice had rolled through his soul. Although I wasn't nearly strong enough for a mind like Zephyr's, grazing his pearl had left me with bits of his memories. Whenever I closed my eyes, I could see Finn in battle. I could feel his horror and utter disgust with the dead at his feet. He had been born into the world as a soldier and had grown into the monster of the Aos Si. He was the bringer of death. He was the most feared. And because of this, he had few friends, even fewer to love him. I could relate to how he felt when he looked in the mirror. He, like me, was scared of who he had become and who he was yet to be.

I dreamed I walked through a field of bodies, all fallen at Finn's hand. My feet squished in the blood-soaked earth. The red liquid burned my feet. I met Finn in the middle, where he warned me that I was being hunted in Elphame. He didn't know who it was, but the energy was familiar. We agreed to draw the traitor out in secret. He reached for my hand, and I pulled back, not trusting his touch. My stomach twisted, and I was yanked back from him. I was dragged over bodies as I screamed for Finn. It didn't matter how fast he ran. He couldn't grab me. I looked behind me once and saw the Gate. I was being pulled toward Whitwick, and for the first time, I fought to not go back. Something in the back of my mind told me I wouldn't survive being forced through the Gate. Finn's hand grazed my fingertips, and I was gone from him.

I jerked awake, my hand gripping the blade under my pillow. My body vibrated with unease and unspent energy. I stood quickly, unable to remain still, and shook my arms and legs until the pins and needles went away. Nothing could calm the beginnings of panic in my chest. Sleep did not come easy, and when I did close my eyes, I woke screaming or ready for a war I knew was coming. I didn't know when or with whom, but it felt like the eve of big decisions and even bigger consequences.

"You smell like Zephyr before a battle." The shadows rolled across the foot of my bed. They were always close by.

"Standing between life and death decisions," I replied. This was how Zephyr felt the night before he had been taken from us, unable to explain his unease. I wound my hair into a tight braid and pulled on my boots. "I can't sit still. I can't just stand around waiting for everyone else to help me. I need to be out there, doing what I can to bring them home. Anything less feels like I'll go mad. It feels like I'm letting them down."

"You're not letting anyone down, Perdi," they replied. "You're doing everything you can."

"Pretty to think," I answered. "But my family isn't home yet, are they? They're being tortured while I'm napping. And before you remind me that I need sleep, can it. I'll rest when they're home."

"You won't be any help if you're schlepping your tired soul from one end of Elphame to the other. Use your tools before you burn yourself up." Their tone felt like I was being scolded. They sounded like Zephyr. As comforting as that was, it also grated on my nerves.

"I plan to," I replied.

"You've been hunted since we returned from the island. You can't afford to make rash decisions," they said. "We need to stick to the plan. Trust that you and Finn will draw the traitors out of the darkness. If you go out there halfcocked, you risk scaring him and losing the very piece of the puzzle you need."

"I don't know how much longer I can do this. Every day that passes is another day our family is chained to a wall. Eventually, it won't matter if we catch our enemies. They'll be dead, and this will have been for nothing."

"It won't be for nothing. Your people will be safer for it. Trust Finn." It was the same thing they said each time I started questioning the plan I had made with

Finn. "Put your mask on, Perdi. We don't know who your real enemies are, and until we find them, you can't afford to show anyone your cards."

"I don't even know why I take the mask on and off," I replied. "I'm so tired of this shit."

It felt like years had passed since I had given Finn two options, when he had taken me from the island. He could find a way onto the island or die trying. The first day hunting him through my territory had ended in an explosive fistfight and the discovery of a mole within my court. As I pinned Finn to the ground, a knife over his heart, we both froze. Without saying a word, we knew we were being watched. The energy was the same as the dread hanging over Whitwick and the island. From that moment on, I knew my enemy was still in Elphame, and my revenge would need to take a backseat. Finn was currently the only one I could fully trust, and I barely trusted a man who could be used as a puppet. Now, I trailed Finn for the sole purpose of finding the person who followed Finn's every movement. And like every other time I stalked Finn, mixed in Finn's trail was a hint of a traitor, the smell of war coming.

Dressed in leathers, I stood on the balcony railing and jumped as Aeden opened my bedroom door. I don't know if he tried to stop me or save me. I was already gone, wrapped in shadows bound to me by the only other Soul-Eater alive, Zephyr. The shadows and I landed twice as we followed Finn's energy throughout the Dark Courts.

The shadows landed in the hills on the edge of the Dark Courts. I could still smell the smoke from the last time I had been there. Finn's cabin was ash, burned to the ground when I'd tried to force him to face me. When I had come to meet Finn, I had been followed. To maintain our charade, I'd lit his cabin on fire. It had been enough of a display to send the traitor away, amused by our hatred of each other. It was also enough for Finn to feel the dark energy in person. We weren't any closer to finding the man, but it was a lead we needed, and Finn spent every waking minute trying to find him.

After scouting the grounds around his once home, Finn's energy still hung in the air. I wondered why he had come back to his empty cabin, why I could feel his magick here again. There was no reason for Finn to come back here. Faintly, a tincture of hate hovered in the air. I knew after I closed my eyes and rolled the smell through my mind that Finn had tracked our enemy back to his cabin. I wondered why our enemy had circled back to the cabin again. There was nothing left standing and no reason to come.

"There aren't many who circle back," I whispered to the shadows.

"A soldier?" they asked.

"It would make sense, wouldn't it? To evade capture this long, they'd have to be trained for this. No one outruns an Aos Si and a Soul-Eater for this long."

"It's not someone from the Dark Courts or the Guard. We'd know by their smell," the shadows replied.

"Golden Court?" I asked. "They've been in and out of Whitwick since the Gate opened, and they've also been to the island."

"But they haven't stepped foot over the river. It wouldn't explain why we feel this energy in Unseelie territory," they answered.

I took that opportunity, alone and away from the watchful eye of our stalker, to feel the energy in the air. Again, it felt familiar, like I had smelled it before, but I couldn't place it. I had found it drifting in the air countless times but couldn't quite remember where or why. It coated the trees in Whitwick the day Zephyr and Nix had gone missing. I'd felt it on the island when we'd landed there—and each day since returning from the island. It was frustrating to know but unable to remember where I knew it from.

I watched the shadows slither through the trees, across every rock, and taste every branch as if they were an animal trailing a scent. They finally pulled back and crawled up my leg. "We still don't know who it is. We cannot draw on Zephyr's memories to place the feel of power, but we have smelled him before."

"Let's keep going," I answered. "I don't like standing around out here. It's making my skin crawl."

We wasted no time and moved on, following Finn from one end of Elphame to the other. I landed once again, and my lungs filled with Summer Court. Wherever I was, it wasn't as strong as I had remembered. The stench of the Golden Court was weak, but it was enough for my stomach to flop. If it weren't for my anger, I'd have taken a few steps back on watery legs.

"We're close to the river and border to the Court of Less. Theofanis is to the North of us." The shadows answered a question that was on the tip of my tongue. "We're in nymph territory."

"Great, because I have such a good relationship with them," I replied.

"Not many have any kind of connection to the nymphs," they said as they fluttered around me, tasting the air as they moved. "Apparently Finn does, though. His scent is strong here, as is the other smell we've been tracking."

I followed the shadows through the dense brush to a stone cabin. The cabin looked old but well-loved. Moss had grown between the stones and only added to its charm. Smoke billowed from a chimney, and soft music poured from a cracked window. I could smell bread and banana loaf. It looked and felt like every other home I had stumbled upon, just out of reach of the court's touch. It was far enough away for them to live a somewhat peaceful life but close enough to still be protected. It was a careful balance in Elphame, not wanting to be included in the chaos of the throne but wanting to be close enough to be safe. I felt that struggle daily.

Through the windows, I could see her. Who I was looking at, I had no clue. I hadn't seen her before. "Who is she?"

"We don't know, but Finn was here just a few hours ago," they replied. "The energy he was following was here just before him."

"Does Finn have a partner?" I asked.

"Not that we're aware of," they answered. "We've never heard him mention someone. But that's not uncommon with the Aos Si, to hide those they love, to protect them. If an enemy were ever to find out about them, their loved ones would be taken and used as a pawn. The Aos Si are the most feared army in all Elphame. To have someone they care for is a token many would risk death to grab. The power that would come from controlling a single Aos Si is worth potential death to many."

"Such is the way of Elphame," I replied and fought not to roll my eyes. Nothing surprised me anymore. "Does her energy feel like anything we should be worrying about?"

"No, she's of no threat and not who Finn is searching for," they replied.

"Maybe he just passed by or tracked our enemy to this cabin?"

"No on both. We can smell Finn's energy coming from inside the house, not just outside. The Aos Si move too swiftly for their power to pool like this. He was here for longer than a simple passing by for us to feel it this strongly. He spent time here, and from the smell, it isn't his first time coming here."

"Why would he leave her unprotected, knowing he's being hunted?" I asked.

"Trust or war games," they said.

"Stupidity," I replied.

"Finn is anything but stupid. He likely doesn't believe anyone would do her any harm if they could feel an Aos Si around her home. His scent is enough of a warning for all," they answered. "But, if anyone were foolish enough to try for her, this would be a trap to lure them in."

"Risky move," I replied. "This is where I would come if I wanted to hurt Finn or force his hand. Hell, if I had known about her the first day back from the island, I'd have taken the cabin down, stone by stone, until Finn came to face me."

"It's probably why he has been here as often as he has been," the shadows answered.

"If we can find her, anyone can. I don't like the idea of leaving her unprotected. A lot can happen between heartbeats. What if Finn can't get back here in time, and she needs help?"

"Finn didn't leave her unattended. The gnomes are nearby," the shadows answered. "She has wee folk in the house. She's probably the safest person in all

Elphame right now, with those powers watching over her."

"They wouldn't be enough to stop me. Why think they'd protect her from our enemies?" I asked.

"They would buy enough time for Finn to get here," they replied. "They're fodder and nothing more."

"I wonder if they know that?" I asked but didn't bother poking at it. We all did things we weren't proud of to save those we loved most.

I watched her move throughout her house through the kitchen window. She was young and beautiful, and her voice, as she softly sang out loud, felt like the calmness of a sunny day. I smiled for a moment, listening to the hum that filled the forest around her home. It was soothing, like stepping into a needed hug or seeing mashed potatoes on the table for dinner. It felt like the small things in life that made life bearable. Then I remembered why I was there and scowled. I was envious that the peace she had would never be mine. Not really. I was a Crow, a Finis, the Queen of the Dark. I'd have to war to have a little peace and quiet. Hell followed me around like a lost puppy.

I leaned against a tree, lowering myself until I sat in the wet moss. The smell of the earth reminded me of the island. The memory gripped my heart and sped my pulse. I was jealous that Finn had this piece of heaven to come home to when I was hunting down the answers to get my family back. As the dark thoughts crept into my mind, my heart sank. When I had been taken from the island, I'd blamed Finn entirely. I'd hated him for it because he was the only one standing in front of me who could take my blame and rage. I had threatened to crumble his world, bringing him as much hurt as I had felt. Sitting in the forest, looking at the one person who probably brought him peace and quiet in a world that screamed in your ears constantly, I felt ashamed for having said those words to him. I shook the thoughts from my mind. I needed to stay focused. I calmed my need to hate and retaliate. There wasn't room for that right now. And whoever stood in that kitchen didn't earn my anger. She was an innocent, and no amount of anger could force me to take it out on her.

The shadows rolled up my back and whispered for only me to hear. "We're not alone. We're being watched—and not by Finn."

"Damn it." I stood. "Let's go. Finn's not here. We're wasting time."

"You're not burning this one down?" The shadows asked out loud, playing the games we needed the rest of the world to see. Everyone thought I was hunting Finn and only him.

"No. I may have threatened Finn with finding those he loves and taking them from him, but it was a threat and nothing more," I answered and glanced around, feeling uneasy. The urge to blast through the forest and grab whoever was following us was intense and made my muscles twitch in readiness. But I couldn't risk failing and losing the only lead we had on our enemies. But it didn't stop me from adding a threat. "Harming her would bring the full attention of the Aos Si, and I'm not that stupid. No one is. The Aos Si have the ear of every power in Elphame. There wouldn't be a hole deep enough for me to hide in."

"Perdi, your threats only mean something when you're willing to follow through with them," they replied.

"I'll do horrible things, but I won't kill needlessly."

"Be grateful that you can't take a life so easily. Save your horrors for war, for when you're given no other choice." They wrapped around me, and we were off.

We moved across the Dark Court, beyond the border of the Court of Shadows, to the caves of the Sluagh. I felt their prickly power roll over me, tasting who had been so foolish as to step into the pits of hell willingly. Their calls bounced off the cliff walls in a warning, vibrating their unspoken threat. Although they wouldn't come for me until they had a reason, I would be a fool not to look over my shoulder. I'd be cautious about how far I'd go while standing in their home. Regardless of who I was to them or why I had come, the Sluagh would not allow me to bring down their mountains to smoke out my enemies. I was sure, however, that they'd forgive a small fire or two.

When the shadows finally zeroed in on the energy of Finn, we landed at the mouth of a cave. It was Finn's home when he wasn't with the other Aos Si. I had come many times these last few days, only to see that I had missed him by mere minutes. But he wasn't the only one I had felt when I'd come. Whoever was hunting us was able to come and go without having to fight off the Sluagh. And again, tonight, that energy was near. It angered me that our traitor didn't fear the Dark Court, that I wasn't someone worth noticing. It rubbed my ego and my anger the wrong way.

"Your enemy draws near," the shadows whispered.

I nodded. I could feel him as well. "Don't go very far."

"Get ready, Perdi. You're going to take one hell of a beating tonight," the shadows replied. "When we can, we will try to get closer to the man tracking you to see if we can find out more. Keep the fight going long enough for us to gather more information."

I shrugged. "I won't be the only one to hurt tonight."

"But Finn was born for this. You weren't," they answered.

"I wasn't born for a great many things. Yet, here I am," I replied. "I'm not worried. Finn will make me earn every inch, but he won't kill me."

I stood at the mouth of the cave and cringed. The thought of fist-fighting with an Aos Si, for any reason, real or for show, made me want to take a step back. Finn matched me in every way. He distrusted most people, raged in ways that made others uncomfortable, spoke without thinking, and like me, would do anything to stay alive and keep my bones from breaking. In battle, Finn was a force unlike any other Aos Si. He could clear the field before Zephyr put his boots on. Finn was who the others sent when the monsters were too scary. Although he held back with me in training, I knew his moves and how he reacted. His ego never let him back down, which was how he had the snot beat out of him day in and day out during training. That I was walking into a cave to see who we all sent to kill the nightmares wasn't just foolish. It was unbelievably stupid. My bravery didn't care that we played games, putting on a show for those who looked too closely. I knew firsthand that games hurt as much as the real thing.

"You might as well ring the doorbell, Perdi. I felt you before I heard you whispering to the shadows." Finn's voice called from the cave's rear, and I paused. "You came all this way, after trailing me all night, you might as well come in already."

"You must be a masochist, Finn. Did I not warn you about stepping foot in my territory?" I asked and finally stepped through the long hall and into the center of his rocky home. It reminded me of the trainee's cave, only it was cleaner and smelled better. It was one massive room, built for the enormous beasts who'd once lived here.

"There's a kink for everyone," he replied and wiggled his eyebrows. Even in the face of uncertainty, he was still the Finn that annoyed us all. "The Court of Shadows is not yours. The Sluagh decide who comes and goes."

"You're not welcome in any of the Dark Courts, Finn," I answered.

"Don't worry. I'm just grabbing my things and leaving. So should you." He stood with a duffel bag in each hand. He breathed in the air and shook his head.

I glanced over my shoulder and felt a slight draft coming down the tunnel, carrying with it the faintest hint of dark energy. I nodded. We weren't alone. I questioned again how they had gotten by the Sluagh. Finn raised his brow and shrugged. He, like me, wondered the same thing.

"I don't care where you go, as long as the land does not belong to my courts or those that I have a treaty with. Though, you'll soon find yourself not welcome anywhere else, either. Who would be foolish enough to harbor you if it risked having me show up at their door?"

"You're so much like Solas. It's irritating," he muttered.

"And you're a dead man," I replied. "Are we going to continue pointing out the obvious, or are you stalling long enough for help to get here?"

"I haven't called for anyone, Perdi. I don't bring war to the doors of my brothers," he answered.

"As if you're that honorable," I answered.

"Why do you think Zephyr chose me on the island?" he asked.

"It certainly wasn't because you're honorable," I replied, and he grinned at my jab. "Do tell, Finn. I'm curious why Zephyr would choose you to die over the others."

"I'm the only one who can survive the wrath of the little Crow. Your pain and hurt would kill everyone else," he replied. When I rolled my eyes, he shrugged. "Fine, I drew the short straw in my ability to suffer greater than the rest. I get the task of dealing with this shit every time there's a power too great for the others."

"Lucky you," I said, my tone flat. "We'll see just how much of my rage you can survive."

He grinned. "Do your worst, but know I've had better than you."

"I've heard that before," I replied.

"Be the bigger person and walk away."

I shook my head. "If you're waiting for me to be the better man, we'll be here until the end of time. There's no room in Elphame for better people."

"Yes, there is. You are proof of that," Finn replied. "But if you choose to stay and fight, you're the only one who will burn for it. I won't feel your flames and don't mind dancing in fire. I was born for this. Were you? Are you ready to truly face someone like me? Are you ready to understand why I'm the first one sent into every room? The first one sent out in war, and the reason so few ever survive meeting me?"

I felt his energy sneak across the floor, inviting me in, convincing me to relax. But that's not all it was doing. It told me to get comfortable, that everything would be all right. I was safe, I was home and I wanted nothing more than to stay here. As his power crept up my legs, it rolled tenderly across my thighs. I felt need and hunger…and desire. My body flushed with heat. I reached for the zipper on my jacket and froze. My Malice tore up from my gut and pushed back. She, like me, would rather die than be touched against my will.

"Finn, if you dare touch me like that again, magick or hands, I'll cut off your most favored body part," I warned him. I didn't care if we were playing games. I wouldn't let his magick roll across my skin like a lover would. "You can twist my soul or break my bones for all I care. But if a single article of my clothing comes off, I'll end you. This is the only warning I'll give you."

"It is not my need that you feel," he replied. "On that, I swear."

"If you push me on this, it will end badly for you. No one touches me like that without permission," I replied. "But if this is the way you want to die, in shame, so be it."

"I'd never force something like that, Perdi." A flash of disgust passed over his face. "I was trying for calm, not romance. I swear."

"Calm is not what you will find here," I answered.

He glanced at my clenched fists. "You won't like what you'll have to do to make me suffer as deeply as you are right now. Many have tried over the years, and very few have succeeded."

"And many have underestimated me, only to die at my hands." I smiled. "I wanted to draw it out and enjoy it, but I find I'm not so picky anymore."

I watched the excitement flash over his face. He was built for war and the suffering of others. I stepped away from the middle of the room, from the blankets and other things that would trip me. I had seen Finn fight many times on the battlefield and in training. I have fought with him myself. He was strong, smart and as dirty as I could be. He dropped his bags and rotated his shoulders. He widened his stance and waited.

"Shall we?" I asked.

He was at my front before I could say another word. His power rolled over me and grabbed at every little corner of my soul. Whether I wanted to or not, my Malice wouldn't let him pass. Whatever type of Fae Finn was, my soul didn't want to be touched by him. But I couldn't fight him and force my Malice to listen. She made decisions on her own whenever I was under threat. She'd eat his soul in one gulp, whether I asked her to or not. I couldn't help but laugh. This must be what Solas and Zephyr felt every time I did the exact opposite of what they told me to do. My Malice was as foolish and determined as I was.

Finn's magick pulsed through the room, eating the dark energy that slinked across the floor. Finn leaned into my ear. "I need one more day, Perdi. Whoever is stalking us is Fae. They're damn powerful, strong enough to hide who they are from me, but I'm close."

"Why one more day?" I asked. "He's outside. I can feel him. Go grab him."

"And risk losing what we need? What if I can't make him talk? What if his mind is too strong and you can't read him? We both felt their energy on the island. If they were there, they would know where the Mages are or, at least, how to come and go on that island. Without them, we won't find a Mage. Without a Mage, we can't get back to the island. You need patience or we lose, and I don't fucking lose."

"If you wouldn't have taken us to begin with, we wouldn't be here," I replied.

"Get over it or die for a misplaced grudge," he answered. "One more day, then we can go back to beating the shit out of each other for choices that were not ours to make. Give me a little more time to smoke him out, and we'll have what we need."

"One more day," I replied. I shoved him away with a nod and went back to screaming at him for the benefit of our spy. "This is *your* fault!"

"I'm sorry, Perdi," Finn said, standing an inch from my front. "Please know, I never would have left them behind if I'd had a choice in the matter. I did everything I could to help you, to give you a chance, but I can't save everyone. After lifetimes in this place, you learn to choose who you can save and who you need to go back for."

I felt those words, and they weren't for anyone else's benefit. Finn truly meant them. "You didn't even try."

"I did all I could," he replied, pushing his power through the room. I felt it slink past me to the opening of the cave. I flinched as it rolled past me. I didn't like his gifts any more than someone enjoyed mine.

"You could have warned me. We could have come up with a plan," I replied. I pulled the shadows from around the room. They danced around us and ate the energy that rolled around the cave, from the entrance to the center, tasting whoever was seeking us. "Instead, you said nothing and blindsided me. You lied to me the moment you didn't come to me with your truth."

I had grown used to feeling the energy of those around me, the explosiveness of those stronger than me, and I drank it like a familiar wine. As soon as my Malice reached out for Finn, he swung. But I had known he would. He was always the first to attack whenever I had used my Malice during training, and I ducked. He had never liked feeling her and certainly wouldn't like it now that I was an emotional wreck. Hell, not even I enjoyed the feeling of her right now.

"I'll take as many beatings as you need, but I won't let you kill me to ease your pain." His voice was calm and even. That he wasn't exerting energy as I was annoyed me in the same way Zephyr always had. Finn blocked my punches with ease. "Does my queen need a whipping boy? You would not be the first royal to use me as such, and I doubt you'll be the last."

"Fuck you, Finn," I growled the words through clenched teeth.

"I thought you didn't want to fuck? Make up your mind. Fight or fuck. Either way, you'll get what you need from me tonight. I'm too tired to do this dance with you all night," he replied and motioned me forward. "It's okay, Perdi. I can take it."

"So can I," I whispered back.

We both nodded. This was a dance we'd do to hide our intent. The stakes were high, the lie we both were living. Finn stopped holding back, and so did I. Malice and magick poured from my body until stones in the wall crumbled to the floor under the force of my anger. I unleashed the fiery pits of hell I had been carrying around in my soul since the day I was taken from the island. All my anger, fear, and utter sadness emptied out of me, fueling my every movement. I was faster than he thought I'd be. But I had been training with another Finis, who was faster than Finn would ever be.

Each punch he threw, I knew it was coming and where he was aiming. I blocked and moved and ducked. When he went left, I went right and hit him with everything I had. Three times, I heard his ribs snap under the pressure of the blows I landed. He backed away and tried to taunt me, a poor attempt to regroup himself. But I didn't give him the space. As he moved back, I stepped forward and kept swinging. When he'd land a blow, I still didn't back up. It wasn't as hard as I knew he could hit, and that would be the only way I'd win against him. He held back, scared of hurting me. I didn't hold back and didn't think I'd ever had the power to truly hurt him. Pound for pound, he could kill me with one blow. All I'd do is irritate him.

When I thought I'd have to take a step back, I let my Malice and shadows lose on him again. He pushed his power over me. Rather than fight it, I pulled it toward me and drank it down. When I was filled to the brim, I gave it back as if I were healing him and brought him to his knees. His broken bones slid back into place painfully slow. The crunch of bone on bone echoed in the room, and I fought the urge to be sick.

"You will never win, Finn." I leaned over him. "Because you have nothing left that's worth fighting for. And the moment you finally grasp anything of worth, I will be there to take it from you, and you will feel the pain I am feeling today."

"I'm sorry," Finn said and spat blood. "I didn't want to leave them. You have to believe that. I swear to you, on any oath, I didn't want to do it."

"But you did. You had a choice and picked your own life over my family. They suffer because of you," I replied. My next question had lingered in my mind for days. "Why, Finn? Why did you do it? Why didn't you help me?"

He looked up from his hands and knees. His eyes glittered with tears. When I saw the pain in his eyes, I stepped back. My heart hurt for him. "I wish, more than anything, I could have brought them all back. But I couldn't. I'm not that strong. I can't grab Zephyr unless he wills it. Nix was in his arms. I couldn't pull him. No one takes from the Finis. And Solas' soul is too strong for me to take unless he allows it. It's why I told you to do it. He'd never fight you like he would me. I tried, but you wouldn't do it."

"I don't care about your wishes, Finn," I replied. "We aren't absolved of what we do simply because we wish we had done it differently. Debts are tallied for our acts, not for what we hoped would have happened had we been given different options."

I stepped forward and paused. I gripped a knife in my fist but couldn't take another step. Although Finn nodded, I couldn't do it. I couldn't stab him for a game. The part of me that craved my family's return begged me to move forward, to give the best show I could. But the piece of my soul I heard loudest told me that I couldn't allow my enemies to reduce me to desperation. What I was willing to do in this world, good and bad, would answer the question as to why Finis were drowned at birth. If I became a monster greater than any other in Elphame, regardless of the reasons, would the Gods ever answer another prayer of mine? Or would I be punished for becoming the monster that has haunted my dreams since becoming a Crow?

"Did you find a way back onto that island?" I asked, and he shook his head. "Did you find a Mage?"

"No. But trust that the Aos Si are searching," he replied.

"Not good enough," I replied. "If you're so sorry, why the hell are you sitting here and not out searching with the others?"

"They're terrified to be caught with me. Aeden is enforcing your law. I can't go anywhere without putting others at risk," he replied. "I came to grab a change of clothes. Mine are covered in crusted blood. Every time you find me, I'm a bloody mess after. I can be smelled from miles away. How can I hunt a Mage if they can smell me coming?"

Finn lifted his finger to his lips, and I paused. He motioned to the tunnel, where we both watched the energy shift. The shadows twisted over his magick as if eating every spare clue. The dark energy we had felt before was gone. I could feel the shadows in the back of my mind, collecting pieces of our puzzle.

The shadows wrapped around us and pushed out a wall of impossible force, as I had seen them do with Zephyr. "Aeden is here. Whoever is stalking you both is gone."

I groaned. "Damn it. Did you get anything off him?"

"We did," they replied.

"If he's gone, why the wall?" Finn asked. "It's not Aeden if that's what you're about to say. I know his energy as well as I know my own."

"No, it isn't Aeden," the shadows replied. "But that's not why we're blocking him out, either. What we're about to say has consequences, and we felt you both would want the information in private. When the traitor arrived, we wondered how he got past the Sluagh. Only those familiar and welcome can come and go with all their limbs intact. During your fight, we inspected his energy. Once we ate his magick, we rolled around in Finn's energy, and they were both similar. We know why the magick was familiar to us all. Your enemy is Aos Si."

"Aos Si?" Finn sputtered as he came to his feet. He clutched his right hand and twisted his fingers back into joint. "Impossible."

"Why is it impossible?" I asked, sliding my middle finger knuckle back into place and shaking out the pain of it.

"We're all oathed. We'd never be able to go against Zephyr or you, even if we wanted to. Why would an Aos Si be hunting you, Perdi? We'd never go against you. It's not even the oaths that keep us from harming you. You saved our Commander. You're the last little Crow. We'd never hurt you."

"That's not true about the oaths, Finn," the shadows said. "Those not yet accepted into the trainee program, those still being tested, are not yet oathed to Zephyr. That doesn't happen until they've been enlisted into the Aos Si. And some of the trainees who came while Zephyr was locked in the Golden Court are not oathed yet."

"You're certain?" Finn asked.

"Yes, we are," the shadows replied. "We do not know who he is, though. We didn't push too hard, or he'd have felt us. But yes, he feels like Aos Si. They smell of Aos Si. What's more, we can smell the magick used on the island. We can smell the Mages on him."

Finn nodded and stared at me for a moment, breathing me in. "When you got here, I thought I could smell trainee and raw magick, but the smells get confusing around you and the shadows. I thought it was you I could smell."

"Why does it get confusing around me?" I asked.

"Because you're Finis, so you smell like all Elphame. Your Malice has a smell that changes depending on your mood and whose energy you consume. And the shadows? I can smell each and every one of them. Together, you both are too chaotic. I'm getting used to it, but it's difficult when your emotions are all over the map. I can find you, track you as a witch, but sniffing you out is harder."

I groaned. "What the hell do we do now? Find every trainee and those being tested and pick through their souls?"

"No. There are too many of them, and none of them are going to line up for either of us to touch them. Give me the day, Perdi. I'll track him down. Now that I know I'm looking for an Aos Si, he'll be easier to find," he replied. "Keep your mouth closed. Tell no one. I'll find you as soon as I have him."

I nodded. "You have one more day, Finn. But come tomorrow night, we start doing this my way. My family can't wait on us. They don't have that kind of time."

"I know. But we protect our territory and people first. They can't wait on us to follow our hearts over our duties. This world doesn't have room for softness. Our duty comes first, I'm sorry," he replied. Although I agreed, I didn't like it. "I have dead men to hunt. Time to kick me out and make it look good."

"Why don't you trust Aeden?" I asked.

"The only people I trust with your life are still on that island, Perdi," he replied. "Zephyr didn't trust anyone but Solas and Nix. I've a mind to follow his choices. We trust no one until we know who our enemy is and pick their minds apart."

"I trusted you," I pointed out.

"If I wanted you dead, you'd be dead the moment you threatened me," he answered. "Unlike the others, I won't warn you. I'll simply kill you."

"We have so much in common," I replied. The shadows pulsed around us. We weren't alone. "You have one more day, Finn."

"Perdi." Aeden's voice echoed into the cave, and I cringed at the continuation of the risky game we were playing. The thought of leaving Finn and facing the Aos Si alone made my stomach roll.

"You're not alone," Finn whispered. "Trust that I see you always."

I nodded. "You have a free pass, it seems. Get your things and get the hell out of my territory. And if you think of going to your cabin, the last wall fell to ash a couple of hours ago."

"I know. I was inside of it," Finn replied and grinned. "Barricading the exits was a nice touch."

"I know," I answered, then tilted my head. "I found her, Finn. I think her cabin would take more force to take down than yours, but it's not impossible. If I found her, someone else can."

He scowled. "That is not a war anyone wants with me."

"I stood twenty feet from her already," I answered. "Figure it out before you're fishing her dead body out of the drink."

"No one is that stupid," he replied. "Run along, Perdi. Your bleeding heart is leaking all over my freshly polishing floors."

"Everyone has the capacity for stupidity. Anger makes us do some mighty foolish things in Elphame. Don't say I didn't warn you. The wee folk won't be able to protect her from everyone." I knew he understood my warning meant something more, but his cockiness still rattled me. He'd either move her or risk her to capture our traitor. I hoped it would be the latter. I wouldn't forgive him if I had to dig a hole for someone who could have been easily saved.

"Thank you for the heads-up," he answered and motioned to the tunnel. "You have people waiting on you."

"You have one day, Finn. You either find me a way onto that island to save my family, or you'll find yourself in a shallow grave," I replied.

"You'll never be the beast you want to be." His tone was smug. It didn't seem to matter how deep we were sinking, he never seemed to lose that arrogance.

"You have no idea how monstrous I can be, how utterly heartless I will become to save those I love," I answered. "I'll break myself in half for them. You're only alive right now because you're still useful. But once you're not, you'll die like everyone else in Elphame who isn't of value to someone with more power. And you, Finn, aren't nearly as valuable as you think."

"I truly hope that you can be," he replied. "As always, it's been a pleasure to see you. Until next time, enjoy your evening."

I turned my back to him and walked to the mouth of the cave to find Aeden shaking his head. "What? He's still breathing. Kill him or let him live. This, what you're doing to him, is beneath you," Aeden said.

"No, it isn't. Finn and I are walking the same path. A path, I might add, he pulled me onto," I replied.

"He didn't do this. Zephyr did." Aeden corrected me as he had before.

"We all make choices, Aeden. This was Finn's," I answered with as much honesty as I could give. "Is your little pep talk why you've come, or is someone else missing?"

"Lily wants to see you," Aeden said.

"What now?" I asked.

"After you left Whitwick, a fight broke out. Lily tried to contain it. She didn't want to bother you again but was injured while trying to keep mortals from crossing the Gate. Many of your kinsmen have threatened to breach the Gate and enter Elphame for war. It seems they won't allow Fae to police them. The Seers have stepped aside and have told them they are welcome to try. They will not stop them."

"What the hell is wrong with them? They inch closer and closer to their own deaths with each passing hour." I groaned at the thought of returning to Whitwick. "Is Lily all right?"

"She is, but she's fuming mad," he replied, and we both cringed at the thought of an angry Seer. "May I suggest, Perdi, you give them what they so desire, or you'll be going back and forth until you're arguing with the next generation."

"And what do you suggest I do, Aeden? It's not like I have many options here," I replied.

"If they do not want us there, why are we there? We cannot protect them from themselves. It is a battle that is not ours to win."

"If we leave, then what?" I asked.

"They either learn to overcome their pain, or they don't. Whatever the case, we are a constant reminder. We are the reason for their agony, and we're standing over their shoulders. Whatever they decide is up to them, unless you are willing to dominate them entirely, which I don't believe you do."

"No, I don't want that," I answered.

"Solas only kept the guard there to protect your people because of you. It is what you wanted, so that is what he did," Aeden answered. "I see the question roll across your face, what he would do in this situation. I cannot speak on what he would do, and it wouldn't matter. Solas is not here. You are. What would you want to happen if you were in Whitwick? If it was your fate we were discussing?"

"I'd want to be protected," I answered.

"By us? The very people who have hunted you?" He asked. "If you had never come here, never loved us as you do, would you still want Fae in your streets?"

"No, I don't think I would," I replied, and I didn't like the answer I had.

"Nor would I," he replied. "It would feel like a slow invasion."

"What the hell do I do?" I asked.

"You either deal with this now, or mortals with no place in Elphame will come through that Gate and die on our soil. They will blame us for those deaths, and no amount of explaining the powers of Elphame will stop them from sending even more to their deaths."

"I don't have time for this." I released a long sigh and rubbed my temples. The tension was making my eyeballs hurt.

"Heavy is the head that wears the crown," he replied. "This is what it means to sit on the throne."

"This feels more like reigning in hell," I replied.

"Now you know why Solas fought tooth and nail to get home for dinner. Being with you is the closest to serving in heaven as he ever gets."

I motioned for the shadows. "Take us to the Gate. If you feel anything different with the island, I don't care what we're in the middle of doing. Bring me back there immediately."

"We are linked to the shadows we left behind on the island. At the first sign of trouble, we will have you there," they answered, wrapped around Aeden and me and brought us to the Court of Less, a place that crawled across my brain like talons.

Chapter Three

Tonight, the Court of Less was swarming with creatures and guards and those we only called in times of war. The wee folk were out in droves. Once word reached the Hallows, the gnomes did as they always did, prepared to war for one of their people. It was uncomfortable to see their beady eyes in the dark, small flashes from the shadows as they hunted for any sign of Nix or the faintest hint of his scent. They moved as silently as the Aos Si but were more terrifying to see. They made everyone uncomfortable, including the Aos Si. Sparkles caught in the moonlight from Orrian and her people. The fairy queen was out tonight, and her squeals said she wasn't happy. Solas and she had been lifelong friends, but her heart was breaking for Nix, who had become one of her closest confidants. It settled something inside me to see her. I gave her a wave. She nodded in return as she whistled to her people to begin another watch over Unseelie lands.

Standing in front of the Gate were Faolan and Oisin. Next to them was a group of ranked Aos Si. They were all likely coming back from a scouting mission. It was unusual to see the Winter Court standing in Solas' territory, but our treaty still stood, and Faolan was holding up his end. Oisin nodded once, all business. Faolan, on the other hand, smiled as he always did. He tried for peace before anything else. But after being in his mind on more than one occasion, I knew he'd do things I couldn't even think about, let alone do. He was a good person to have on your side for that very reason.

"Any news?" I asked Oisin.

He shook his head. "Not yet, but there are places in Elphame we can't walk into anymore."

"Need me to set some fires?" I asked.

"It may come to that, Perdi," he replied. His voice was tired. "We're going to try the Aos Si way and see if that has better results."

"War?" I asked.

Zeno, Zephyr's number two in command, leaned around Oisin. "We'll try for peace first but will do what we must. Let's regroup at the manor in a couple of hours. Orrian is coming with her people. They can get in and out of every territory without much issue."

I nodded. "If you need help…"

"We will call you right away," Zeno finished my request. "Lily is waiting for you and Faolan."

I frowned. "Why Faolan?"

Faolan stepped forward. "Because they're demanding we leave Whitwick. If you decide to pull back, you will need someone to second your decision. There is an oath between the Unseelie Courts and mortals. If you're withdrawing that oath, you'll need the only other king in the Unseelie court to witness and agree."

I groaned. "Would you withdraw the oath?"

"That's not a simple answer, Perdi. If they want us to leave and threaten war unless we do, we are left with very few choices. We can stay and risk killing them to protect ourselves, or we can leave and hope they don't try to follow us into Elphame. Four mortals have already stepped through and had to be carried back. What happens if one of them dies here while we still have our people on the other side? They will be at risk. Either way, I have no stake in Whitwick. They are your people. I won't make this choice for you, but I can support you while you make it."

The shadows followed Aeden, Faolan and me. We stepped through the shimmering wall, and I wanted to stay hidden inside. It felt horrible to remain within the Gate, but it was still a better feeling than anything I'd face on either side. Sadly, my brain didn't agree with my heart and pushed my feet into action. My body, starved of air, made decisions I didn't want to make for myself.

In Whitwick, we stepped straight into the middle of arguing. The tempers from both mortal and Fae rented the air and left behind the stench of burning flesh. The screams boiled the rage in my stomach. I felt pulled in too many directions. My heart and soul were sitting on an island, and I was standing in Whitwick, dealing with fools. I understood why Solas returned home some nights and looked like he wanted to smash a window—or why he had walked home slowly, releasing his frustration before seeing me. The annoyance of pettiness and idiocy, when dozens of other things demanded my attention, dragged claws down my patience until my last nerve snapped, and I was inches from losing my temper—a temper I could never afford to unleash—not entirely and not here. I'd never be able to kill them all, and that was the rule for Soul-Eaters.

Kill them all or walk away, lest you wish to be hunted to the ends of the earth.

"Enough!" I screamed, and the entire crowd came to a dead silence. I felt the ground tremble slightly under the force of my anger. Self-control was finite, and I barely had any on a good day. Today, it felt out of reach. Having to return to Whitwick, again, made it all the more worse. "What the hell is wrong with you people? You're going to cross the Gate? Are you out of your minds? Do you have any idea what that Gate does to you? Even halflings can die from the power that will roll your body into slop. If you cross, you will die, not because I or anyone else wants your death, but because you're not meant to be in Elphame."

"She is telling the truth." My father, who stood nervously between the crowd and me, spoke up. Every time I came back, I pitied him a little more than the last time. He was caught between a rock and a hard place. "Had it not been for Fae magick, I would have died when I crossed. You will not receive the same assistance I was given, when I went to fight for Whitwick."

I was able to stop myself from unleashing hell on them, but I couldn't keep myself from yelling. My anger needed out, and I was perilously close to letting it go. I closed my eyes and breathed beyond my need to punish them for their foolishness. I could smell their anxiety and panic. It was a familiar smell. I had grown up with it. Fear makes us brave, but it also breeds ignorance and repression. That repression breeds hate and menaces stability. Without control, it would burn and blister us all.

"Crossing that Gate will solve nothing. Do you hear me? Four of you have already tried, and I fear they'll never fully recover. Instead of listening to warning after warning, you keep sentencing more of your neighbors to a horrible fate. Their deaths will not be on *our* hands, but *yours.* We will not be responsible for your bad decisions."

A young man I had known in school, stepped forward. "We want the Fae guards gone. They are nothing more than a reminder of the control the Fae have had over us."

"Peter?" I asked, and he nodded. "Do you understand what you're asking? What it truly means to ask us to leave?"

"Yes."

I shook my head. My impulse was to argue, to keep fighting for them, to keep warning them, to help. But they didn't want it, and I couldn't force them to take it. I turned back to the Gate, to the Seers. "Go home. We are no longer wanted here."

Lily shook her head, not in a stand against my order, but because she, like me, knew what it meant. After a long moment of frustration, she agreed. "As you wish."

"I don't wish for any of this," I replied. "But it is what they want."

"Thank you." Peter smiled as if he had won some invisible fight.

"Don't thank me, Peter. Don't any of you thank me for this. I will not be responsible for what you've done to your people." I let out a shaking groan. "There is no one left to protect the mortal lands from whatever Elphame decides to spit out. I cannot control every bloody Fae in Elphame. Some will come, and you will be powerless to stop them."

"We can protect ourselves," Peter answered.

I laughed, thick with sadness and pity for them all. "No, you can't."

"Soon, Perdi, you'll see how well we can protect ourselves from your kind," Peter replied and stepped forward. "Your kind isn't welcome here."

Aeden moved in front of Peter. "Young Sir, if I may offer you your last piece of advice, for I fear your life will be too short to be given another chance to learn. One person was standing between Fae and mortals, and you've asked her to step aside. I see you inching closer to her, step by step. You hold hate in your eyes, and it's directed at only her. What do you think will happen next? If you touch her, what do you think I will do? There is no one left to protect you from me or from my brethren."

Peter stared but didn't answer.

"It was a question," Aeden said. "From where I'm standing, I'm speaking to a dead man who hasn't enough sense to lie down."

"Don't threaten me." Peter's words weren't nearly as intimidating as I knew he wanted them to be.

"That, young man, is not a threat," Aeden answered and looked out over the crowd. "I understand what it feels like to feel fear so great you want to hide, but the fear has crippled you and won't let go—terror so sharp, you can't scream, you can't breathe, you can't cry out for help, grief so utterly pure and deep that your soul drowns in oceans of tears. If what is on the other side of that Gate can make *me* wish for death, what do you think it will do to *you*?" he asked everyone in the crowd. "Your fear of us, I understand, but you've allowed it to seal your fate. Those of us who killed our own people for you will no longer be here to protect you. We stood at this Gate to ensure you had freedom, that not another mortal would suffer at the hands of Fae, and you've thrown it away. The next Fae to walk through that Gate will not come to offer you aid. Those who we never allowed to cross the Gate, for fear they'd swallow you whole, will come, and they will feast. They will come for your children, for your wives, your husbands, your blood, and nothing you do will stop them. And we won't stop them, either."

"Let's go." I touched Aeden's arm. "There's nothing more we can do here. They must walk their own paths."

"What a rocky road it shall be," he answered.

"We don't need you either, Perdi." Peter looked me in the eyes. "Take your people and go."

Faolan smirked, which turned into a full laugh. "You most certainly will need her. If you believe nothing else we say, believe that she will be the only one who comes. I will hear your screams from my lands and won't come to help you, and we won't come to help her save you again. You have torn up the only agreement that said we would come to your aid." Faolan's voice was filled with the same disappointment I felt in my heart. "Your fates were once to suffer at our hand, and when given the freedom to choose again, you've decided to walk that same path. May the Gods have more mercy on your souls than we will. Because from where I'm standing, we're talking to a graveyard."

"We have a new oath…" My father stopped his sentence as he realized the oath meant nothing if only the Fae were upholding it.

I nodded slowly as I watched him come to terms with their new future, one they had been fighting to have, however short it may be. "Once we leave, that oath is broken on your part. You've asked to end the protection we've offered. You've sent it away. There is nothing—no oath, no army—stopping Fae. And I cannot stop them on my own. I won't give my life for this. I have given it once already."

"This is not the way." My father tried, in desperation, for his people to understand, but not a single person would listen.

"You've sentenced your children to the same fate as every other Crow," I replied. "You will die, and people will step over your bodies to save themselves, but there will be nowhere to run. You'll never run fast enough, and there isn't a corner in hell where a Fae will not find you."

I looked at each face, committing them to memory—not for retribution but to remember those who would die for no good reason. I couldn't fight two wars. I couldn't save everyone. So, I chose, and the mortal world didn't win this time. I had always picked them, and each time, I'd paid dearly…but not today. I wouldn't stay here and force them to listen or live. I had my family to save, those who counted on me, who would come for me and who always picked me first.

"I will ask one more time. Is this what you want? Because when I leave, I will not come back for this." I finally spoke, once the grief of it all settled into the pit of my stomach. "Is this what the entire community wants? Because once we step through that Gate, you are at the mercy of Elphame. By nightfall, all Fae will know that you stand unguarded by those who are the very justice of Elphame. You will be alone again. You will have nowhere to hide…again. And when the fog fills the streets, you will kill each other as you once did." My breath caught in my throat as I remembered that fear. The screams echoed through my mind, followed by taunting and laughter. "There will be no Taking, only death. I have tried so hard to keep this from Whitwick, from the mortal world, but I can't save you from yourselves. You will sentence everyone to a bitter and terrifying end."

"Go and take the rest of your kind with you," Peter answered.

"They will be gone before the sun rises again," Faolan answered.

I glanced at my father. "I'm sorry, Dad."

"I love you, Perdi." He dropped his eyes from mine and walked away. I saw his defeat. I felt it along with him.

"Let's go." I turned and left the mortal world to the fates they decided. I stepped through the Gate and screamed until my throat hurt. But I didn't cry. I had no tears left for Whitwick.

"My lady." Lily approached me.

I looked back to the shimmering wall and watched as little creatures returned to Elphame. They should have already been home, but the wee folk were prone to doing what they wanted. "Our people come home. Those are the only ones who cross into Elphame."

"And if mortals attempt to follow?" she asked.

"Give them a warning to return to Whitwick. If they don't listen, send them back in any way you deem suitable," I answered. "If my father comes…" my voice hitched in my throat.

"We will not take his life. We will offer him sanctuary, should he wish. But he will be the only one we will show mercy to, as he is the only one deserving of such things." She answered, and I nodded. "Do we guard Elphame against entering?"

"They have said they can protect themselves. Let them learn," I answered. "For now, let them try it their way."

"I do not see this ending well," she answered. "I can feel it in my bones. This is only the beginning of a very big problem."

"I feel it, too," I replied. "I can't stop it from coming, Lily. Each hour brings a new reason for war. I don't want to be one of those reasons, with my need to save them. As hard as I try, I think my help only speeds fate along."

"I understand," she replied. ""I'll meet you at the manor shortly. The Seers have a few ideas on how to breach the wards."

"We need a Mage for that," I replied. "Do you have one handy?"

"Not yet," she replied. "But we can discuss our ideas to find one if Zeno turns up empty-handed."

I walked back toward the manor, feeling my shoulders slump with the weight of what I had just done. Although I stood on familiar soil, my mind was still at the Gate, with those who had forgotten that they were the hunted and not the hunters. How had they grown so cocksure? Before becoming a Crow, we shuddered at the thought anytime someone mentioned a war against Fae, but that fear was now gone. People did not find that much courage overnight. I wondered where their newfound bravery came from. It tickled the back of my brain like only pending doom could. Whatever they had planned, I'd find out sooner rather than later.

"Are you okay?" Faolan asked, pulling my mind out of my dark thoughts. "That must have been difficult."

I shrugged. "I don't know how you guys do this, going from one fire to the next. It's one problem after the other. It never stops, does it?"

"It is why so many kings go mad over time. They grow tired of it all." He sighed as if he, too, had come close on occasion. "Kings do not simply lead, Perdi. We share the duties and burdens with those we trust. Had I been in your shoes, I'd have sent Oisin. He would know what I could and couldn't live with and would have made decisions on my behalf with that in mind. More than that, he would have weighed the choices against the safety of our people. I share my burdens, as should you. You may not have the luxury of sending Oisin, as I do, to deal with the Gate or the mortal realm, but hundreds of other problems will come up over time. You need to be willing to relinquish some of that control to someone else."

"I usually share those burdens with Solas," I replied. I felt a twinge inside my soul. I was homesick for my person, the one who was my home. My eyes watered at the very thought of my other half.

"I may not be Solas, but I care that you're hurting right now. What would you honestly do if Elphame invaded the mortal realm? What would your heart tell you to do?"

"Help them," I answered.

"If that is the line in your soul, of what you can and can't live with, why allow the mortals to cause the very problem that'll require you to leave the search of your people? You could stop the fire from starting now before the flames reach your home. If you're only going to protect them in the end, why wait for it to become a blaze that can't be contained later?"

"Punishment, I think. If mortals don't want us there, why should I do a damn thing to help them? I thought, if I pulled us all back, maybe they'd remember why we were there to begin with."

"Have you forgotten what was done to you? As a child, as a young woman, a year ago?" he asked, and I shook my head. "They've not forgotten either. And every time they see Fae on their lands, it is a bitter reminder that the Fae were able to kill their people, and there is no punishment for what was done to them."

"How do I help those who don't want it?" I asked. "They don't want us there. The longer we're around, the worse it gets. What started as a spark of anger has turned into an inferno of hate. Hell, I can feel the heat from here."

"I have a suggestion," Aeden spoke up, always a foot or two away from me. "You don't need to stand at the Gate in Whitwick to protect them. Your threat alone is enough to scare most Fae. Who would dare risk your wrath? You carry the weight of Solas and the entire Dark Courts. You're the friend of the only Soul-Eater and Commander of Aos Si and the family of Nix? The gnomes are often overlooked, but they have the ear of every power in Elphame. I would stand against you, Perdi, before him, in a heartbeat. You will bring war and certain death. It will be quick and clean. Nix would slowly destroy all I have built, from the inside. I would sentence generations to come to his very long-living memory."

"So, I should threaten Fae?" I asked. "That sounds like I'd be picking a fight with a different group. One, might I add, I don't want to fight, either."

"Then let them die," Aeden countered as if it were a simple decision. "Perdi, respectfully, you must choose. I'm sorry that this is your reality, but you either want them to live or don't care if they die. You cannot have both. The world does not allow for such things."

"I can't choose," I answered.

"Yes, you can. You just don't want this decision to be yours," Aeden countered. "If you don't want to threaten Elphame, forbid them from using the Gate. It is yours by law, just as much as the land it stands on is yours by law. Enforce your lockdown on your courts. If anyone steps foot into the Gate, they forfeit their lives. It is within your right to limit who touches your soil and for what purpose they do so. You don't have to kill anyone for people to fear you might. Treat the Gate as if it were your own backyard. I've seen what you do to those who aren't invited into your yard, Perdi."

I nodded and smiled at the simplicity of it. I knew what he was doing. I couldn't choose between the life and death of mortals but could decide not to be a part of their fate. And I wouldn't suffer guilt for it later.

I motioned for the shadows. "Go tell Lily of our conversation. She is to ensure that all of Elphame knows that the Gate is off-limits, and no one is permitted to cross it. Our people can come home, but our people can't leave. The Seers are to decide who touches our land and who does not. We will do nothing to protect Whitwick from a fate they chose, but we will protect ourselves from the fallout."

"You cannot save them all, but damn it if you're not going to try." Faolan laughed. "War follows you, Perdi."

"I'm trying hard not to, but every day feels like I'm one step closer to the inevitable," I answered.

"That is the way of Elphame, to teeter on the edge of oblivion," Faolan answered. "I'll see you at the manor. I'm meeting with Oisin and Zeno. Hopefully, we'll have good news to bring you."

"Thank you for coming with me," I replied and waved him off. Although I appreciated his help, he was a poor substitute for Solas.

Aeden walked at my side. "I don't envy your position, Perdi. You're straddling two worlds—both which you love dearly. On one side, your mortal family. On the other, Fae. It is not a place I'd wish anyone to be."

"You are both Fae and an Aos Si. Doesn't that get hard?" I asked.

"At one time, I'd say no. That they are the same thing." He sighed. "But yes, it can be difficult but not for me in the same way as it is for you. I am Fae, a Fae Aos Si, in an army on Fae land. My priorities are Fae, pure and simple. I will never be forced to choose between mortals and Fae. I'm not forced to choose between my brothers and my family. It is much simpler for me than for you."

"The more time I spend in Elphame, the less divided I become. Sometimes it feels like I'm betraying them somehow," I replied.

"You're not, if that helps," he answered. "One day, they'll understand you did everything you could to protect them. And if they don't, that is on them, not you. You have fought and won wars in their name. You've literally given your life for them. What more could they want that can be given?"

"I fear what they'll need to suffer before they understand anything more than their own pain," I replied.

"I doubt anyone who could do serious harm will dare cross into Whitwick. Most of those creatures are already oathed to you through your throne." His voice whispered across my shoulders, and calmness settled in. "I think it is you who will be forced to endure when you're made to finally choose."

"War?" I asked. "It's always war."

"It wouldn't be Elphame if it wasn't."

"I'd be forced, no matter which side I stood on, to fight against my own people."

"That is the burden of being a king or queen. It never matters which side of the field you stand on. You're still responsible for the deaths of many." He grimaced. "I have only ever stood with the Aos Si, but I've killed those I care for in the name of war because they stood on the other side. It doesn't get easier, Perdi. Nothing about it gets easier. If anything, each time I prepare for battle, it eats at me a little harder than the last time. And when it's over, I grieve deeper than the last time."

"I don't think I'd be able to fight if it came down to us versus them."

"That you see an 'us' and 'them' tells me you've already begun that fight. You just haven't admitted it to yourself. One day, you'll have no choice but to decide. We're all forced to choose at some point in our lives. And I pray, Perdi, you choose yourself and stop leaving pieces of your soul all over this cursed land. You're too good to suffer as greatly as you do."

Chapter Four

The manor felt empty, even with two dozen people standing in the dining room and even more roaming the halls and yard. It was the kind of emptiness that couldn't be seen, only felt. The rooms were too big, too cold. I sat at the table and ate a bowl of mashed potatoes with Orrian and a gnome. They went back and forth on the merits of simply waging war on every other territory over our plan of questioning and releasing the innocent. Orrian was of the mind that no one in Elphame was innocent. She thought waging war instead of investigating would solve future complications. The gnome, who I agreed with, said new problems would arise with the death of kings, and it was better to keep the monsters we knew, rather than have to learn how crazy the new ones would be—though he couldn't argue her point of innocence. No soul ever survived Elphame without doing unspeakable acts.

Zeno had returned without a Mage. He and Lily were arguing over our next move. It was a common sight to see, the Aos Si and Seers fighting over plans and consequences. The Aos Si didn't care about the fallout, while the Seers thought about how far-reaching each decision could be. Solas and Zephyr were usually the ones who would make those decisions, weighing the risks and rewards. Left to their own devices, Lily and Zeno had no one to step between them. I certainly wasn't going to be the referee. I had enough problems as it was.

I tuned them out and finished my dinner. The shadows roamed the halls and grounds for any trace of our traitor. They'd warn me of his coming, the moment he turned up. So far, no sign of him. Whether Finn had a plan or not, I'd grab the bastard the moment he stepped foot in the manor and damn the consequences.

I cleared my dishes, made myself a cup of tea and leaned against the wall, watching them each take turns picking the other apart. I was not the only one who was entertained. Both sides had gathered in the room to watch the two strongest members of their group. I was pretty sure the Aos Si were placing bets on who would win this disagreement today. I put my money on Lily. She may not be the storm that was Zeno, but she was a force all on her own. She survived a lifetime of Solene, the very terror of Elphame. She didn't back down for anyone. She wasn't about to start now—with Zeno, of all people.

"It was you, Lily, who told Perdi to take the fucking trainees to the island," Zeno said. "If you would have kept your mouth shut, like Seers should, we'd probably be back with all of our people."

Lily laughed. "Don't blame me because your men were too weak to fight Zephyr's pull."

"Because of you, the one person I need is being hunted all over Elphame by a pissed-off Soul-Eater," Zeno countered. He eyed me once and turned his attention back to Lily. His stare made me uncomfortable but not enough to speak up. "Had you not meddled, I'd have Finn, and this shit would be dealt with."

"I'm not taking the blame for Perdi, either. I don't control her. None of us do. If you want her to do something, ask her, but don't pick at me because you're a chickenshit," she replied.

"I'm standing right here, you know." I raised my hand. "Don't talk about me like I'm not in the room."

Lily's eyes zeroed in on me from across the room. "Enough of this, Perdi."

"Everyone needs a hobby. Mine is hunting Finn," I replied.

"Is digging holes for your family and planning burials also a new hobby I don't know about?" she asked, and I blanched. "I didn't think so. You have two choices. And this time, it's solely on you to decide. We're running out of time. Every hour we spend off that island is an hour our people are at the hands of our enemies. How many hours do you think they have left?" she asked. When I didn't have an answer, she continued. "My thoughts exactly…not many. The longer we're away, the more creative their captors will become. It is the way of war. With time at a premium, we need to find a Mage. We need Finn for that. Without a Mage to help us, you will need to do a spell to break the wards, and it'll likely result in your death."

"Why Finn? Why can't you find one without him?" I asked. "What's so special about him that he is needed for this?"

Zeno shook his head. "Finn can find a freckle on a fairy in all Elphame with one glance. I think the Mages are either hiding themselves with magick or are being hidden by someone powerful."

"He said he's been looking but hasn't found one," I replied, and that was the truth. They didn't need to know what else he's been doing. "What would be so different? If Finn can find someone hidden with magick, why can't you guys?"

"Finn is much like Nix in how he can sense energies and magicks used by others. It's why you've yet to sneak up on him during your hunts."

"I'll have to try harder next time," I replied. I said I'd give Finn a day, and now I didn't think I'd be able to buy him the hours I agreed to. "He obviously can't help us, or we'd have a Mage."

"Sometimes I forget how young you really are. You're still attached to your anger and need for vengeance, like a child would be." Lily sighed. "After decades of this, you'll learn to let go for the greater good or you'll be dead and I've wasted my breath on this conversation."

Her words stung. They were true in most cases for me but not this one. I was angry, but I had stopped stewing in it to save my family. I had let go of the need for revenge against Finn the moment we stood on common ground. "Why hasn't Finn found one yet?"

"Finn has been hiding out, searching as he moves from location to location, remaining out of sight. He's trying to do what he can while respecting your pain and what he thinks you would want from him. Finn won't do what is necessary for fear of how you'll react. He doesn't want to rock the boat any more than he already has," Zeno answered. "Let him loose, and he'll smoke out a Mage. And if he doesn't find one, they aren't here."

"And if they're not here?" I asked.

"Send him to Whitwick to drag one back or kiss the island goodbye," Lily replied.

My eyes widened, and my stomach flopped. "Set Finn loose on the mortal realm?"

Zeno nodded. "That will be the cost of saving your family. You either will do everything you can to bring them home or you don't. Whatever you decide, you need to make that decision now. You have the entire Unseelie courts wreaking havoc to find our family and enemies. If you're not going to do what it takes, we must pull our people back and focus their attention on securing the Dark Courts. We need to plan for the possibility of war with the Seelie Courts and with the mortals. We are at last moves, Perdi. It's time to decide or you risk us all."

"We're not pulling back," I replied. "But we do need to plan for war, regardless. I doubt the Seelie courts will come. My money is on the mortal realm trying something. But let's ensure they all have plenty of reasons to remain on their side of the lines."

"If you're not pulling back, we need the Mage. They can show you how to break the spell," Lily pulled my mind from the dark thoughts of sending a monster into Whitwick and the war that would follow. "You can use the collective power of the Aos Si again, and Jare can help you redirect the power. You can fill him up with all Elphame magick, and he wouldn't so much as twitch. The Seers will be there to keep you from frying your brain, in case things get too heavy for you."

I wouldn't risk using all the Aos Si until I knew who had sold my family to the enemy. I needed Finn. We needed to move now, or we risked our enemy disappearing from our grasp.

"Then Finn is back on my shitlist," I added.

"Not so fast," she replied. "You'll need him on the island. Finn is the only Aos Si who doesn't have an oath with Zephyr. He needs to be there to keep you from being manipulated and tossed off the island again. Finn can keep the others from being pulled into your dreams and can protect you from the oaths the others may be forced to fulfill."

I groaned. "I don't think I'll ever fully trust him again. He lied to me."

"Too bad," Zeno answered. The words felt like a slap. "I get it. You're pissed off. We all are. But your anger is misplaced. Finn didn't do this. Zephyr did. Fix your shit before it kills three good men. When we get them home, you can do as you please with Finn. Until then, suck it up. You do not want to face the rest of us if your anger and stubbornness are why our Commander is dead."

"Don't threaten me, Zeno," I replied. "I hear you, but if you threaten me again, they'll never find your body."

"It's not a threat. It's a warning," Zeno turned to face me fully. His arms fell to his side, ready for whatever would happen between us. "You don't have what it takes for me to step back, little Crow."

I smiled. It wasn't friendly. I relaxed my arms and body. I wouldn't be bullied into doing anyone's bidding. "And you don't have what it takes for me to take your shit."

"You both beating on each other isn't going to solve anything. You're only going to waste time we don't have." Lily sighed. The tension in the room was thick enough to chew on. "Which do you want more, Perdi, staying angry or saving your family?"

"The safety of my family," I answered. "Revenge is a luxury."

"A luxury you can't afford," she replied. "Do it for them—and take it out on Zephyr's hide when you get them home. But bring your people home before you spend your time on your anger."

I nodded, and Zeno scowled. Their truth felt uncomfortable, but it was the truth, regardless of how it felt. I doubted I'd ever trust Finn fully again. It didn't matter that we were working together today. Later, when I was broken in half, I'd remember the part he played, and it would be difficult to overcome. My mind understood his position, but my soul wouldn't care for excuses later. I closed my eyes and thought of Solas and his last words to me to keep Finn close. I had, in a manner of speaking. But I doubted Solas had meant I was to hunt him down, torment him, hatch a plan to lie to everyone else and search all of Elphame for one of Zephyr's people.

Lily then glanced at Zeno. "And you can stop taking your shit out on everyone else. We get it. You're frustrated. But intimidating those around you makes you look weak, nothing more."

"I'm not bullying anyone. We don't have time to tiptoe around the truth of the matter, and Perdi doesn't need to be coddled," Zeno replied. "We need Finn for this. We've tried to do this without him and have come up empty every time."

I finally caved. "I don't know where he is."

"Try his cabin?" Lily asked.

I felt my face heat. "I burned it down the other day."

Lily cleared her throat, trying to hide a laugh. "Remind me not to piss you off."

"He's at the Aos Si training camp," Aeden spoke up. "It's the only place not officially owned by anyone."

"How is there unclaimed land in Elphame?" I asked.

"Would you try to claim it?" he asked. "You'd have to fight the entire Aos Si."

"Good point," I replied and grinned.

"Don't," Lily cut in. "I can see the wheels moving behind your angry eyes. Don't even try to claim it. You'd have to fight them all, and I doubt you'd win."

"I think I would," I replied, then shrugged. "It was just a thought."

"Always the warmonger. Solas would be proud." Zeno grinned. "Go get Finn. He won't come if it's one of us that goes. He won't trust that it is you who wants his help. He's hurting, Perdi. Tread lightly. There's no reason to keep cutting him up."

"You're certain there isn't a different way?" I asked, still holding out hope that I could buy Finn that extra day.

"We would have found it if there was," Zeno answered. "The longer you stall, the longer you're away from that island. The longer the Mages go unchecked in Elphame, the higher the risk is to your people. We need one to find the others."

I groaned and motioned to the shadows. They curled around me, and we were gone to a place I had yet ventured into—a place where Zephyr had grown into a man and a nightmare. When my feet touched the earth, they sunk into black-as-night mud, and I was filled with the sensation that Zephyr was just around the corner. I could feel his energy rolling across the ground as if he had just been here.

"Zeph," I whispered.

"He's spent the better part of his existence in these hills," the shadows replied. "His energy has stained every square inch, from the roots of the trees to the walls of the caves. You can't go anywhere here without feeling his presence. It calms the trainees."

"I wasn't prepared for how much this would hurt." I hissed out a breath and pressed my hand into the center of my chest. My heart felt heavier. It hurt more to feel Zephyr and not see him.

"It's why the majority of the Aos Si, who aren't on duty, are here," they answered. "To be closer to Zephyr."

The first twinge of guilt started. I was so wholly wrapped up in my own pain and war games, that I forgot how utterly horrendous this would be for those who had spent centuries with Zephyr. At least the Dark Courts had me, the reminder and tether to Solas. Since Solas had gone missing, our people had moved a little closer, joined in on the searches and had a purpose. But the Aos Si only had Zephyr.

I glanced around the dark forest and breathed in the scent of rain and pine. Under the earthy odor, I smelled sweat, winged beasts and leather. Without being told, I knew we were close to the Court of Blood and Bones. I could sense the creatures that protected their court. Their presence tickled the back of my brain and told me to run. I could taste the salty ocean lingering in the mist, and it reminded me of Solas when he returned from the caves. Just beyond that, I could feel Zephyr's island hum in my veins as if I were walking up a long path leading me home. I could feel the tension leak from my weary muscles and bones.

Around us stood an old-growth forest. Trees of every species, shape and color, stood towering over me. Mosses grew up the trunks and across the ground. It was as beautiful as it was terrifying. The trees held years of scars from swords and bodies and bitter fights. Massive stones were broken and scattered. The sight of them and the knowledge that someone had picked them up and thrown them sent a shiver down my spine. Training up here was as deadly as war.

"Why not bring me all the way?" I asked the shadows.

"We did. We're standing in the middle of the training camp. It's a few hundred acres, all forest, cliffs and tunnel systems. Finn is in a cave, thirty feet to the right."

"Do you think he knows I'm here?" I asked.

"No. It's hard to feel anything other than Zephyr here. The grounds are spelled to keep the men from using their Fae abilities. Zephyr doesn't allow them to train in hand-to-hand combat with their powers. He trains them not to count on their magick."

"Why?" I asked.

"Really? They'd kill each other within minutes, Perdi, if they could use their power while training," they replied. "One of the Aos Si can turn someone inside out. Another can boil your blood from the inside."

"Makes sense." I huffed a laugh.

"They learn to control their abilities, fine-tune them but never depend on them. It's the same reason Zephyr is the one who trains you. You learn to fight with more than your Finis abilities. You learn to outsmart and outthink your opponent. If ever you were without your

Malice or your Fae powers, without training, you'd die out here."

"Why do I still have access to my abilities?" I asked.

"Because you're Finis and not just Fae. Your Malice is harder to control," they replied.

The breeze carried dread in the air. My arms prickled in goosebumps. A silent warning from my Malice. "He's here, the traitor."

"Explains why Finn is here," they replied.

I followed the shadows through the trees, slipping and breaking branches along the way. The ground was roots, rocks and slop. The lushness of the forest only made it look hospitable. If I had to run, I'd have broken bones in my attempt. Every now and again, I'd grab the trunk of a tree to keep myself standing, only to pull my hand away and see someone else's blood and hair and other parts I didn't want to look too closely at.

The shadows led me through a tunnel and into the back of a cave. It was smaller than the Sluagh caves but had the same feel to it—large, smooth, warmer than you'd think and covered in trainee clutter. Weapons and leather and empty wine bottles littered the floor. Finn was in the rear, curled on his side, on a thin bed of hay and blankets. For a split second, I felt like garbage for chasing him out of his home. It didn't matter the reason. He had been treated like a monster his entire life, and I had done the same in the name of love and desperation. The expression on his face was frozen in lines and sadness. My heart skipped as I watched him suffer in ways I knew he didn't deserve. His eyes fluttered, and his lips pursed. Whatever he was dreaming of had left him looking like he was drowning in grief.

I'd never be the monster I threatened I was. I would do monstrous things to survive and keep those I love alive. But at that moment, I wanted to hug Finn and squeeze all his broken parts back together. Seeing this pain in anyone and not doing anything about it was very much beneath me and who I really was. I stepped to Finn's front. Several things happened at once as I reached down to wake him. Finn's eyes flew open, a knife came out from under his pillow, and I was jerked back by an unknown hand. I didn't fight the grip on my shoulder. I pushed my head back and connected with something that sounded like a breaking nose. I had seen and heard enough of them crunching under fists to know precisely what it sounded like. A gruff curse echoed in the room from my attacker.

I didn't have a chance to spin away from my assailant. He picked me up and tossed me through the air. The shadows grabbed me before I hit the ground and dropped me behind the man who had a hundred pounds on me. I jumped on his back and wrapped my arms around his throat. I didn't think I'd be able to choke him out, but I could give Finn a chance.

My Malice poured from my body, always ready and willing to eat the souls of those who crossed me. The energy she tasted rocked me to my core. I held on to my enemy, the man who had been tracking us. As he twisted and turned with me on his back, I read his soul like an open book. Unfocused and unable to use his magick to block me out, I saw flashes of his memories, his truths and unspoken hate. His great-grandmother was a mortal, a witch turned Mage when she was lost to Elphame. He was born with Mage and Aos Si blood in his veins. Below all the layers of hate, I saw Solene. He had been feeding Solene information about the

Dark Courts, about Solas and me. He had been the mole Solas could never find. And tonight, he planned on killing Finn to get to me, in the name of retribution, for killing Solene.

"Finn!" I screamed as I jerked back from the man's mind. "Run! Run, Finn."

"Perdi?" Finn's voice cut through the cave.

"Don't just stand there. Run, damn it!"

Finn tackled us. The force pushed me off the man's back and crashed into bookcases. Books fell, glasses shattered, and I jumped to my feet as the shelves came down. I launched myself at the man again as he got back up. I grabbed his lower body and pushed him face-first onto the stone floor.

Finn picked me up by the neck of my leather jacket and shoved me toward the tunnel. "Run, Perdi!"

"Finn, I came to help," the man who grabbed me said.

"Cal?" Finn asked. "I don't need your help. It's Perdi."

"She's here to kill you," Cal replied and reached for me again.

"I left her family on that island. I get what I deserve," Finn answered and grabbed Cal, pulling him back from me. "Go—and don't let anyone else in here."

"Are you sure?" Cal asked, but he still moved toward the exit. He looked back a few times before I lost sight of him.

I motioned to the tunnel. "I'm not the one who came here to kill you."

"I figured you weren't here to kill me since you tried to save me from one of the trainees. He doesn't have what it takes to end me," Finn replied. He lit a candle on a table and took a seat. He lifted his finger to his lips and motioned to the tunnel. We were still playing our cat and mouse game. "Are you hungry?"

I nodded. "You're offering me food, after I've been hunting you?"

"You haven't been hunting me. You've been harassing me. If you wanted me dead, we'd be having a different conversation right now." He leaned in. "Ask the shadows to follow Cal and report back when they find his hideout."

I nodded and motioned to the shadows. Half of them slinked across the floor and were gone from sight. The other half pushed themselves into the cave's opening, creating a door no one would dare cross, not if they didn't want to burn off all the hair on their hands and arms. Oisin had tried once and burned both of his hands.

"It's him. He's the man we've been looking for," I said, my voice still hushed. "I read his soul."

"I tracked him here and have been waiting for him to come," Finn replied. "We'll follow him and snag him when his guard is down. Cal is damn strong and hard to track. I don't know what kind of Fae is mixed in with his Aos Si line. Whatever it is, he would have been a damn good Aos Si. Were you able to find anything of importance when you read him?"

"Yes, and I'm not as shocked as I should be. I guess nothing surprises me anymore," I replied. I sat at the table and told him what I saw with my Malice.

"Everything will circle back to that bitch, Solene, for generations to come," Finn answered. "It makes sense why he's stalking you and me. He wanted to bring the Dark Courts to their knees. He went after the two people everyone blames."

"People blame you and me?" I asked. "It was Zephyr and me who did the deed."

"Solene sympathizers don't see it that way. It was me who helped get you into Blood and Bones and me who was sent into the room first. And it's me who has been hunting down her supporters since you killed her. It looks like Cal went unnoticed."

"Ain't revenge sweet?" I rolled my eyes.

"It will be when we wring his neck for this," he replied. "Have some dinner, Perdi. You look like skin and bones. You can't rescue Solas looking like you crawled out of a hole. How un-romantic of you."

Finn pulled out his white bag and started to pull out enough food for an army. He pushed a bowl of mashed potatoes toward me. I didn't complain this time. My eyes watered as I looked at the butter melting on top. It was how Solas served them to me.

"I'm sorry you're hurting," Finn said. He slid a handkerchief across the table.

I closed my eyes and sunk into my seat. "I could say the same to you."

"I'm used to the torture," he replied.

I shook my head, disappointed this world taught us all how to grow used to pain. "I wish more for you."

"We can wish as much as we want, Perdi, but there's no room in Elphame for such things. Hell comes whether we're ready or not. And after a few decades of this, I'd rather be ready for it than crumble under its touch every time."

"I'm not used to it, and I hope I never get to that point," I replied. "My heart and soul are already broken. I can't imagine lifetimes of this shit."

"It wouldn't be Elphame if it didn't fucking hurt." Finn slid a white teacup of red wine toward me and lifted his glass in return. "To broken souls and those who broke them."

"Why would you toast to the person who broke your soul?" I asked.

He smiled. "Those brave enough to try to break me were desperate enough to risk their own death for it. We both know what it feels like to be between two impossible choices. I don't begrudge their desperation. My heart hurts for them to have been pushed into such a place, only to die at my hands in the end."

"You don't strike me as an easy target," I answered.

"I'm not, and neither are you," he replied. "But we suffer when we choose to, for those worthy of our blood."

"What an uncomfortable thought." I clinked my cup against his. "To love."

"It's the only thing worth dying for in this soul-sucking realm," he replied. "So, tell me, what sent a little Crow to the worst place on earth? You didn't come to check on me, and you didn't track Cal here. He was here before I got here."

"Contrary to what the others say, you obviously don't get around. If this is the worst place on earth to you, you need to get out more," I teased. It felt good to carve out a slice of happiness. It had been far too long since I had laughed or felt anything other than the pressure of finding my family, staying alive, and keeping my people alive on both sides of the Gate.

"It's the worst place for people like me and most of the trainees and full-ranks. Most of us look to Zephyr as our father, our soul, the very reason we live. Without him here, the camp is the only place where each breath hurts more than the last. It feels like coming home, but everyone you love isn't here. To me, it feels like what I imagine the manor feels like to you," he answered, and I knew exactly what he was feeling. "But if we're talking physical pain, I'd say the water is the worst place to be. I'd take war over being caught in the water for too long."

"I hate the water here." I shivered at the memory of swimming from Zephyr's island back to shore. "It feels like Zephyr here. It feels wonderful and horrible, exactly like how the manor feels. Full, but empty of everything I want and need. At home, I can smell Solas and feel a hint of his energy lingering. It feels good, but it also feels like the end of the world and being the only one left alive."

"The best and the worst place, for that reason alone. Those we love aren't there, but we can feel them enough to have it constantly remind us." He breathed deeply and winced. "What brings you to the training camp? I thought I had one more day? What has you speeding up the timeline?"

"I heard it was unclaimed. I was thinking of claiming it before I left, to teach Zephyr a lesson."

Finn grinned. "As much as I'd like to dare you to try, I don't think we'd both make it out of here alive. No matter their rank, all Aos Si are oathed to protect these lands. They'd all come."

"I'm pretty sure I'd fare okay. You, though? I'm not sure if you'd make it out of here in one piece," I replied.

"If we had the time, I'd take that bet. But as usual, business before pleasure."

"Ain't that the truth. We have no moves left. Zeno wants you out hunting down one of the Mages responsible for the wards on the island," I answered.

Finn scowled. "Fuck."

"He wants you to look in all of Elphame, and if one isn't here, go into Whitwick and drag one back."

Finn nodded. He knew what I was asking and, within seconds, had resigned himself to being a monster. "And what do you want?"

"Does it matter?" I asked.

"To me, it does," he answered.

"At one time, I didn't really care how much anyone else had to suffer for me to get my family back. But when I stepped into this cave and saw you, I knew you already felt that and more. I can feel it in the air. I can taste your tears on my tongue. I felt sad for you when I saw you sleeping. I could see the pain on your face. Without having to even touch your soul, I already know you've been a pawn in a game you will never win. You'll always be the monster they call on, Finn, but I don't want you to become one for me. I don't want you to scar your soul more than it already is."

"It will save our family," he answered.

"At what cost?" I asked.

"I owe you."

"No, Finn, you don't. I held you responsible because you were the only one I could point fingers at. I needed someone to hate, someone I could name if things didn't work out. You were an easy target. It wasn't fair to you, and I'm sorry."

"I wouldn't blame you if you hated me. I'm easy to hate and used to it."

"I don't hate you," I said. "I'm angry that you were used, that I was lied to, that we were forced to do something we didn't want to do. I'm angry that Zephyr did what he did and put us all in a position of choosing between duty and love. I'm sorry that you were forced to make an impossible decision. And I'm sorry I have you chasing all over this damn realm, helping me. I know you're hurting and feel alone, and I've offered you no help or care. I've been ignoring it, hoping you'd find me a way back to my family."

"*Our* family." Finn's eyes glittered. I didn't push the handkerchief back to him. The Aos Si ignored tears. "Zephyr did what he thought was right, and I don't blame him. You're the only other Finis he has. I'd do so much worse for my family than what he did. We're a protective bunch, and it often clouds our decisions. You know as well as I do what we will do when we feel backed into a corner and have few options. Zephyr did what he could with the few options he had."

"Speaking of being backed into a corner, I'm sorry I burned down your cabin. I didn't know what to do when Cal showed up. I didn't want to risk losing the only lead we had." I tried to look sorry but grinned at the memory of him roasting marshmallows, standing inside the fire, completely unfazed.

"You wouldn't be the first to burn it down." He smiled. "I'm too mouthy to keep the damn thing standing."

"Where the hell have you been staying?" I asked. "You haven't been up here the entire time. Have you been staying with the woman in the forest of the Golden Court?"

"No. She's a friend I met when Zephyr was locked away. She carried messages to Zephyr for us in return for Aos Si protection. With our enemies at large, I've been checking on her. She's still under our protection, but with everything else going on, she's been bumped to the end of the list of things to do. I didn't want to leave her at risk, given all she risked to help us with Zephyr," he replied. "I've been staying at the manor.

I've been sleeping in Zephyr's room, right under your nose."

I turned my focus to the shadows. "You didn't feel him?"

"No. Finn's energy is already everywhere in the manor, as are the rest of the Aos Si. Finn's energy is chaotic and temperamental. It's difficult to read," they replied. They were nervous. I could feel it vibrate against my soul.

"It's all right. I'm not angry, just surprised," I answered. "I didn't think of it, either."

Finn barked a laugh. "It will take centuries for you to learn how to hunt an Aos Si. Don't beat yourself up. Most of us who are more powerful can hide for decades. It's why Cal has been so hard to find. But I let you find me when you needed me. Every time you've left the manor, I've been close by. And when you were tucked in bed, I was below you, listening to you snore. It sounded like sleeping beside the Sluagh."

"Asshole," I replied and winked.

"You owe me a cabin," he replied.

"Put it on Zephyr's tab," I replied.

The other half of the shadows rolled back into the room and joined their brethren. "Cal is in the Golden Court, near the coast. We could feel the same energy that created the island wards. He is hiding someone. The Mages we seek are close by."

"Let's go hunting," Finn said. He stood with an ear-to-ear grin as if it were Christmas morning and he was getting a pony.

"Dead or alive?" I asked.

"He doesn't get to see another sunrise, Perdi. After we're done with him, he's dead," he replied. "We don't have dungeons here. It is the way of the Aos Si. It is the way of the Dark Courts."

"It is the way of Elphame," I replied.

* * * *

I staggered into the dining room, cleaning blood from my nose with my sleeve and picking twigs from my hair. I leaned against the wall and gripped my nose, twisting it until I could breathe again. The shadows inched across the room slowly, drained of energy. They flowed out of the back window and into the garden, where they'd eat the extra power from the soul garden I had collected. Those in the room stared in surprise.

Zeno stood from the table. His eyes widened, and his mouth fell open. "Are you all right, Perdi?"

I nodded and motioned behind me. "I had a slight accident."

Finn stepped into the room, dragging a potato sack behind him, not a single scratch on his body. "*Slight*? That's one way to put it. But it certainly was the highlight of my evening."

"What the hell happened?" Lily asked. "Did Finn do that?"

"Not me. This was all Perdi." Finn laughed. "She fell out of a tree and hit every branch on her way down, landing on her face."

"Why were you in a tree?" she asked.

"I was waiting for Finn to smoke out a Mage. He told me to take cover, in case the Mage used his magick. I climbed up to get a better view of what was going on and fell," I replied. "I landed on the Mage and hit my nose on the back of his head."

Finn hauled the sack to the middle of the room. "He's unconscious, a few broken bones from a Crow assault, but he'll live."

"For now," I replied. "Solas was clear on this. The Mages don't make it out of Elphame alive. If they live, they'll keep hunting me."

"Your nose isn't straight. Take a deep breath." Finn stood in front of me and gripped my nose. The grinding of bone on bone made me gag. He glanced back to the room. "It took us less than an hour to find one. What the hell have you guys been doing these last few days?"

"Keeping Perdi from knowing you were in Zephyr's bedroom," Aeden replied. "You're welcome."

I glared at Aeden. "You knew?"

He nodded. "Yes. We all did, and we also know about your sneaking around with each other, hunting someone together. No one said it out loud, since we, too, didn't know who we could trust."

"Finn is the only one who can help you if you lose control of your Finis abilities," Zeno added. "I wasn't going to risk you eating our people during a temper tantrum, so I kept my mouth shut and was thankful he was sleeping below you and not me."

Finn shrugged. "I don't know why they put their faith in me. I'd rather watch it all burn with you over stopping you from setting the fire."

"You're uncomfortable to be friends with," I replied.

He grinned. "As are you, little Crow."

The shadows returned, filled with new energy, and spat Cal onto the floor. He wasn't dead yet. I nudged him with my foot and got a groan back. "Zeno, Cal here has a few things he needs to get off his chest before the sun rises."

Zeno frowned. "What's happened?"

Finn vibrated beside me. The pressure in the room increased, making my ears pop. He couldn't bring himself to look at his fellow Aos Si. "Where do I start? He's a Solene sympathizer and has been selling our secrets since stepping foot in the Aos Si. When Solene died, he began plotting against the throne. While on duty at the Gate, he allowed the Mages into Elphame. He accepted payment, knowing why they were coming. He knew our family would be taken, and he did nothing to stop it from happening. He knew Perdi was being lured and agreed to help ensure she went to the island. He's been tracking Perdi and me since we got back," Finn explained. "He's been in contact with the Mages since the beginning. He had them weaken the wards just enough for her to break them and trap us there the first time. The island was a one-way trip. We all were to die on that island. If it weren't for Zephyr, we'd all be trapped there or worse, Perdi would have broken the spell for us to leave and would be dead. When we returned from the island, Cal has been trying to get Perdi alone to finish the job. He's been hunting her day and night but hasn't found her without me, the shadows or one of you. Knowing we'd return to the island, he hid one of the Mages to trap us when we went again."

I cringed at the memory of Finn forcing Cal to admit his traitorous ways when we had trapped him in his hole in the ground. When we found him, he was surprised and filled his dirt hovel with enough power for me to feel like I was being boiled alive. Finn hadn't flinched but did laugh. I don't know what was more uncomfortable, that Finn had suffered worse and the boiling hadn't bothered him or that he had laughed at it. Finn grabbed on to Cal, and the blistering heat stopped in an instant. Minutes later, Cal was unconscious, broken and bloodied from Finn's wrath, and we were out chasing down a Mage. With Cal down and out, the Mages were no longer warded by Cal. Picking one off was easy enough.

"You will die for this!" Aeden's scream rattled in my chest. He blasted through the room and grabbed Cal off the floor. In a blink, he was gone from the house.

"Where's he taking Cal?" I asked.

"To carry out his sentence," Zeno replied. "He is your Royal Guard. It will be up to him to take Cal's life."

"Oh," I whispered. "I didn't ask Aeden to do that. I would have done it."

"You wouldn't have been able to stop him," Finn replied. "It is his duty. If he didn't, the rest of us would fight over who got to do it. This way is faster and cleaner."

"What about the others?" I asked.

"Others?" Zeno asked.

Finn pulled a slip of paper from his pocket and handed it to Zeno. "Here's every name we could pull from his mind, mortal and Fae. Cal has rounded up a lot of support over these last few months—those without oaths and those close to the throne."

"We'll clean house," Zeno replied and eyed the list.

Lily peered from over Zeno's shoulder and grinned. "My, my, Zeno, you certainly have a messy house. Most of these names are Aos Si or friends of your ragtag crew."

"This coming from Blood and Bones? That's rich," he asked but winked playfully. "This will be dealt with before the sun kisses our hills again."

"Now what?" I motioned to the sack on the floor.

"Now that we know who helped and they're out of our way, we go back to the island. The Sluagh will know what to hunt, once we're done with the Mage. They'll track them while we're searching the island," Zeno replied. "It'll be harder this time. If they weakened the wards the first time to allow us onto the island, it will pack one hell of a punch this time around."

"I should add, Theo is still camped out on the shores." Oisin moved from the table. I hadn't noticed him when I'd first walked in. "He and his men haven't left. I don't think we'll get away with not hauling them with us again. I don't know what part he's played in this, but I think it would be wise to consider him an enemy to the Unseelie courts."

"I have bigger problems than Theo, but I agree with you. He is an enemy of our courts," I replied. "If he wants to come, let him suffer the same fate as the rest of us. I'm not leaving that island without my family, and I'll use his body to beat down the door to get to them if I need to."

"When do we leave?" Faolan stepped into the room. He smelled like he had just come from Winter Court. I smiled the moment the smell of Christmas filled my lungs. "I offer not because of our treaty but as your friend and a friend of the Dark Court."

"Now," I answered. I appreciated Faolan's offer to help me again. I turned back to the others and waited for someone to object. "Unless any of you have a problem with that?"

Lily raised her hand. "Perdi, I know you don't want any of my suggestions, but…"

"It's okay, Lily. I don't blame you for any of this."

She nodded. Although she kept her face neutral, her shoulders visibly relaxed. We all carried guilt for what happened the first time we went to the island, each for their own reasons and actions. But I felt like what we were all feeling, the uncertainty and guilt, was but a drop in the bucket. When we went for a second time, we would leave with new nightmares and better reasons to want to fade into the shadows. We'd come home with shame and regret and fresh blood on our hands.

"I recommend you take the trainees and leave the ranked Aos Si," Lily said. Her words cut through the silence like a knife. "With the mortal world the way it is, there may be a war. If you don't want us slaughtering your people, we need enough manpower to send them back with bruises rather than missing limbs. Although you don't believe the Seelie courts will wage war, I'm not nearly as trusting. If both were to come at once, we'd have to call the full-ranking Aos Si back from the island. I don't want to call your rescue to a halt because we didn't plan accordingly. And, to be blunt, I still believe the trainees are who you need to have beside you. I can't explain it, Perdi, but I'm telling you that you need to keep them close to you. Those relationships are how you will stay alive, not just today but in the long term. They are where you'll find support when you didn't even know you needed it."

"I don't like that idea," Zeno said. "If you'd had us ranked members with you the first time…"

"We'd still be standing here, having this conversation, after I tormented you instead of Finn." I interrupted him. "It wouldn't have mattered who I had with me the first time. Zephyr would have used you as he used Finn. I'm not leaving here without them."

Zeno frowned and finally nodded. "If things start going south, you'll call on us, and we'll rain fire down on them."

"It went south weeks ago, Zeno. We just didn't notice," I replied. "Okay, boys, go home, grab your gear, kiss your family if you have one and meet me at the island in one hour. Let's hope I don't fry my brain."

"It wouldn't be the first time, and it won't be the last. You're a Soul-Eater, with shadows, and you still fell out of a bloody tree," Finn added on his way to the table for food.

"I can't really argue with that," I replied and left to prepare for another trip into possible war. This time, I had my bag packed and was ready for this very moment. My hands shook, and my stomach twisted. I closed my eyes. Although my family couldn't hear me from here, I still whispered to them. "I'm coming. Just hold on a little longer."

The shadows rolled through the room and twisted around my legs as I paced. "They'll hold on, Perdi. Nix will keep them going. He's utterly fearless and puts his heart and soul into believing in you. He will be the last to give up his faith in you."

"I hope you're right."

"Let go of the anger. Let go of your need for revenge. Focus on keeping your lands safe, your people safer and our family safest," they replied. "Are you ready to break yourself in half to bring them home?"

"Yes," I answered and pulled my bag onto my back. Feeling a little taller than I was just moments ago. "It's time to burn lands and eat worlds."

Chapter Five

I opened my eyes and closed them just as quickly. My brain sloshed around in my skull with each movement. My head pounded to the same drumming in my chest. I groaned and tried to turn onto my side. The motion brought my last meal to my throat. My stomach churned, and my mouth watered with the need to be sick. A groan escaped my lips. Even that small protest hurt. My throat was raw, as though I had screamed it to the point of chapping. Every muscle was tense and sore…and exhausted. The smell of Christmas filled my nose, and I knew it was Faolan holding me. My warning came out as a gurgle, but it was enough for him to lean my head to the side, and I was sick.

"It's okay, Perdi," Faolan whispered.

I groaned as the feeling in my body shifted from heaviness to pins and needles. I could taste blood and earth. The insides of my cheeks were chewed to bits. My tongue felt like I had rolled a lump of hot coal around on it.

"What…happened?" I asked.

"You don't remember?" He asked.

"No. I was standing in my bedroom, getting ready, talking to the shadows—and now everything hurts," I answered.

"Give yourself some time for it to come back," he replied. "Your mind and body have been through a lot."

"Did I work a spell?" I asked. "This feels like I paid a debt for magick."

"No spells," he answered. "But it did take far too much power to break the wards."

I slowly opened my eyes to swirls of light that smelled of campfire. I was sick again. "Nothing good ever comes from waking up inside a cave."

Faolan helped me slowly sit upright and gave me a jug of water to clean my mouth. "We're on the island."

"I don't remember any of it," I replied, but still smiled at the knowledge that I had made it back, somewhat in one piece.

"That's probably because you damn near died, Perdi. When we got to the beach, Finn held down the Mage, and you read him. You needed much more energy than we had thought. The Aos Si had to give you a steady flow of power to break the wards. Jare held on to you to ensure you wouldn't cook your mind in the process. When the wards came down, it killed the Mage and stopped your heart. You were thrown across the beach and into the trees. It took Jare and the Seers to bring you back."

"How'd I get here?" I asked.

"Finn," Faolan replied. "He didn't let us so much as clean the blood off your face. He tossed you on his shoulder, called the shadows and brought you to the island before anyone could suggest otherwise. Finn's nervous Zephyr will use one of the other trainees to send you home and is questioning every decision made until you're fully awake. You've been in and out of consciousness since last night. Don't worry. Finn stayed with you while the rest of us scouted the island during the day."

"Where are the shadows now?" I asked. "Are they okay? Did they find those we left behind?"

"We're right here, Perdi," they answered and rolled across the rock floor. "We found the others as soon as we got here."

As soon as the shadows touched my legs, the cramping in my body calmed down, and the gaps in memories eased back in. They flowed, like reading a book, rather than a flood of information that came like a punch. I breathed through the disorientation and allowed them to give me back what I had lost when I was thrown into the trees twenty feet from where I had been. I remembered the pain and desperation when I knew I'd die for the island but held on anyway. I had told myself that even if I died, the others would be able to get to the island and save my family. The moment I was thrown and my heart gave its last thump, I smiled. Life or death, I would still win.

"Well, that's not one of my better days," I said. "But also, not one of my worst."

"You and Cas are on the first watch." Finn came into the cave with his gear, dropped it by the fire and motioned at Faolan. "The shadows, me, you and Oisin are on Perdi duty. We're the only ones without oaths to Zephyr or Solas. We can pull her out of her dreams without suffering too much for it."

Faolan stood and stretched out his back. "Get some rest, Perdi. Tomorrow, we will teach you how to hunt."

"I can hunt," I replied.

"Uh-huh, then why am I still alive?" Finn asked, back to his usual cocky self. The Finn I got to see in private was not the Finn everyone else saw. No one stayed above ground for too long in Elphame by showing the world their vulnerabilities and cares.

"If you had been a better Aos Si, a little Crow wouldn't have had to take pity on you and let you live," I answered.

"In your dreams." Finn glanced over with a playful smirk.

"I don't think you want to hear what I've been dreaming of doing to you," I replied.

Faolan chuckled. "Good night."

"Thank you, Fao," I replied and curled into my sleeping bag.

"I wouldn't tell the others you've been dreaming of me. It'll make them jealous," Finn joked as he unrolled his bed and climbed in. "If anything happens, I've got your back, Perdi. I won't let Zephyr send you home again. You have my word. Even if it is just me and you left on this island, I won't let you go."

"If it's life or death for you, let it happen. We'll come back as many times as it takes," I replied. "Don't die to keep me here."

He glanced over once and smiled. "You're a better person than I am. I'd let you die to save my family."

"I hope you can still say that about me when we get home," I replied. "Good night, Finn."

"Good night, little Crow," he answered.

Aeden checked on me once before going to bed outside. The room grew darker as exhaustion sucked me back under. As I drifted to sleep, Finn's hand rested on my ankle, ready to pull me from my dream if needed. The shadows blanketed me and filled my lungs with the familiar scent of home. As they had before, they replayed memories not of my own and coated me in smells from places I had never seen. I fell asleep to the scent of strawberries and the memory of Zephyr. Now that I was back on the island, the anxiousness that plagued my mind had settled.

"Little Crow." Zephyr looked up from a stone wall. "I have done everything I can to keep this from you, and you come back? Why did you not listen to me?"

"I never listen. Why does that continue to surprise you?" I asked.

Solas breathed me in from beside Zephyr and smiled. "She is not yours to command, Zephyr. I don't know why you continue to try."

"Hello there." I smiled. Relief filled my chest and calmed the knots in my stomach. Solas' voice washed away the layers of fear and sadness that had dirtied my soul. "How many times do I have to come to this island to rescue you?"

"Twice should do it," Solas replied. "What took you so long?"

"The usual. I've been gallivanting around all night, smoking out Aos Si traitors and keeping the mortal world from dying on Elphame soil," I replied.

"Aos Si traitors?" Solas asked. "This keeps getting better and better."

"You guys have been getting lazy if it took a wee Crow to find moles in our court," I teased. "I want a raise. This promotion doesn't come with many perks."

"I'll show you perks when we get home," Solas answered.

Before I could comment, I felt a slight tug against my pearl and smirked. "Not so fast, Soul-Eater. You can't get rid of me that easily."

Zephyr pushed against my dream and groaned. "I see you have Finn with you. I thought he'd be dead by now."

"You and I are going to have a very long chat about this, Zeph, when I get you home. And I will, Zeph, bring you all home," I replied. "Don't make me hurt your people to save my family. Do not make me do things to your men that I'll regret later. But trust me when I tell you that I'll do horrible things to stay here. Your wanting to protect me is not as strong as my need to bring my family home."

Zephyr shook his head. "You never learn."

"Neither do you," I countered. "And, since we're on the topic of Finn. You owe him a cabin. I set it on fire with him inside of it. I'll do the same to this island if I must. One way or another, we all go home together. You can either make it hard for me, or you can accept that this is the choice I make for myself."

"I do enjoy your fires." Solas looked into the room and wiggled his eyebrows. "See you soon, little Crow. We have company, and it would be rude not to entertain them."

"Wait," I said. "Let me feel them. Please. If I can feel them, we can track them. Do not push me out yet."

"They'll feel you," Solas answered. "Are you ready to be hunted?"

"I was born to be hunted," I replied.

"Scorch it all. Take no chances this time," Solas said. "Set it all to burn when it is time. They pay for what they've done to our people. No one takes from the Dark Courts and lives to tell the tale."

I nodded. "I hope the flames find you last."

"Close your eyes, little Crow," Zephyr said. "If you're not going to listen to anything else, please shut your eyes for this. It is not something I wish you to remember. There's no reason for us all to have this memory. You'll have enough reasons for nightmares, so do not add to them if you don't have to."

I shut my eyes and waited. The shadows pressed against the glass, drinking down the energy in the air, tasting and remembering. I could finally feel the Satyr as they crossed into the room. The energy pulsed through my chest and reminded me of every time I've stood on the brink of decisions. It felt almost desperate, yet lacked empathy. They would do what they needed to do, to get what they wanted, at the expense of any who stood in their way. I knew that approach well. I cycled between running from the monsters and trying to be the bigger one. And with my family on the other side of the wards, I knew I could be the biggest monster on the island. It should have bothered me more to know who I could become to win…but it didn't.

The magick holding my people was familiar in several ways. It smelled of the Mage we had captured but also of mortal blood. They not only built the wards that protected the island but also helped build the very dungeon my people sat in. I breathed the energy in and focused on the power behind the spells. I felt the anger, hate and fear flowing through each line, holding the magick together. Beneath the emotion, I felt the stain from several touches. It had taken many to build, which is why it almost killed me to break. To get into that room, to rescue my family, I would have to break several spells at once. It didn't feel greater than the wards hiding the island, but breaking this spell would leave me as vulnerable as it had when we came here the second time. I couldn't fight if I was clinging to life again.

When Solas and Zephyr laughed, I pulled back from the dream. I didn't hold on this time. I didn't want to see what would come next and knew it would hurt them more that I saw. I woke in the cave and turned onto my back, but I didn't cry. The shadows twisted over and over, swirling and dripping mist like tears. I could feel their anger.

"You need to warn Lily." I finally said to the shadows. "Mortals and Mages, on Elphame soil."

"There is one thing you've not yet questioned. Mortals were granted safe passage into Elphame by Cal, but who in Elphame collected them once they were here? Whether this was their first time coming or not, who helped them with their Fae sickness? Who housed them? Who brought them to the Satyr?"

"Good point, and I have a few guesses," I replied. "Go let Lily know, please. Whoever helped them suffers the same fate as those who did the act."

I sent half of them to warn Lily and Zeno of what we'd felt in the dream and the pending questions. Those who had stood against us were likely still in Elphame. And like the rest of our enemies, they would die on the same soil. I climbed out of the cave. Finn was still asleep but no longer dead to the world. As I moved from the back of the cave, I heard his breathing change, lifting his awareness up to follow me. I sent the other half of the shadows to keep a watchful eye on Theo and those who would go bump in the night. Outside, I stretched my chilled muscles and plotted my next moves. I stocked the fire in my stomach and would wait until I found those I'd set it loose upon. Soon, I'd find my family and the world would tremble at my anger. I'd let it all out, all my worry, pain and fear. I'd let it burn the island to ruin. Any who stood in my way would fall. That was the way of Elphame, the only way to survive this land.

"Can't sleep?" Faolan stepped from the edge of the tree line. I wouldn't have known he was there if he hadn't spoken.

"Wear a bell or something. I didn't even smell you." I smiled, then shook my head. "Dreams."

"Drink?" he asked, pulled a small canteen from his pocket and passed it over. "Your mind is miles away. That's why you didn't feel me here."

I took a sip and swallowed hard. It burned like fire. "Bloody hell, what is that?"

"It is made from potatoes," he replied.

"One more reason to dislike potatoes." I coughed. "It goes down like boiling hot razor blades."

"Do you need me to get you anything?"

"No, but thank you. I just couldn't sleep," I answered. I glanced over at the men and smiled. They were tucked tightly together, each one watching over the next. I knew not all of them were fully asleep. One word from me would have brought them wide awake and running for war as they cleaned the sleep from their eyes. "I'd have given anything to have friends like this growing up. Life would have been a lot easier to have someone at my back. Elphame would be a hell of a lot less scary if I had more friends."

"You can still have it," Faolan replied. "We live far too long to not have friends."

I shrugged. "Easier said than done. I'm not exactly skilled in this area."

"I heard your conversation with Aeden the last time we were here. You questioned why the others didn't talk to you as he did. May I suggest, if you want to make friends, you behave like a friend would first? Maybe don't send them away so quickly? As you navigate how to get closer to them, they're doing the same with you." His smile caught in the moonlight and reminded me of the many nights we had spent talking about the little things that mattered most. I missed those days, before war, before death. I didn't regret becoming a Crow, but I would rather not have the memories of becoming one.

"They don't strike me as wanting to be all that close to a Crow," I replied.

"If you were only a Crow, they'd have been in the cave with you. But you're a queen—and not just any queen. You stand between the greatest powers of Elphame, Solas and Zephyr. You sit on the throne of nightmares and death. You have surrounded yourself with those who would take lives for you without question. Wouldn't you be hesitant where you stepped or what you said, when standing in front of someone who could end your very existence?" he asked, and I nodded. "I know it's important to you to be accepted. But it really is life or death for those who do not sit on the throne. One wrong move by you, and all is forgiven. One wrong move by them, and it could mean their life. It's a dangerous position to ask them to willingly stand in."

"Fair point. I didn't think of the consequences of being my friend," I replied. Although I wouldn't take their lives, I knew they'd suffer at the hands of Zephyr and Solas, and nothing I could say or do could stop them. "I'd try to protect them, even if I couldn't do much more than suffer with them. And before you call me a bleeding heart, I know. But for those you care about, you should be willing to bleed for them."

"You'll get no argument from me on that one. It's one of your better qualities and why they chose to follow you. You'll suffer with and for them. You're willing to bleed for them, yet, you still haven't asked all of them what their names are. I have never seen you sit with them. You hover on the outskirts, removed from them. You don't interact with them outside of war talk and updates. Aside from a few, you don't even know what magicks each of them are. The last time we were here, you only interacted with them to keep driving them forward. Back home, you hunted their brother and demanded answers. Those are not acts of someone who wants to earn their friendships."

"I don't even know where to start," I answered.

"How about you try to get to know them? That's usually where people begin."

"I think I'm scared," I answered.

"Of what?"

"I'm scared of being rejected. I know it sounds very childish, but I didn't have friends growing up because I wasn't mortal enough. Halflings didn't stick together because we died too quickly to form bonds. And here, I feel like I'm not Fae enough. Rejection is hard to overcome. Somehow, it feels much worse than anything else I could face here. It feels like I'm not good enough."

"That's the risk you take when you try to get close to someone. Do you want friends who accept you as you are or those who tolerate you despite what you're not? Being vulnerable is never easy, but it's worth it, when you find others who will care. The closer you bond to them, the better your chances of surviving this realm."

"It sounds nice and simple, coming from a king, who is *Daoine Uaisle*. You are royal born, from the original Gentry. I doubt you faced much rejection in your life."

He huffed a quiet laugh. "Perdi, you rejected me repeatedly, long before you came to Elphame."

"Eventually, I didn't."

"Eventually," he replied. "But it didn't bother me because I'm used to it. Kings face more rejection than anyone else. To be close to us means a very likely death for those we love. Who the hell would willingly sign up for that?"

"It appears the same fate is mine as a queen," I answered.

"Yet, here you are, surrounded by those who will die in your place. They're not here for duty, Perdi. They're here for love," he replied. "Life will always be what you make it. Make friends when and where you can. They'll help you weather the storms. They'll make all other rejections mean little to you because you'll have them to soften the blow. If you want them to see you as more than a queen, show them who you are under that prickly new crown. Perdi, if you want to win, you need friends and family. They are the only ones who will put you back together when we're done here. You need those who will stand by your side out of love, not duty. Love pushes people into action quicker than duty ever will."

"Thank you, Fao." I could hear the others whispering behind us, and I turned. "Since we're all awake, we might as well have breakfast and pack up for the day."

A collective groan filled the forest. I turned back to Faolan and smiled.

"This is not how you make friends," Faolan laughed.

"Close enough," I answered and walked to the cave to pack. I gave an update to Aeden about my dream when he came in to complain about waking up so early. The shadows returned, and we packed up our camp within the cave. The shadows informed us that Lily would hunt down any stragglers not belonging in Elphame, and the Sluagh would hunt for the magicks we'd felt in the dream. And they'd all suffer the same fate as those who helped take my family…death.

It was always death in Elphame.

* * * *

I stood in front of the Aos Si, their eyes forward, heads high, waiting on my usual demands. The morning had started with official titles, tipping of heads, stepping back and clearing space for me, silence at my approach and eyes on the ground. The crown felt like a curse. It pushed me away from everything that mattered most to me, family, friends, love and freedom. And every time I got too close, it felt like I was taking away what they needed.

I reminded myself that they weren't tools any more than I was. They deserved to be treated like they were more than the monsters we sent to war. They were souls, and as battle worn as they were, they needed the same thing I did—love, care and reassurance. Although Lily's last comments about them echoed in my mind—that they were who I needed to survive this land—they, too, needed the same chance in a world that only took from us. They were more than a life raft. They were Zephyr's family, and I wanted to pull them all a little closer and call them my own.

Before I could do that, I'd have to be the one to extend the first branch of friendship. The problem was, I didn't know how to put it into words without sounding desperate. People skills weren't something high on my list back in Whitwick. Survival was. It wasn't worth having close relationships when those people could die the next time the Gate opened. But now, it felt as important as survival. Friendships were the very key to my survival. Family would keep me alive. They would keep me from becoming a monster who needed to be hunted and imprisoned. They'd keep me from turning into the very beast Zephyr feared I'd become.

I had spent the last week running them into the ground, making demands and ignoring anything other than the answers I was seeking. I had been the one to turn them into tools, into weapons. I had taken the easy route. Tools couldn't hurt you or deny you the care you sought. But they weren't objects for me to use. I knew what it felt like to be used and abused. Even if they saved themselves and refused to step closer to me, I'd still walk away a little lighter. I'll have offered. Even if they couldn't reciprocate, they'd know I cared.

"I'm sorry, guys. I'm nervous as hell." I swallowed what felt like a rock. Anxiety tightened my throat. My hands wouldn't stop sweating, no matter how many times I wiped them clean. "I admit, I don't know how to do this. I don't know how to be something greater than who I am or someone worthy of wearing a crown. I wasn't raised to be anything more than what you see. I literally was raised to become a Crow one day."

"And a fine Crow you've become," Oisin added and gave me an encouraging wink.

"Thank you." I smiled, yet still fought to remain calm. "I know how to be the Crow of the Dark Courts. I don't know how to be a queen or act like anything more than who I feel I am. I'm trying, but I keep hitting a brick wall. It feels scratchy. I just want to be me, the me I've always been, the me I desperately cling to. Although I'm sure it's a great honor to be queen, that is not who I am, first and foremost."

I looked at Faolan, who motioned for me to continue. "Truth, Perdi. Only the truth."

"The truth is, I'm uncomfortable being something else. It makes me feel like I'm lesser than I am, not more—like I'm pretending to be someone you need, not someone I want to be. You are Zephyr's family, and through him, you are mine. When I'm treated differently, it makes me feel like who I am doesn't matter to anyone but me. I'd like to ask that you stop treating me like a queen and treat me like a person. For you not to hold me above you, but beside you, and I will do the same."

Finn, standing in the middle, was the only one who risked a glance. The others stared straight forward or at the ground, at my feet. "Ma'am, may I ask a question?"

"I'm surprised you're even asking, Finn. But yes, please, ask away," I replied. "Also, I thought we were over this 'ma'am' business? Perdi…always."

"Old habits die hard," he replied. "But, always? Even in front of others?"

"Really, that is my preference," I answered. "My friends call me Perdi. That's the point I'm trying to make. I've been called many things here, but my name wasn't one of them because I wasn't anyone's friend. I came here as a Crow, and that's all I was. I fought to become Perdi again, to become 'little Crow' to those who love me. I can't go back. And each time I don't hear my name, it tells me that I'm not real, I'm not me and that no one sees me anymore. They see me as an object, a tool, someone not worthy of a name. When you call me by my name in private and don't do it in public, it feels like I'm not a person when others can see. When you stop talking because I've stepped too close to the group, it feels like you don't trust me with your stories and that I'm not worthy of joining in on the conversation. Perhaps, one day, being called a queen will roll off me or will become a term of endearment. But until then, I need to be Perdi."

"Very well, Perdi," Finn answered. "My question is—and I cannot speak for anyone else—but I wonder what your wish is. I don't fully understand what this talk is about? What I mean is, have we done something wrong?"

"You must be in a lot of trouble, often, for your mind to go there first, Finn," I answered.

"Nearly every day," he replied.

"No, no one is in trouble. This talk is because I would like to be included, to be part of your group. My gut tells me that we won't win if we're not in this together."

"Perdi, you lead us," Finn replied. "You are the first to lead us in the absence of Zephyr, and we choose to follow you. You are as much a part of the group as the rest of us are. Have we not been welcoming, or have we done something to make you feel like that?"

"No. What I mean is…" I started, then groaned.

"May I?" Oisin stepped forward.

"Please," I answered with begging eyes.

"Stop treating her like a queen and treat her as your friend, your family. That's what she's seeking and what she needs. The Dark Courts are not like the other courts. It is much more of a family than a court. When we stuff her in a cave and we feel her discomfort, she would prefer we invite her out of the cave until she's settled, to be with the rest of us rather than sending someone in to fix her. She can fix herself or ask for help when she can't. She is not delicate and does not wish to be treated as such. She may be a queen, but she's your family first. You wouldn't leave your sister alone in some cave. Why would you leave her? We may think we are showing her reverence, but she sees the distance, and it hurts. She gave her life to be here with us. We can at least try to make her feel it was worth it. She's asking you to care as much as she does."

I smiled. "That sums it up nicely."

"May I speak bluntly?" Finn asked.

"Do you have any other way of speaking, Finn?" I asked, and he grinned. "Of course. I may not like it or agree, but it would save a lot of time if we didn't beat around the truth."

"Thank you. Bluntly, never mind what Zephyr will do to us. We're used to his temper. What if Solas should hear of this? He's not exactly friendly or even the slightest bit understanding when it comes to you. We're not allowed to talk to you informally or be near you without a damn good reason. Hell, we can't breathe the air Solas believes you may need. He, like Zephyr, is protective of you. We're caught between a rock and the boulders of hell. And to be honest, I'd rather be beaten to death than deal with the fallout. What are we to say when he asks us why we tossed protocol in the trash? *'Because Perdi told us to'* isn't going to be a good enough reason, and we all know it. He wasn't exactly thrilled when we were drinking in the caves with you or that we brought you into Blood and Bones. We've been warned, and we only get one warning. You're asking us to spend it."

"You can send him my way," I answered. "Solas doesn't own me, and neither does Zeph."

"This is true for you, but Zephyr certainly owns my ass and will do with it as he pleases. I'm already on his shitlist. I don't need to add fuel to the fire," Finn answered. "Are you going to take my beating?"

"You can hide behind me if you'd like?" I asked. "Or you can simply tell him I ordered you all, and I'll deal with it. I'm fine with either."

Finn grinned. "I'll hide behind you. And when he beats me to death with your limp body, I won't be the only one to feel the burn of a Finis. If I suffer for this, so will you, since we're family and all. A pound of flesh for a pound of flesh."

"He must beat the snot out of you every chance he gets." I rolled my eyes.

"He does...and he will," Finn replied. "Know that what you're asking of us has consequences for us all. Some of us have too much to lose for a maybe. If you're willing to pay them with us, I'm more than happy to invite you to sit in the mud with us. But if you're not, I'll keep my head down, hope for the best and come out of this with all my limbs."

"When in war, we're in this together. When we need the formalities, we will follow your customs, and you can bow until your back breaks. And when Zephyr or Solas blow their lids, I'll come every time. I may not be able to do much to protect you, but I'll certainly be there to take it with you. Does that work?"

"Yes," Finn answered. "Out here, we are soldiers. We simply didn't think you'd wish to sit with us. Aside from Solas, you'd be the only royal who wanted to sit in the muck while we do. It'll take some time to get used to, but I'm sorry you've felt left out. That was never our intent."

"And I didn't think you'd want to sit with a Crow," I answered. "So, I never tried all that hard. I was scared I wouldn't be wanted."

"*Little Crow,*" Finn corrected me. "You are the Crow that ate the world. We're honored to be with you and to be given this chance. And I will be honored to share a meal with you, when we have to hold you down for a break later."

I laughed and felt the ease from the others roll off them. "All right. Now, next order of business… I spoke to Solas last night. I have a few things left to cover here. When we got to the shores of the Golden Court the first time, we suspected only Mages to have built the wards. We've since learned that mortals were aided by Cal. During my dream, I could feel Mages *and* mortals in the room holding our family. Together, they were here and wove the spells holding Zephyr, Solas and Nix. This begs the question, who helped nurse them back to health from Fae sickness? Whether they've been coming and going or this was their first time, someone had to help them. Someone had to collect them and house them. More than that, someone had to bring them here, to the island, to the Satyr. It wasn't the Unseelie court."

Oisin motioned his head to Theo and his men, lingering twenty feet behind. "I'll give you one guess."

I nodded. "The mortals came here to kill me, and, in the process, I think they bit off more than they could chew and ran. Now they can choke on it. I've sent word to Lily, to send the Seers and Sluagh to find them. Keep your eyes and ears open. I don't know what other wards or spells they've cast upon this island. I know for certain that the dungeons have similar wards, but that's about it. The last time we were here, Solas had told me they were being held by a few hundred Satyr. I'm guessing those numbers have increased. Solas doesn't know where they are, but the Satyr will be expecting us. I was able to feel them. I'll be able to hunt them down better now. Are you ready? I'm sorry, guys, but I'll be running you into the ground again."

They all looked me in the eyes and smiled. The very notion we were going into war excited them, as I knew it would. This is what they were built for, not tracking down kidnappers but killing them. Oisin was grinning ear to ear as though I had given him the gift of a new cave filled with unknown monsters to outrun. Faolan, like me, felt the pressure of what we were about to do. He felt the consequences of being a leader, the responsibility of decisions, not the excitement of being a soldier.

"Perdi, I'm sorry for asking this, but if this does not go as planned, what is plan B?" Faolan asked as we made our way through the trees. "The Dark Courts are known for planning. I'm hoping very much that you have one?"

"Leave," I answered plainly. "When I tell you to leave, I need you to go—not argue to stay."

He nodded. "And if you return burning, what do you want us to do?"

"If I am a ball of flames, things here did not go as planned, and I've lost my family. If that's the case, I won't return to the Dark Courts until I'm calm. The shadows will take me somewhere else until it's safe for me to return. Protect our people, Faolan. Swear to me, you'll do everything you can to protect both our courts."

"No one will touch your lands, I swear."

"They won't live long enough to do much damage. They'll be hunted down by those we keep in the shadows. But even one life lost is too many," I replied. I stopped walking and faced him. Looking him in the eyes, I saw centuries of burden looking back at me. It both hurt and gave me courage. He held his morality in a death grip while the monster within him circled like a vulture. I felt that struggle deep in my soul. "Will you try to take the Dark Courts if one of us isn't there to protect it?"

"No, *never*," he answered, a hint of surprise that I had asked edging his voice. "Solas could have taken my land several times over. He never has. And it has nothing to do with it being too cold in the Winter Courts. He is not the warmonger people think he is. He's had ample opportunity to kill me, and for good reason, but he's not tried a single time." His usual calm was eaten away by memories that made him flinch as if he could close his eyes and will them away. "After my father…" He paused and took a deep breath. "When I killed my father for his crimes, for what he did to my mother and sisters, my people and countless innocents, I lost grip on my calm. I hunted my lands for those who had acted in my father's favor. They were hideous and terrible men who deserved what I did to them. It didn't happen overnight. It took me ten days to cleanse the land of the horror that was the old king. Solas could have used that opportunity to take my throne, but he didn't. And others, who came for my crown? He stopped them before they reached my border. He never once stepped foot into my territory, and neither did anyone else. I am safe. My people are safe because he won't allow anyone to cross. The only time I've ever faced him in war is because I've been stupid enough to go. So, Perdi, your court, his court, will be taken by no one. I will not allow them to cross."

"If I don't come back, swear you will shelter them all until I return," I asked.

"I swear, Perdi, I will keep everyone safe until you return. I give you my word."

We walked silently for hours before Theo got the courage to walk by my side. He hadn't said much to me since coming back to the island. Theo had pushed his way back for a second time, and little by little, I understood why. He was nervous and scared. I wouldn't have questioned feeling those emotions on anyone else, but on him, they were misplaced. The reasons were darker than pending war.

"What will become of the Dark Court without an heir?" Theo asked. He was curious what I would do if I couldn't get Solas back, if my family died on the island. His interest was uncomfortable and insinuated outcomes that would leave me alone and unprotected.

"Heir?" I asked. "Why would the Dark Courts need an heir to rule?"

"War would certainly come if a queen were left to rule."

Aeden snorted a laugh, entertained by the little king. Whenever Theo opened his mouth, Aeden enjoyed toying with him until Theo finally regretted it enough to leave us alone again. "There will always be war. Let it come. Without the calm touch of Zephyr and the level head of Solas, imagine what my queen would do to your lands. Zephyr and Solas are the only reason you still live. She was born to burn this world, and her armies were born in the bellies of war. Were you?"

"I d-didn't s-say…" Theo stammered.

"You didn't have to. I can smell it on your skin. That is the thing about being bred for battle. We know when it's around the corner," Aeden continued, and I didn't stop him. I didn't like Theo any more than Aeden did. He breathed Theo in and scrunched his nose as if smelling something awful. "I taste your defeat, and we haven't even drawn the first line in the sand. What choices will you make, Theo?"

"I make no choices."

Aeden smiled. "That's too bad. I would like to feel the sun from your hills as I tilled your land as my own and set fire to your flowerbeds. Any act against our queen, the very heir you speak of, and I will plot my gardens from your bedroom window, with your bones as land markers."

"Get a handle on your boy, Perdi." Theo moved away quickly and bumped into Faolan as he retreated.

"You will find no allies once you cross the river." Faolan grabbed Theo's arm. "There is nothing but death for you in *all* the Unseelie courts. When it comes to protecting the Unseelie lands, we stand as one. Do *not* come, Theo. We just got the lawns looking nice again."

"You are beginning to sound like Solas." Theo pulled away.

"No. Solas is much calmer than I am. I would kill you for no other reason than you're pissing me off right now. It has nothing to do with war or land. I just don't fucking like you. You've managed to wear away at my calm in a short amount of time. You don't want to see me when I've lost my temper. I'll burn your entire kingdom to the fucking ground simply because I hate the smell of it," Faolan called out to Theo as he stormed away.

Aeden laughed. "He scares easily."

"The proud ones always do," Faolan replied and laughed with him.

Chapter Six

My Malice jerked in my stomach as my skin suddenly prickled with panic. I turned as a hot wave of emotion pushed against my back. The shadows blew through the trees like a nightmare of thick black worms in the night. They smashed into me at full force. They wrapped around my entire body, covering me in darkness, and lifted me off the ground as if I had been shoved. I was gone without them asking. My fear spiked until my feet landed on the sand on the other side of the island. I could still feel the others, but it was cloudy, like miles rested between us.

"We didn't have time to ask." They could already feel my anger about being snatched. I had always hated it when Zephyr had done it to me. "You had to see this, and we didn't want to say anything in front of Theo. You've said he cannot be trusted. We don't know how to talk to your soul yet. So, all would hear us if we spoke to you."

"Next time, just tell me if you need to talk to me in private. Don't steal me." I followed them to a hollow in the earth. Inside, bodies over bodies, tied, gagged, tortured. "What…the…hell?"

I jumped back and covered my mouth. I didn't know if I would scream, vomit or cry. Every emotion washed over me, from rage to grief to disgust. I didn't want to breathe them in, but holding my breath only made the world tilt a little more to the right. I shook my head, hoping to send the images from my mind, but I knew they'd stain my memory forever. It was odd how horror did that, stayed with you always, preserved in the goriest of detail. Later, when this was over, they'd warp and twist and distort into nightmares that weren't real. I didn't want to see them again, scared I'd give my mind more images to beat the crap out of my soul while I slept.

I forced myself to look again. It was a mass dump of bodies, not even a grave. Broken limbs and discarded parts, bloated and bruised… Some looked weeks old, rotten to the bone, bugs and worms already moved on the next. Some were fresh enough to stink of new blood, a week or so before we had gotten there they had suffered this fate. They were fresh enough that I could still see their expressions twisted and frozen on their faces. Fear, pain and prayers gone unanswered. I knew that look well.

"What happened to them?" I asked.

"We don't know." The shadows swirled around the ground.

"Who would do this?" I muttered, more to get the words out than find an answer.

"It smells of Fae, but so do the dead. We can't distinguish who has done this. There are too many smells to overcome," they answered. "And there are more bodies elsewhere, Perdi, many more that we've found. In total, well over a hundred. After scouting the island, we've found only a fraction of the dead."

"What did they die from? Someone didn't do this to them, did they? Who would do this?" I asked and shook my head. "Why would someone…?"

"They died from what you see. Some were beaten to death, some starved and some killed themselves. Each body we've looked at is like this. We believe they have died of torture."

"Torture? You're certain?" I asked.

"We have seen torture, Perdi, many times, and this is what it looks like."

"Have Zephyr or Solas ever done this to people? Is that why you've seen it?" I asked.

"No. They've never done anything like this. Neither has a use for torture, not when one can read a soul faster than this could possibly take and the other can scare the truth out of the devil. They end lives. They don't prolong them like this." I watched as they twisted in what looked like a shiver. It reminded me of when porcupines raised their quills. "We have seen the fallout of many wars. Those who did not make it home from enemy lines looked like this when they were dumped over their border or retrieved by the Aos Si."

I was relieved to hear Zephyr and Solas weren't the monsters many thought they were and disgusted this was done at all. "These men didn't drag themselves in here to die. They were put here."

"Someone killed them and hid their bodies. The Satyr bury their dead. They don't dump them. We have found graves marked with names and shells, cordoned off from the rest of the island. A place to grieve. They honor their dead. They wouldn't have done this. It is why we brought you here. The Satyr are not the only ones hunting on this island. If whoever did this is still here, you're in more danger than we first thought. But more than that, how could they come and go, on this island, with the wards in place? They were either here before the wards or are still here. This is not the work of Mages. They'd never corrupt their souls with this type of dark magick. And it wasn't mortals. They're simply not strong enough to kill this many Fae with brutal force. One, perhaps, but not over a hundred."

"Take me back, please," I asked, if only to escape the stench.

On my return, the others were setting up camp. I glared at Aeden, who had used this opportunity to stop for the night without having to listen to me complain about it. They had moved quickly, knowing I'd have tried to make them pack it back up. I motioned for Aeden to follow me into a shallow cave, where I saw my gear sitting and a small fire already burning. I sent shadows to inform Faolan of what we'd found. Faolan would know how to spread the message around to our men without Theo hearing. In the back of the cave, I told Aeden what the shadows had found.

After Aeden got over the shock of it, he was speechless. We both sat in complete silence, trying to find something worth saying. Whether the Satyr had my family or not, what had been done to them was beyond belief, beyond punishment of this sort. Even in my most profound hate for those who had taken my people, this was outside of what my rage would be willing to do. Torture was not something my soul could ever consider.

"Jayde would know what happened," he finally spoke.

"Who is Jayde?" I asked, surprised. I hadn't heard that name before.

"Sorry, I forgot myself." He jerked as if I had scolded him. "We're not here to talk about our personal lives. We're here for war. We leave everything else behind, so we have something to return to." It sounded like he was parroting what he had been told several times.

"It's okay. It's actually kind of nice to talk about something other than war. Any other time I ask someone a question that has nothing to do with why we're here, they just sort of blink at me as if they didn't understand," I replied. "And it's not like my bleeding heart hasn't soaked you all a few times by now."

"It's how we're trained. But some of us want more than war."

"Are you one of those people?" I asked.

"Now, yes. Very much. I will always be Aos Si, even long after I'm gone from the ranks. But Zephyr allows life outside of Aos Si. He encourages it. He believes it's hard to fight in a war when you have nothing to fight for and nothing to lose. We just don't talk about it. It really is easier to face the viciousness of war when we leave the softer parts of ourselves behind."

"I can understand that. But I also believe the softer parts of us are what keep us from doing the unspeakable. Some things aren't worth doing, not even to stay alive," I answered, then prompted him again. "Who is Jayde? Just for tonight, let's let the light in a little. I need a bit of home right now, after what I've seen. I don't have enough war under my belt to muster like everyone else. And truthfully, I don't think I ever want to feel at ease with war and death."

"I hope you never do, Perdi." He answered. "Jayde is my oathed partner of...wow, I can't even remember. I'll deny ever saying that, so you know."

"I'll never tell a soul. Days seem to bleed into decades around here." I laughed. "You said something about knowing what happened? How?"

"Jayde... He can feel impressions left behind, kind of like, I don't know what would be similar in the mortal world? Almost like what you are."

"A witch?" I asked and smiled.

"Close enough, for the sake of me butchering this with information that I don't really understand myself. Jayde is empathic, with a little more. He can taste memories left behind—feel them, see them, touch them. Nothing like you or Zephyr, but Jayde has a way with emotions and memories. He can sense things that others can't. He can see the truth in a memory, like being able to see a dream and know what parts are real and what's fear. He can see the imprints left behind. If he were here, he'd know exactly what happened, as though he had been there and watched it happen."

"What a horrible skill to have," I answered. "To see nightmares with perfect clarity."

"Nightmares only haunt the keepers of the memories. He has almost perfect control, unless there is war. Too many wild emotions...and he feels them all. During war, he stays with the Sluagh. It's hard for any emotion to make it all the way to the caves," Aeden replied. "For this, if we had warned him ahead of time, he'd have been prepared, and it wouldn't be as it was for you, a sudden assault on your heart and mind. He'd have been able to tell you who was responsible, if he had met them before."

"Sounds like we should have brought him with us."

"I thought about it, but love makes you stop thinking of the greater good and start thinking of what you would do if you lost them. He could have sensed what had happened here and given us a heads-up, but I couldn't bring myself to ask him or risk his life. He's not of this world, not like we are."

"I felt that one in my soul, the drive to protect those you love most," I answered. "Solas feels that, I think, every time I do something crazy."

"That I would not agree with. Solas is a different breed altogether. He feels pride when you stand in the face of danger and don't flinch. It is why you are both so good together. Your softer parts are protected by the rougher sides of each other. If Jayde were here, I'd be losing my mind. Solas, on the other hand, would clap and dare the world to try its best to stop you. I've seen him watch you go toe-to-toe with Zephyr. The first time you met, Solas clapped and told Zephyr to figure it out on his own. From the first day you came, he's known you can protect yourself. His face literally lights up with pride the moment your temper flares."

"I scare him, trust me. He fears a lot of the choices I make."

"Fear is different. It isn't based on reality, not really. We all fear many things, but that doesn't mean Solas doesn't get a thrill from seeing you charge into a battle, ready to eat the souls of anyone who passes."

I cringed. I was still ashamed of every pearl I had taken and trapped. "Who told you I would do something like that?"

"No one. But, Perdi, we've spent entire lifetimes with a Soul-Eater. We have lived and breathed his energy. We know it when we see it. And we've seen you do it plenty of times."

"Do the others know?" I asked.

"Yes. Your back garden is filled with shadows. And since they're not trailing behind Zephyr, we knew the only other person who could have made them was you. Zephyr has not confirmed it, but there's been no reason for us to ask what we already know," he answered, then smiled. "I can see the thoughts fly across your face and the uncertainty of which questions you want answers to."

"I didn't mean to do it…trap the souls," I answered, embarrassed.

"I know. I see your shame, even now."

"Does it scare you what I am?" I asked. Although others fearing me had been a benefit, I never wanted to step into a room and have people move away from me. I saw that happen with Solas and Zephyr. Although they didn't flinch at it, I saw that it hurt them a little, each time it happened.

"It would if my soul was on the menu. But no, not generally. I respect who you are and hurt for all you've had to become. War is a cruel bitch and bends us all to her will. But you fought back and held on to who you are deep inside. You didn't let the cruelty of this world force you into becoming a monster. You are the last Crow, and you did that, Perdi, against all odds. Be proud of who you are. It's the only thing that can't be taken from you. Your enemies can take your life, your love, your faith and your home. But they will never take who you are. No one has that power, not even fate."

"You remind me a lot of Zeph."

"To hear you say that is the greatest compliment."

"Whatever happens, Aeden, whatever we find, swear to me you will protect the one who needs the most protection, whether it is Solas, Zephyr or Nix."

"What about you?" he asked.

"Never mind me. If we get to the point where you must choose, do *not* pick me over my family."

"But you'd still be alive, even if you hated me."

"You do not want me to hate you," I pointed out. "Finn wasn't a fan of it."

"Even if your hate took my life, you'd still be alive. I'm sorry, but I cannot make that agreement. That is not who I am, and I couldn't live with that decision. Like you, I can't be forced into doing something that will stain my soul."

"I appreciate that you're being honest and didn't make some agreement and break it."

"I'd never do that. You'll always get honesty from me, even when you don't like it."

"Okay, how about this? If I can still fight, you will protect the others. You will not sacrifice their lives for mine unless it must be done."

He nodded. "I will not sacrifice them unless I must. In return, you will not try to bind me to choose what I can and can't live with. At the end of the day, I have to be able to live with my choices, not you."

"Deal." I finally agreed and understood his position. I had made many decisions I wished I had never made and had to live with every one of them. I didn't want to force that on him.

"This was a very uncomfortable conversation. I can see why Zephyr returns from you frustrated."

I grinned. "You have no idea how stubborn I can be."

"I have a pretty good idea. Jayde is as stubborn, and by God, I've wanted to drive my own head into a wall every time he digs his heels in." Aeden smiled at the very mention of his partner. "But it's worth it all."

"Why are you here, Aeden? And not at home with Jayde? If I had a choice, I'd be home with Solas," I asked. "When you speak of Jayde, your eyes light up, and your body relaxes. Any other time, you're tense and on edge. Sometimes, standing next to you is uncomfortable. But right now, your energy is soft and inviting."

"I'm here because I want to be. I want to be of service to you and your family. I want to bring our people home. But too many years of this, Perdi? It wears and shows in ways that tire me out. When I think of Jayde, it offers me solace. He reminds me of why I am here and willing to sacrifice—family, love, the future."

"If you could be anywhere else, doing something entirely different, what would it be?" I asked. "It can be any dream. Sometimes, it's those dreams that bring us home. In a perfect world, where would you be?"

He smiled and relaxed into the dreams he held on to, as we all did when thinking of the perfect life we wished for. "Jayde and I always wanted a chunk of land and a massive house. One of those houses where when you walk up the path, your first thought would be how utterly ridiculous and excessive it is...something even kings would think is garish and extreme. And we'd fill the land with animals and gardens and ponds and creeks. And the overly excessive house would be filled with children with nowhere else to go. All you'd ever hear, as soon as you stepped foot on our land, would be laughter, joy and happy screaming from children who wouldn't have had another chance in this world. We'd fill the yard and every room with happiness, and they'd only ever feel cared for and not the harsh hand of Elphame. We could teach them of love again and how to live in a world that yearns for blood and death.

If I could make any dream real, that would be it. And that would be where I would spend my days. Jayde and me, away from wars and courts and the risk that one of us wouldn't come home that day, living out eternity, making sure others were given a fair chance. Whenever I feel the world pressing down on me and I'm away from home, that's where my mind goes."

"That is a damn fine dream." I could almost picture it in the back of my mind. Hints of laughter and love wrapped around my heart and warmed every inch of me. "Why haven't you done that yet?"

"Fear, I suppose. Aos Si is all I've ever known."

"You may be scared of that dream but think of how much scarier it would be to come to your very last breath and realize you've not lived it. But, if you arrived at your last day, surrounded by all those you had given a new beginning to, imagine how soft that death would be, how full your heart would feel. Easing into your final moments sounds like a much better way to go than fighting for another step. War isn't pointless, but the death it causes very much is. And you, Aeden, are meant for giving life, not taking it," I answered. "Don't take this the wrong way, but I hope one day you're just not here anymore. I hope I wake up and you're gone, and I hear of how many children are loved because of you and Jayde. I hope I find you again, chasing children through your fields rather than chasing war."

"I think that's the kindest thing anyone has ever said to me."

"You're more than war," I answered. "You're the peace that comes after."

"Speaking of war, what do we do about the bodies?" he asked, then laughed at his poor segue. "Sorry…

There's no way of moving from the topic of peace to war. It always comes out brash."

"I don't know. I think we need to be careful. Whatever is out there hunting the Satyr is likely also hunting us." I cringed at the memory of twisted bodies piled over each other. "Keep everyone a little closer tonight, and pay special attention to Theo. Every time I look at him, I dislike him for new reasons. Tonight, just the thought of him makes my skin want to crawl off."

"That he offends your very skin is reason enough to kill him," he answered, then smiled. "It's just a suggestion until you ask for his life. Then I'll gladly deliver."

"And you say my topics are uncomfortable," I laughed. "No wonder Zephyr never dumped me with you guys alone. You have too many ideas I like and he'd hate."

Chapter Seven

Our break would last exactly twenty minutes. I was assured by Aeden that it would not be a minute longer. My legs didn't protest like my soul did at the needed stop, and I slumped against a tree with my eyes closed. The swooshing of my pulse in my ears was replaced with soft voices, the crunching of apples, the faintest bird songs and small critters scurrying to get as far away from us as possible without swimming to a new shore. At the farthest reaches, the ocean lapped the land. It was the only thing that didn't care we were there.

I ate my lunch while the shadows returned to Elphame to scout for any issues and check on the progress of hunting Mages and mortals. Having them out there didn't sit right and ate at my mind like a task unfinished. And as much as I didn't like killing those who had done this, I'd sleep better knowing they were dead. That ordering their death came easily was about the only guilt I'd feel for their demise. The regret I'd feel had nothing to do with their worth and everything to do with my desperate grip on my humanity. Little by little, I shaved it off and told myself it was for a good reason. The pain of it told me I had lied to myself each time.

I smelled Faolan before he got to me. The smell was strong and spicy, like Christmas and winter and candy, all rolled into a tiny ball. It made me stop to think of the times I had met with Faolan in secret, only to return to the manor. Solas would have known just by the smell. The entire time I sneaked around, I had worried that someone would tell him when I had carried the evidence home on my flesh. I could see why no one could keep a secret in Elphame.

"Faolan, what do I smell like?" I asked.

He leaned against the tree above me and grinned at the odd question. "Sweat. Dirt. You smell like the rest of us."

"No, I mean, you smell like winter, like Christmas, like mint and candy I can actually stomach. What do I smell like to you?"

"You smell of home, the Dark Courts and more." He breathed me into the bottom of his lungs and smiled. "You smell of magick, like the air before lightning strikes. You smell of Solas and Zephyr in that way. But under all of that, you smell like home, like the good parts of home. You smell like crawling into bed, hugging a loved one—or if laughter had a smell, it would be you. You smell a little like my mother, like a fresh breeze, and like apples and lavender."

"That's a lot of things to smell like at once." I laughed. "Do I smell the same to everyone?"

"The energy part, yes. It pricks the back of our minds and tells us to back up, lest we wish to be struck down by lightning. Zephyr smells the same as you, only stronger. Smelling him on you is what makes most of us think twice about approaching you." He breathed in again, and his body visibly relaxed. "The home smell, no… It's not the same for everyone. That's a personal attachment I give to what I smell, sort of like how you smell Christmas when I'm nearby. Others have said I smell like the forest by a lake they once fished or like a cabin their family had. Some say I smell like an avalanche when I'm verging on anger. But we attach something personal to it when it's a familiar person. It's also why you smell of apples, because I attach the smell of Nix to you. It is so rare to see you without him. I can't help but think of him. The lavender that grows wild through the Dark Courts is why your smell makes me think of Solas. The parts of you that smell like my mother is because you remind me of her, the part of you that refuses to become a monster. You'll play one to protect those you love from bigger beasts, but you'll never really be one." He crouched down. "Why do you ask?"

"No real reason, just wondering. I could smell you before you got to me. I was wondering if others could smell me as well."

"Yes, we can. But more than that, we feel you…especially right now. We all feel your need and fear. Your fear smells like tears. To me, it feels like when someone cries and you hold them. Their body vibrates as they shake in grief. I feel that vibration in my chest. For your men, they likely feel it against their souls. They're bonded so closely to you that they taste your tears instead of smelling them."

"I'm trying to keep it from leaking all over you all."

"Don't bother," he answered. "Fear isn't something to be ashamed of. If anything, it is keeping your men rallied. They feel your love. We all can. Someone who fears nothing is uncomfortable to be around. Those who do not fear are usually the ones who will cause your death."

I smiled. "You were coming over here for something? I'm sure it wasn't to chat about smells."

"Can I borrow you for a moment?" he asked and pushed away from the tree.

I glanced up. "Depends. If it's to move a dead body, you already know how I feel about that."

"No bodies…yet." He laughed, and I flushed, remembering our first and only date in his library. I had come so close to crossing a line with him in search of the truth. "I want to show you something."

I stood and followed him away from the men, where we met Aeden and Oisin. Aeden looked like he had slept a solid eight hours and had just climbed out of bed, fresh-eyed and bushy-tailed. Oisin looked rough around the edges, but he always had that just-climbed-out-of-a-cave look. They were both bent over, inspecting the ground.

"What's up?" I asked.

Oisin popped up with a worried look. "We've been finding trash, wrappers and containers scattered around the island."

Aeden held up a sock, inspecting it closely. "And pieces of clothing."

"They've obviously been off this island," I answered and gave Faolan a look that said he had just disturbed me for nothing. "Is this what you wanted to show me? Garbage?"

Faolan leaned into my ear. "I do not think they have been off this island."

I frowned. "What do you mean?"

Aeden motioned for me to follow him and pointed at the ground. "There are boot prints here, Perdi."

"And, what, Satyr go barefoot?" I asked.

"They do not wear boots," Aeden replied. He started laughing when he realized I didn't understand what he was talking about. "Perdi, they have hooves, not feet."

"Oh." I felt my face heat and flush. When I had seen their bodies, I hadn't noticed much beyond the horror of torture. I scolded myself for missing such an important detail. Solas wouldn't have missed it. The brief thought of Solas cleared away my embarrassment, replacing it with sadness. "Sorry, Aeden. You were saying?"

"It's okay, Perdi," Aeden replied. "Do you understand now why these boot prints are out of the ordinary?"

"We already know we're not alone on the island," I countered.

He nodded. "Not all tracks are fresh. Weeks of prints and waste. Some are older than others."

I nodded. "Who?"

Aeden motioned back to the ground. "This place reeks of those we brought with us. Some smells are far too old for them to claim it is because they are here today."

"Golden Court?" I asked, and he nodded his head. "No wonder they wanted to stop me, then forced their way to come with us."

"Do you want us to kill them?" Oisin asked as he and Faolan moved to my front. He said the words like they were as simple as pushing a table out of the way.

"Not yet," I answered. "I have other plans for them."

"There may come a time where the choice is them or us," Oisin added.

"I know. And if that time comes, always choose us. If it comes down to the wire, kill them," I answered. "I think our break time is up."

"If ever you were to lead men into battle, you'd exhaust them before the war started." Oisin teased.

"You've seen us touch the battlefield, Oisin. If this was an actual war, we'd be done already," Aeden replied. "We would have been home in time for dinner."

"This treaty with Perdi is starting to look better and better." Oisin took a healthy step away from Aeden, who noticed and laughed.

With my gear back on, we traipsed through the trees and soggy earth. We weren't fifty feet from where we'd taken a break before the shadows returned with news from home. Elphame was still standing, and to my surprise, so was Whitwick. Morrow and his people offered aid to anyone in need—food, shelter, or healers—should they be needed. He allowed the Aos Si to enter his lands and walk the borders between his territory and the two other Seelie courts. Morrow didn't fuss or send his own men to ensure the Aos Si weren't up to something more nefarious. He simply said yes and brought food and drinks to the camps. He said he was taking the first step in repairing relations with the Unseelie courts, but I bet fear played more of a role in his offerings than good tidings. I didn't care for the reasons behind it and respected him a little more for facing his fears and doing what he could, through peace, to protect his people.

"Perdi, there is trouble in Whitwick." They had saved the best for last.

"I'm not surprised. What trouble?" I asked.

"Something is happening in Whitwick and with the Gate. We can feel Fae, but we also feel something other and do not know what the 'other' is," they answered. "Do you want to go back?"

"No," I answered. "I do, but I can't."

"We fear you will regret this," they answered.

"I know, but so will they," I replied and rubbed the center of my chest. I could feel it in my soul. Something was wrong. "I will not leave my family here to go and help those who don't love me and don't want me. I can't save everyone. So, I will choose who I can and will save them."

"Something is off in Whitwick. We do not feel you should ignore it."

"I'm not ignoring it, but I can't deal with it right now. I will go once this is over. I can't be in both places." I felt the first tickle of irritation, being pulled in two directions at once. "I can't risk leaving again. What if the wards go back up?"

"You'll be kicked off the island, regardless," they replied. "We will keep an eye on the Gate."

"Tell me if Whitwick invades. The rest can wait," I answered.

"You are wrong. The rest will not wait for you, Perdi. But you will pay just the same, as will your people," they answered, then paused as if they were thinking of what to say. "You asked us before what Zephyr would do because you trust his judgment. You ask what Solas would do because he is a master of many things at once and never loses. Both of them would go look. If either felt something was off, they would investigate it. Ignoring a problem will only allow it to grow. And ignoring us and our warnings will burn you later."

"Well, Zephyr and Solas aren't available at the moment," I answered and sighed. "I can't leave."

"Yes, you can." Aeden stepped to my side. "I understand you don't want to, but your people depend on you. Protecting the Dark Court is your first priority, always. And as much as it hurts to realize that you and your needs come last, it is the crux of your crown, to live in service of your people over yourself. To do both, you need to delegate, or you'll tear yourself in half." He smiled weakly, seeing my frustration. "I'll remain here. You take one of the Aos Si. I know what you would want, and we will keep searching. Just because you are here on the island doesn't mean the rest can wait. I'm sorry, but this is what it means to lead from the front. Trust in others. Perdi, you can trust me. You go, I stay."

"I forfeit being queen," I grumbled.

"Sorry, but Dark Court laws are pretty clear. You should know, at this point, the only way out of this is death. And, as I've heard you say, many times before, they would need to pry your life out of your cold, limp hands," Aeden answered. "With Solas gone, you are the only one left."

"Death would be easier."

"Even I can taste that lie without trying. If you wanted death, you could have simply stayed dead. From where I've stood, you've been given that option more than enough times. Hell, you could have come here alone, if death was an option you sought. But you fought for this. And now, you must walk the walk," he countered, and I groaned at his truth. "Who are you taking with you? I could suggest a few if you'd like?"

"I'll take Finn. He's growing on me."

Aeden raised his eyebrows. "Not my first pick, but it makes sense."

"What makes sense?" I asked.

"Finn doesn't grow on anyone. But I understand why you've chosen him," Aeden answered. "You picked the one who matches you in temper. Finn is the least likely to tell you not to do something you most certainly should not do. He is also the one Solas would have picked for that same reason. Finn is the last one who will grow tired of your anger and will clap at the carnage. He's also the last one Zephyr would suggest. He's kept you two apart for a reason. You are both walking war and will hide bodies for each other."

"Solas and Zephyr can't agree on a damn thing," I replied and called out to the man who probably brought the marshmallows from the manor for the fire he was waiting on me to set. "Finn, let's go."

Finn moved to my side. His energy swirled off him in waves of excitement. From his eyes to his aura, he radiated dark possibilities—all of which I'd probably like, but none of which we should act on. "Where are we going, little Crow?"

"To the Gate," I answered.

"For peace or for war?"

I appreciated him asking for the rules upfront. It was very Aos Si of him. "Try for peace, but war if that's not an option."

"To war we go," he replied, and when he saw the look on my face, he grinned. "The world is filled with fools, Perdi. It only takes one of them to step forward, and the rest will follow."

The shadows wrapped around us, and I snarled in frustration. I didn't like having to be in two places at once. I understood why Solas left early in the morning and fought to get home for dinner. It was the only peace he ever had. When my feet touched the ground in the Court of Less, I backed up quickly, wiping magick from my arms. The shimmering wall between both worlds felt off. I stumbled back, wanting to be as far from it as possible without actually running away. My back smacked into Finn's chest. Unlike me, he wasn't scared of it. Or, he was, but was just better at hiding it than I was.

I saw Zeno first and waved. "Remember when you said you wanted to retire? I bet that's looking pretty good right about now."

"We don't retire here. We die. But digging a hole is starting to look more and more appealing," Zeno replied as he slipped from his men and eyed Finn first. "Zephyr is not going to like this. He's told you both to stay away from each other. Seeing you together is bad news. Terrible ideas follow you both around."

Finn shrugged. "If you have an issue with it and would like to bark new orders, our queen here has a few choice words for you. Let me warn you… She doesn't like being bossed around."

Zeno glanced back at me. "Zephyr thinks you both together will lead to trouble. But I'm not brave enough to say much more than that. How are things on the island?"

"Still hunting. How are things here?"

Zeno put his fingers in his lips and whistled. "Lily knows more about that."

Lily saw us and quickly stepped from her cluster of people to our side. "Do none of you have manners?"

"I was tortured in your basement," Zeno replied. "Kiss my ass, Seer."

Her smile ate up her face. "If you were a better soldier, you wouldn't have been caught."

"And you say I have no manners?" He gave Finn and me a nod and walked away, grinning.

"Is everything okay between you two?" I asked.

Finn laughed. "Can't you smell him on her? Things are more than okay between them."

"Oh, *ooh,* that was you in the cave the morning I came to ask Zeno for help, when Zephyr and Nix went missing?" My face flushed when she smiled. "All right then. I'm sure that's not why you've called me here. What's up?"

"Thanks, Finn." Lily rolled her eyes. "Didn't Zephyr tell you to stay away from Perdi? I think it's why he picked you to pull her off the island, so she'd hate you, and this friendship would never bud." Lily asked, then shook her head, motioning to the Gate. "Do you feel it?"

I nodded. I closed my eyes and focused on the energy. The air was tainted with something more than the usual Gate, as if magick could rot. "It's awful. What's wrong with it?"

"I don't know. It's your Gate, so you tell me," she answered. "We didn't touch it. It started doing it this morning. It's getting worse as time passes."

"Has anyone stepped in to check it out?" I asked.

"Not on your life. I never liked being close to the damn thing to begin with. I'm not going in there now," she replied and extended her arm toward the Gate. "If you're curious, feel free to look for yourself, but I'm staying out here."

My stomach flopped as I stepped forward. "Finn, are you coming or staying out here?"

"Today looks like a fine day to die," he answered and rotated his neck. He stepped forward with me, without a care for what came next.

I grabbed his hand. "Don't let go. I don't know what we'll find in there."

"You not knowing about your own Gate? That's an uncomfortable thought," he replied.

"Isn't it, though?" I asked, grinned, and pulled him in with me.

We stepped through the wall and stood between realms. It looked as it always did but felt unlike it ever had. I could feel the energy twisting and turning and reaching out for any life it could grab. It pulled on my arms and pushed at my back. It felt like too much of one thing and not enough of another. Ahead, where we would step out into Whitwick, the wall shimmered with thick streaks of black. The usual white mist felt sticky and wet and heavy. My stomach flopped, and the little hairs on the back of my neck stood in a warning. Finn took another step forward, and I pulled him back. Whatever was inside the Gate now should not be there and was placed there by someone else. It was new magick, unstable and angry. If you could see revenge, this is what it would look like, tinted with black and starved of life. I pulled Finn with me as we backed out onto Elphame soil.

"What the hell was that?" Finn asked and rubbed his arms. "It's all over me."

"Magick," I answered and looked at Lily. "I suggest you bring a lot more people here."

"Is Whitwick planning to invade?"

"They've been preparing for that since before I was born," I answered. "As to what they're doing right now, I don't know what's happening, and I'm not sticking my head out of the other side to find out. Whatever they plan to do, someone very powerful in Whitwick is helping. It isn't more Mages. The magick is too strong for that."

"Were there more witches in Whitwick that we don't know about?"

"No. I was the last true witch. But they did threaten to find some, to help build a new Gate. They'll never find another full-blooded witch, but God only knows what other magicks are out in the mortal world," I answered. "Whatever I felt in there wasn't a new Gate. It was something worse, something built of fear and hate."

"That's what the rest of us thought. It felt like things that shouldn't be there."

"The shadows felt Fae when they had come earlier. Have any Fae entered Whitwick?" I asked.

"Yes, and they haven't returned. They're either wreaking havoc or are dead."

"How did they get by you?"

She stared at me as though I had just accused her of not doing her job. "If Nix were to run by you, could you catch him?"

"No, but I'm also not fully Fae or a trained killer." I pointed out.

"I'm not sure if you just lied to me or if you're still lying to yourself, on both accounts," she replied. "But to answer your question, there are other things here, Perdi, that are a hell of a lot faster than Nix. We can't catch them all, and I'm not planning to die here to keep them out."

I pursed my lips and forced myself to release a heated breath, deflating my temper. "I'm sorry. That wasn't fair. I'm just tired and frustrated that I had to come here."

"Your first sit upon the throne still chafing?" she asked with a grin, and I nodded. "How are things on the island?"

"Where do I even start?" I took a long, rueful breath and tucked my stray hair behind my ears. "Mortals and Mages came into Elphame to hunt me down, then warded the island for the Satyr to help them lure me to my death. On the cursed island, someone has been hunting and killing the Satyr. Their bodies have been left to rot in the sun. I disagree with what they've done to my family, but I can see why they're pissed off. And to make things exciting, I'm pretty sure we're towing around those who have been doing the hunting."

"Be careful over there, Perdi. Not even the Seers have ever been able to see that island. I do not see how it will end, but I feel it. It feels like ants crawling all over me." She motioned back to the Gate. "What the hell do we do about this?"

"Beats me. Stay out of there and be prepared for something to come through from Whitwick."

"I will call for more guards. Thank you for checking it out for us."

"Have you heard anything of my dad? Do you know how he's doing?" I asked.

She smiled. "He was brought to Faolan's land, to his healers. Your father suffered Fae sickness when he came again. He's doing better, but it'll take time. Don't worry about him, Perdi. He is safe where he is."

"It must be bad enough there for him to think he's safer here."

"But we do war and death so well. Why wouldn't he want to be here?" She huffed a small laugh.

"And the parties," Finn added. "No one does a banquet quite like Fae."

"Have you been to a banquet here?" I asked. "I'd rather be lashed again than attend another Seelie banquet."

"Unfortunately, I have, and like you, I'd take the lash," he replied. "You don't live as long as we do without seeing the underbelly of every court in all their hellish glory."

Lily shivered. I squirmed. Finn didn't flinch.

"Thank you, Lily." I waved as she walked back toward the Gate.

"Perdi, before we go back." Finn motioned me to the side.

"Make it quick. I didn't want to leave the island to begin with. Each moment I'm away… I don't know. I just don't like it."

"Entire lifetimes are lived between moments, I understand," he said the words I couldn't find. "My mother was a Seer, my father, an Aos Si."

"Do you see a bad outcome?" I asked.

"I don't see this path because I'm on it with you," he answered. "My mother taught me the history of the Finis, as she did every other Fae. I have been with Zephyr since I was a child. I've seen what he does when someone stands in his way. I truly fear what will happen once you're backed into a corner."

"So do I."

"The cost will be greater than you think."

"It always is. Are you planning to help me or hinder me?" I asked.

He wiggled his eyebrows and grinned. "I plan to hold down whoever you need to kill for answers."

"Although I like your answer, is that why you've pulled me aside?"

"No." He motioned to the Gate. "It's about the Gate. When we were inside, was it just me or did you feel it too?"

"The magick being off?"

"Not just that, but I mean, did you feel the emotion in there? It felt like we're waiting on decisions to be made on whether we are going to war or not. There was so much rage and terror. The only other place I've ever felt that level of wrath was standing on the battlefield with bodies at my feet. Christ, I felt it on my skin like splashed blood. It was hot at first, then sticky and cold. It was uncomfortable, more so because it is mortals on the other side, and it's directed at Elphame, at you. The moment we stepped inside, the energy was for you and you alone."

I tilted my head for a moment and thought about it. I hadn't really stopped to feel the emotion in the air, only the magick. Although I had felt it, initially, I hadn't focused on it the way Finn had. I closed my eyes and let my Malice eat away at the lingering emotion. Little bits had escaped the Gate and hung in the air around us. It held an edge of unease until you pushed at it a little and twisted it around in your mouth to gain the full flavor of it. My Malice pulled back on her own, not liking what she ate.

I opened my eyes and shivered from my head to my toes. "It feels like being locked in a dungeon, waiting for your door to be opened next, and everything you hear and feel while you wait for your turn. It feels like waiting to die, that dread and fear that takes root."

"That's a terribly accurate way to describe it, but yes. I don't have a good feeling about what the mortal world is planning next. Truthfully, though, I don't really blame them."

"Me neither. We were expecting them to get creative, and I think we just found what their fear has twisted."

I motioned for the shadows, who pulled us both back to the island. My mind raced with the possibilities of the Gate and what Whitwick was doing. Were they closing it or about to send thousands through to their deaths? Whatever they planned on doing, it would hurt and would come sooner rather than later. I sent up a prayer to whoever still bothered to listen, that whatever came out of the mortal realm would wait until my family was back safely at home. I could deal with the nightmares of Whitwick once I was no longer standing ear-deep in the nightmares of Elphame.

"I didn't need to go there for that," I scolded the shadows. "It was a waste of my time. You could have reported back what Lily's thoughts were."

"We disagree. You now know what the energy feels like, and you can't get that secondhand. That alone will be a warning. You will be prepared. Elphame will be ready. Protecting our people is not a waste of time." They admonished me with a tone that made me sink a little deeper. "Staying alive means knowing what is around the corner—or have you forgotten everything you've been taught? You have watched Solas prepare for battle. There is not a ditch in Elphame that he doesn't look in. And there certainly isn't a shadow Zephyr hasn't bent to his will. Secondhand information will kill you and your people."

"You're right," I answered. "Damn it, you're right. I'm so focused on finding my family that I'm not paying attention to anything else."

"No, Perdi, you're not." They twisted around my legs in jerky movements. It wasn't often I felt anything but kindness and guidance from them. And right this moment, I felt their anger and disappointment. It felt very much like being chastised by Zephyr. "This is about more than just our family. This is about you staying alive long enough to be of any use to any of them. This is about ensuring your people stay alive, even as you search. If you die because you didn't stop long enough to think, they all die with you—our family and our people. Their fate is tied to you and your throne. We're sorry, Perdi. We wish you never had to experience any of this. But this is where you are, and now you must do better. There are no second chances."

"Your bedside manner needs a lot of work," I replied.

"You've said the same thing before and will probably say it again," they replied. "You need to take care of yourself, take breaks, eat and connect with those you're counting on or this is all for nothing, and we might as well go home. At least you'll live, as will the others who came with you. If you don't, don't bother getting to know them."

"I get the point. I hate it, but I hear you," I answered. "This had nothing to do with the Gate, did it?"

"Not entirely. Although we still believe you needed to know the threat. This was about you stopping long enough to focus on more than running through the forest to your untimely death. This was about you learning that a one-track mind will be your end and the end of those you love. Even Solas stopped for dinner. He always came home to you to reconnect, to ground himself, to remind himself why he fights every day."

"Thank you," I replied. "May I suggest you work on your delivery?"

"No. We feel we delivered the message in the only way you would understand. You don't listen when someone takes the soft route. You only hear us when we push it in your face, and you can't ignore it. But if you'd like, we'll start adding a 'please'."

I laughed. "Are you this way with Zephyr?"

"Yes."

"I bet he's enjoying the break from you," I replied.

"Most certainly."

Faolan stepped to my side. "Finn has filled us in about the Gate."

"Is it easy for you to bounce from trouble to trouble while in the middle of chaos? I know I have to delegate, but even then, I can't imagine it is any easier," I asked. "It feels daunting, like nothing ever gets done because there's always something else to deal with."

"Yes. But I have decades upon decades to get used to the constant demands. Go easy on yourself. This is your first week," Faolan replied. "Speaking of bouncing from problem to problem. What do you think it means, what you felt in the Gate?"

I smiled. Faolan was the type that could tell you your house burned to the ground, and you'd appreciate how calm and friendly he was about it. "The last time I was in Whitwick, I could feel something coming. And whatever I had felt, I think it has arrived. It's powerful. And hate doesn't cover what I felt inside the Gate. It's so much more. It's focused and unrelenting. It's awful."

"I need a vacation." He groaned.

"The beach is just over there."

"No one gets in the water here, Perdi. You'd have to be crazy to try it," he answered with a laugh.

"Actually, during the Last War, on one of the days I took off, I ended up swimming my way back to shore."

He frowned for a moment until he realized I was serious. "Jesus, I'm surprised you weren't eaten."

"Oh, they tried, trust me." I laughed, remembering my arrival at the manor and the look on Solas' face. "I had to bribe my way across, but they got a few chunks out of me first."

"You live the oddest of lives. I'm both happy and scared to know you."

Oisin called out from thirty feet ahead. "Are you two coming, or are you guys going to hold us back for the rest of the day? Aeden says we could stop for a break if you're tired, Perdi?"

I jogged up ahead and left Faolan behind. "No breaks."

Chapter Eight

Growing up under the constant threat of becoming a Crow, I was taught to walk the line between anxiety and calm. Somewhere in the middle, I learned how to distinguish the survival instincts that caused anxiousness and the calmness that came with recognizing the inevitable. In Whitwick, we never really evolved from that constant state of stress and worry. Although it made us more resilient, it also left us with poor social skills. We adapted, we mainly got along, but we never really had the ability or the desire to make friends. The problem was that your friends usually ended up dead, or you were willing to trade their lives for your own. And now, after almost two decades, I had to learn how to make friends, and the idea of it was terrifying.

"Can I join you?" My voice was small and hitched with each word. I stood at the edge of the group with my lunch bag gripped in my sweaty hands. I was nervous, which was odd, considering it was my idea to be included. I glanced around and knew I looked like a scared deer, my eyes darting, looking for an escape. Aeden caught my eye, and he motioned for me to move forward.

Finn smiled from his perch on a fallen tree. "Of course, Perdi. Pull up a chunk of ground."

"Thank you." I sat cross-legged, my pulse a little speedy. My mouth was bone dry, and I tried, in vain, to keep my hands from shaking. It felt like trying to make a friend for the first time. Up until now, it had been all business. The change made my stomach flop. I wasn't sure what to do next. I hadn't planned anything beyond asking to join them.

"What did you get in your lunch?" Finn asked. He winked once. I knew he could sense my unease. They all could. But I appreciated him ignoring it.

I opened my bag. "Fruit and vegetables, mashed potatoes and a crispy square that smells like pure sugar. Why do I always get potatoes?"

"To remind you of home," he answered. "I'll trade you for your crispy square? I have three fruits, two cheese sandwiches, soup, mashed potatoes and sauce, three baked potatoes, vegetables with dip, cake, juice, coffee and tea. Take your pick."

"That's what you have for lunch? I don't even eat that in an entire day."

"I ate my crispy square first, then my stew and buns already," he answered.

"No wonder you all say ten minutes isn't enough time." I tossed the square over. "You can have it. I don't really like them. They're too sweet for me."

"Elda will be crushed." He groaned when he bit into it. "Tastes like eating lunch in the sun, on a perfect hill, with the world in perfect order, back home."

"It's apples for me. They smell like my back garden growing up." I smiled at the memory. "Nix grew several types of apples. He hoarded them like a troll and their trinkets."

"A few times, when I was guarding the Gate, Nix brought small apple turnovers. He said they were your favorite," he replied.

I nodded. "My mother used to make them for my dad and me. Nix found her recipe and started making them."

"Did your mother come across to Elphame with your father?" he asked.

Faolan cleared his throat and shook his head side to side wildly. When he noticed me, he had enough respect to drop his eyes and blush. "Sorry, Perdi. I thought everyone knew."

"Did I step in something?" Finn asked. "Do you two not have good relations?"

"Do you live under a bloody rock?" Faolan mumbled.

"No. We just don't gossip as much as the rest of you," Finn answered. "I'm not part of any inner circle, which means I'm not privy to the details. Perdi isn't a topic Zephyr will willingly discuss, especially with me—unless she's burning villages and starting wars. And I don't pry to learn what I'm not told."

"It's okay, Finn." I winced at the awkwardness he'd soon feel. "My mother was hanged when I was a young child. Fae had other plans for my family, and her life was taken to ensure I'd end up in Elphame."

"I'm sorry. I didn't know that," Finn replied and flushed red with embarrassment. "I'm only half Seer. My mother was a Seer, and I didn't learn much from her before I left. It's not a power I've mastered. You're in this gray area because you're tied to Zephyr, and he is tied to us. It's hard to see the life of those who I will walk the same path with."

I shrugged. "Not much I can do about it now."

"You are much more forgiving than I am," he replied.

"Oh, I'm not that forgiving, Finn. If I knew who'd caused her death, I'd kill them with my bare hands," I answered. "I hate them for taking her from me. But more than that, I hate that they took her from my dad. He never really recovered from it. He's always been a little empty after her death. It's like this light went out inside of him the day she died, and it's never come back on."

"I'd do the same thing," Finn answered. He passed me his apple and smiled. "I hope, one day, you get to do just that."

"I'd settle for knowing they died horribly. I'm not picky." I smiled and took the apple. "Sometimes just knowing they're gone and can't hurt another person is enough."

Sitting in the dirt and rocks with others, I finally felt like I was one of them. I wasn't more or less, just Perdi. I leaned against a log and listened to them tell stories, most of which had me laughing until I cried. And for the briefest of moments, we weren't in the middle of chaos. We had carved out the smallest space inside a nightmare, to not be the monsters. We were family, and not one of them thought I was more or less than they were. Somehow, being teased along with the others had made me feel like I was one of them, made me feel valued and loved. I didn't grow up with siblings, but today felt like I had found my long-lost brothers. The feeling scrubbed off the pointy parts of a crown I didn't want to wear. I understood why their breaks were important. It wasn't just to rest their bodies but to rest their hearts and souls.

"Okay, Perdi, if you had to pick between fighting Solas or Zephyr, who would it be?" Finn asked, and I laughed. "If no one could use their magick, which one would you go toe-to-toe with?"

"I've trained with them both and have lost to both of them more times than I can count," I answered. "But if I had to fight one of them tomorrow, I'd pick Zephyr, hands down."

"Why Zephyr? He's stronger than Solas," Finn asked.

"But he's not as dirty of a fighter as Solas is," I replied. "Physically, Zephyr is stronger. But Solas wouldn't hesitate to rip off my arms and beat me with them. Zephyr would stick to some moral code you all follow, one that Solas just doesn't have. It's why Solas always wins against Zephyr."

"I'd pick Solas," Finn answered. "Solas, at least, would end my life faster than Zephyr. Zephyr would draw it out, trying to teach me some random lesson in the process."

"Same," Faolan added. "Solas would just kill me. Zephyr? He would drag it out until I finally begged him to let me die. Even then, I've pissed him off enough times that he'd lock me in a cage and pull me out for banquets."

"This is probably the weirdest game I've ever played," I answered.

"No, there are other games, but we just don't feel comfortable playing them with you here," Finn replied and winked. "And before you get all up in arms over it, if I won't play them with my sister, I sure as hell don't want to play them with you. I don't need to know who you'd rather sleep with."

"I appreciate that, thank you." I huffed a laugh and rolled my eyes.

I grabbed Finn's leg as the world tilted just a little. He froze under my touch. I jerked my hand back when I realized I had touched him. I didn't fear touching him, but he'd fear the consequences of my scent on his body. "Nix..."

"Not Nix. I'd fight whoever the other person is." Finn laughed. "I've been attacked by a gnome before. He bit off my ear and chewed it in front of me. It was...utterly horrifying, watching someone eat one of your body parts. I'm not doing it again. Pick someone else."

I pressed my hand into my chest. My heart was pounding for no reason. "No, I feel... I can smell buttercups."

"Perdi?" Finn asked. "Are you all right?" He grabbed my hand and squeezed for my attention. "Perdi, look at me. Tell me what you're feeling."

I shook my head and stood in one fluid movement. I pressed a hand harder into the center of my chest, trying to keep my heart from breaking through my ribcage. "No...it's...awful. Oh God, it hurts." I felt a twinge in my stomach. It pulled from my belly button to my core, slicing my soul in the process. Every inch of my skin felt suddenly raw and throbbed in pain.

"Perdi..." The voice made my ears twitch. I stopped scanning the forest and turned from the group.

"Nix!" I screamed and ran toward the smell of buttercups. I pushed my legs as fast as they would go. The shadows grabbed me and pulled me through the forest, following the echo of a voice.

"We feel him." The shadows released me from their grip. "He's alone."

I landed beside Nix's broken body. He looked like he had dragged himself through the forest after first falling off a cliff and hitting every rock on his way down. He was puffy and purple as a grape. I dropped to my knees and screamed for the others. It would take them a breath to find me. I picked Nix up carefully, and his tiny body flopped as if it were made of only liquid and pain. I could barely feel the life within his pearl. Faolan arrived at my side first, on a breeze of icy wind. The rest circled around me as I knelt on the ground. I felt their grief thick in the air and tasted the saltiness of their sadness. A few gasps were followed by a gust of collective rage that dulled Faolan's icy anger.

"Hold on, Nix." I choked on the words. "Please, don't leave me."

With my Malice, I carried him pieces of my own life, my energy. But I didn't have his pearl. I couldn't force him to live. I ran my Malice through his mind, and a jumble of answers came back. Between his fear and injuries, I only caught flashes. It was enough for me to understand what had happened, why they were taken and why they'd die if we didn't find them soon. The horror of it all made the first crack along my soul, for what I knew I'd do to the person responsible for harming Nix.

"My Perdi," he whispered. His voice was scratchy like he had screamed for more hours than his throat could take. His eyes fluttered as he tried to focus on my face. "I knew you'd come. No matter what I said. I told Zephyr you'd come back."

"I'll always come for you," I replied. "Nix, before you fall asleep, I need to know where Solas and Zeph are? Please, Nix, where are they?"

"Solas, Zephyr, they're going to die. Solas got me out, but he will surely die for my survival," he answered. "The Satyr felt you the moment you got back here. They're coming for you."

I cried. "Where are they?"

"Not up here. Below. Go below." Nix was fading again. "Solas…"

"What, Nix, what about Solas?" I asked and fought the urge to shake him awake.

"He said…burn them all…do your worst." Nix squeezed my hand and shook, fighting to stay with me. "Zephyr warned them. They wouldn't listen to him. He said… eat…their…fucking world, little Crow."

"Hold on, Nix. I love you," I whispered to him as he fell into a deep sleep that I wouldn't be able to wake him from.

"Is he… Did he?" Aeden whispered. His voice was soft and pained, and his one hand clutched his chest, a move I made whenever my heart was breaking. His eyes watered. "Oh, little Nix."

"He's not dead yet. He's asleep," I answered.

"Can you wake him?" Finn asked. "Can we help?"

"No. Once Nix goes into his deep sleep, I have to wait for him to wake up on his own," I answered. "Gnomes go into hibernation when they're injured."

"That's not a good defensive mechanism," he replied.

"No, it's not." I sobbed out my words. "He's so weak. I don't know if he'll wake up again."

"Send him to Elda," Finn answered. "If anyone can help him, it'll be her. She's brought back many of us from the call of death, including myself, even after a pearl couldn't bring me from the brink. The magick of the Sluagh is different. They will help him. Jare will be there. He'll be able to find the energy needed to feed him a steady flow. Please, Perdi, send him for aid."

I motioned for the shadows to take Nix. "Take him to Elda and tell her what has happened. Ask for her and the Sluagh for aid, then return to the island."

"Perdi"—they swirled around me—"we do not wish to leave you, not now."

"When you return, you will take the others away," I answered. "I will do what Solas and Zephyr have asked. Please, just do what I've requested without arguing with me." I swallowed back my need to scream at someone. "I'm sorry. Please, just do what I've asked."

"Very well." They picked Nix out of my arms and were gone.

"Solas and Zephyr are underground." I stood and debated what I could say out loud. I didn't want the world to know I was Finis, and having the Golden Court so close, I didn't want to risk it. I leaned in and whispered. "I was able to…read Nix. Fae, who are not Satyr, have helped hold Solas and Zephyr. They are still here. Once the wards were in place, they helped the Satyr hold my family in return for my life. The Satyr don't care who kills me, as long as I'm dead in the end. The Fae who helped—Nix doesn't know who they are—but they plan to invade Unseelie territory once I'm dead. They plan to kill everyone and take the courts as their own." I turned from the group and dry-heaved until I screamed. Nothing but anger came up. Oisin passed me a water bottle to wash out the burning acid.

"This isn't funny, but that plan certainly is." Oisin shook his head. "The Unseelie courts are the most guarded and terrifying territory in all Elphame. It won't fall because they simply want it to happen. They have to kill Solas and Zephyr, all of your people, the armies, the Aos Si and Seers, before they could try for the Winter Court. And any who try to invade our territory would have to face those not even Solas will house." Oisin shook his head, a look of surprise on his face. The rest of the group had the same look, utter disbelief anyone could be that stupid. "Solas has kept his territory small for a reason. It's the easiest court to defend and the strongest in all Elphame. And, to be brutally honest, if anything were to happen to you, Perdi, it wouldn't weaken your territory. If anything, the darkness would eat every blink of light and burn all Elphame in your name."

"Our suspicions that someone has been here, Nix has confirmed it. They are the ones responsible for the bodies we've found," I answered and motioned toward Theo. "Those who came with us hunted the Satyr. Because of them, we stand here at the brink." No one turned to look at who I was referring to. They already knew who I was talking about. We had suspected wrongdoing from the start. "The Satyr want my head for what's been done to them. They blame me for it. And the Fae who have helped are happy with any one of us dying if it weakens the Dark Court."

"Send Theo and his people to Solas' dungeons," Oisin added.

"The Dark Courts have no dungeons," Aeden corrected.

"You're serious?" Oisin asked and stared at me as if I had suddenly grown extra eyeballs. "You have no dungeons?"

"Yes, I was serious. We don't house our enemies. If you are our enemy, why would we spend our resources keeping you alive?" I answered.

He laughed until he saw we weren't joking. "Send Theo and all his people to the caves, to Oberon. If you want them dead, they won't survive ten minutes."

"I may still need them later, Oisin. And the dead can't be tortured to tell me their truths."

Faolan smiled. "We'll take them until you come for them. The Hallows have dungeons no one has ever escaped from."

"Make it hurt. And trust me when I tell you, I really want you to make it hurt. This isn't an idle threat," I replied and looked to Faolan. "No one dies yet, but they all suffer for this, for what has been done to my people and my family."

"People die in dungeons every day, Perdi," Oisin added. "But we will try to keep them alive until you come back."

I tried not to laugh. It wasn't funny. But Oisin had this way about him. "Solas and Zephyr, they've sent a message with Nix. *"Burn it to the ground."* It's time everyone leaves."

I stepped away from the others. Theo and his men stood about thirty feet away, waiting. They were always hovering, trying to gather information that would never come. Under their stone faces, I saw the slivers of nervousness they tried to hide.

"Theo, I'm giving you the option to leave," I said calmly, with my friend's blood drying on my hands.

"And if we choose to stay?" he asked.

"So be it. But you'll die with everyone else on these lands. I'll be destroying the island. You can leave with the others, or you're welcome to stay here and die. I have no preference. Though, if you died here, I wouldn't be bothered by it."

"What about Zephyr and Solas?" he asked, and I watched him fight the grin that jerked just below the surface.

"I've received word from Nix, I am to burn the island to the ground. I'll return to the mainland once I'm done," I answered. It was true enough.

"You do not know where the rest of your people are?" he asked.

"No, I don't," I answered honestly. Part of me didn't care if he knew I was lying. It wasn't like he'd have the opportunity to run or hide. "But this island will burn, just the same."

He nodded. "When you return, you have safe passage back to your lands through my territory." He tried for condolences, but it didn't pass for anything more than a sad attempt at hiding his scheming. Torching the island would burn the evidence of what he and his people have done to the Satyr.

"Thank you." I didn't bother telling him I'd be putting a match to his throne the next time he and I crossed paths, even if I had to bring his kingdom to the ground in the process. "The shadows will be transporting everyone back, then returning for me. Gather your gear. You leave now."

Theo stood with his men, and when the shadows returned, they grabbed Faolan, Oisin and the Golden Court. I would have given just about anything to have been there to see Theo land in a prison cell, demanding freedom he didn't deserve and would never taste again. But more than that, I'd have given my right arm to see their faces when Faolan lost his temper. I had a feeling it would be more terrifying than if the Dark Courts had our own dungeons.

"It's your turn," I said to Aeden.

"No, respectfully, we won't be leaving," Aeden answered. "We are a kingdom of our own. The shadows may grab us, but we'll be back before they are. You can have them waste precious energy or face the fact that we'll be staying. If that means we're at risk of your losing control and eating us in the process, so be it. At least our lives will give you the power you need to rescue Solas and Zephyr," he answered. I looked to the others, who clearly had no plans to leave, either. "We will not leave when we're this close to getting our family back. We cannot, whether we disobey you or not. This is where we have chosen to be."

"I can't ask this of you," I replied.

Aeden's smile was soft but determined. I knew that look well. He had dug his heels in on the matter. "Perdi, Zephyr is all I've ever had, all most of us have ever had. He is the father we don't have. We, the Aos Si, will never leave him or our king. More than that, we won't leave you, and there isn't a power in the world that could make us. Unfortunately for you, little queen, on this matter, your orders mean nothing to any of us."

"Do the rest of you feel that way?" I asked. "I will not force anyone to endure what I'm about to do, what we'll all need to do."

They all fell in line and tipped their heads. "As our queen commands."

"I do not command you. I'm asking you," I replied.

Finn lifted his head and looked at me with the same ice-blue eyes as Zephyr. "It's just a saying. We come freely, Perdi. We come to burn worlds with the last Crow."

"Why do all of you look so similar?" I asked. "Same parents?"

Aeden laughed. "No. Could you imagine the poor woman who signed up for that? We look similar to you, but we all look different to each other. It's the same reason all mortals look the same to us. But when you look closer, some of them have wings, little Crow."

"All right, let's burn the island to the ground. When the time comes, hold nothing back. Do your absolute worst. But don't say I didn't warn you of the cost. We're leaving pieces of our souls behind."

"I've never been told to do my worst," Finn replied. He moved from foot to foot, energy coursing through his veins and leaking into the air like static. "Is it just me, or is anyone else a little excited about the prospects?"

"I don't think it's just you. You're just the only one willing to say it out loud," I answered. "Warmonger."

"I'm in good company, Soul-Eater."

The shadows returned, and we moved through the island. I let my rage out and felt the ground tremble as we pushed forward. Between the Aos Si and me, the very earth knew it would bake under our fury. We moved between every tree, over every hill and through the caves and tunnels. We backtracked and cleared every den and dark corner. We left nothing untouched, until the night finally came, and we were made to stop. Only this time, none of us wanted to, and we forced our bones to settle. Since coming to the island, this was the first time they were content with hunting in the pitch black of the night. Had it not been for the shadows reminding me that I needed rest, I'd have kept going.

We built a fire in a cave big enough for us all and slumped down, defeated by the night and exhaustion. We weren't happy about it, and the air felt heavier from our frustration. When we finally had dinner in the middle of the night, we shared small pieces of ourselves in an attempt to will the unease from our bones. Short stories circled the group, each offering a memory of their first war, their first love, their first brush with death. Some of the stories were funny, and others tugged the tears from my eyes. When it was my turn, I didn't know what to say. There were many firsts, all of which I didn't want to say out loud. I remembered so many moments from the day I was Taken until the day I died, but those were mine to hold. The scabs had just healed, and I wasn't ready to dig in the wounds quite yet.

"Okay, I have one," I finally said. "I once tried to put a leash on a Sluagh. I have a scar on my thigh from where I was bitten. The scar won't go away. Solas says it has something to do with Sluagh magick, it being different from Elphame. And whenever the Sluagh are nearby, my scar tingles, which is an improvement from when my leg would go completely numb, and I'd limp until they went away."

The entire cave went silent. Finn was the first to break the silence and laugh at me. "How the hell did you think that was going to end? Why would anyone be foolish enough to even go near one? I live in the abandoned caves of the Sluagh, and I'm scared enough to live at the edge of them."

"First, Nix rode on the back of one to pull me from the Gate. So, you're just a chicken. Second, Solas dared me," I answered. "When we were going to meet Faolan, before the *first* war I caused, I had asked to have one, so I'd look scarier. For weeks after, I tried to coax a wee one with food. It eventually warmed up to me and would follow me around. Solas then gave me a collar and leash and dared me to try, since I was so cocky and sure that I could keep one as a pet."

"I take it the thing attacked you?" Finn asked.

"Nope. He was fine with the whole thing. He didn't seem to care. He just trotted along beside me. Unfortunately, I didn't think a small one would be an infant. I thought they came in different sizes, like the animals in Whitwick," I answered and felt my face flush, a little embarrassed it had ended exactly how Solas thought it would. "His mother, on the other hand, had a big problem with it. She swooped down, bit my leg and tried to carry me off. She would have eaten me if it weren't for the little guy and Solas. She finally spat me out, and I broke a few ribs in the fall. I think that was probably the most scared I've ever been since coming to Elphame."

"That's probably the stupidest thing I've ever heard someone do." Finn laughed with the others until the cave echoed with teasing and joking.

"Long story short, I'll never try that again," I answered.

"But you won the bet," Aeden laughed.

"It was worth it. You should have seen Solas' face." I laughed in return. "Zephyr just stood there and stared, muttering how I was a '*foolish little Crow*'."

We each took turns telling stories of dares and the breaking of bones. I stared at the ceiling in the warmth of our shared experiences and prayed I'd have more days like this. This time, sleeping in the back of a cave wasn't as bad while surrounded by friends. The shadows settled on top of me, and I slowly drifted to sleep with Solas on my mind.

When I walked through Solas' dream, I knew I wouldn't be able to come back again. I could barely feel him. His smell was weak, like I had walked into a room he had visited days ago, just a hint of him left lingering behind. He was too broken for me to be rattling what little energy he had left. When I saw him, I fought the urge to cringe. He was bloodied and bruised and in worse condition than I had found Nix.

"Perdi." He didn't open his eyes. "Did you find Nix?"

"Yes. I sent him to Elda," I answered. "Hold on, please, Solas."

"I'm counting Nix as a win on my end." He smiled and winced at the movement. "God, this is why I don't have dungeons."

"You don't like to clean up the mess?" I asked.

He huffed a laugh that looked painful. "That, and I don't like the screaming. Zephyr, here, screams like a little girl afraid of the dark. I've never heard his voice pitch so bloody high. I swear he's part siren. He's making my ears bleed."

"Do you know how long it takes to regrow fingernails?" Zephyr groaned from beside Solas and pulled himself sitting. "Little Crow, why did you not take your little gnome and leave?"

"It's not my fault you're a shitty Soul-Eater," I teased. "Now, a little Crow and your trainees must save you."

He tried to smile, but his jaw wouldn't line up correctly, and the end result was more terrifying than it should have been. I sucked in a breath and winced. "Perdi, you will not *like what you find here, what you'll find inside yourself if you come. I tried to warn you. I tried to keep you from this."*

"So you've said before. But I wouldn't have liked what I'd find inside myself if I didn't come," I answered.

Solas sighed. "Today looks like a good day for war, no?"

"It will not be war, only death," Zephyr muttered. "None of you listen to me. Why do I even bother?"

I laughed. "You two are like oil and water. I don't remember a single time when either of you agreed on anything."

"He wants to save the world, but I'm fine dancing in the flames as it comes to an end," Solas answered. "Are you ready to light some fires?"

Zephyr finally gave in, but I knew it hurt him to do it. If a broken heart could be heard, I heard in his next words. "Burn it all, Perdi. If you're going to tear your soul in half, make them pay for every piece you leave on this island – and there will be many. Make them pay for what you are about to do to yourself. You will never be the same after this. Make the cost theirs to bear. I'm telling you that you will hate yourself tomorrow."

"I'll worry about tomorrow, tomorrow. Today, it's worth it," I answered.

Zephyr pulled his eyes open, just enough for me to see the pain in my decision reflecting back at me. "No, little Crow, I don't think it is. My life, Solas' life, is not worth that pain. It is why we sent you Nix, so you would leave."

"Speak for yourself, Zephyr. That's not why I did it," Solas piped up. "Gnomes are flammable."

"Good thing I'm the one in charge, then, Zeph. Since I'm not the one chained to a wall, I call the shots. See you soon." I answered. My thoughts pulled back to the sound of shuffling around in the cave.

The dream snapped suddenly when I felt a hand on my mouth and smelled Finn. If arrogance and love had a smell, it would be Finn. He reminded me of crossing paths with a bear and her cubs. The beauty of watching something wild and free and the warning that shot up your spine when the beast noticed you watching her young.

I opened my eyes to Finn's face inches from mine and his finger to his lips. I nodded my head, and he removed his hand. He motioned to the mouth of the cave. The Aos Si were all awake but not moving. Whatever was out there was there to see, not harm.

Finn pointed to the shadows, then outside. With a nod, I motioned for the shadows. They knew what we wanted without having to tell them. They burst from the cave and surrounded our stalker. The Aos Si were out of the mouth of the cave before I stood. I ran behind and jumped from the rock room to the front of a kneeling half-man, half-beast. With curled horns on his head, he looked up and met my eyes. I stepped back into the chest of Aeden. The hate in his eyes, for me, was enough to feel it like a slap. The Aos Si surrounded us, but the man feared not one of us.

I looked closely at his leathery flesh and saw bruises and bites, claw marks that only a gnome is known for leaving behind. I had seen what Nix could do to a man, and this beast held the welts from an angry gnome. Nix, who was purple, marred by violence, had fought for his very life. I hated this stranger more for that reason. It took several tries, but I finally found my voice again. "Why have you done this?"

"Does it matter?" he asked.

"Yes, it does," I answered. I released my Malice into the air. "You can tell me, or I can dig it out of your mind."

He smiled, and it wasn't a pleasant expression. "For you to suffer as we have."

"How have I caused your suffering?"

"When you interfered with the Gate, you changed the balance of power. When Fae could no longer hunt you, who do you think they began to hunt?" he asked. "If they couldn't kill your people, whose people do you think died in your place?"

"Until now, no one even knew you existed on this island. How am I responsible for that?" I answered.

"The Golden Court has been hunting and killing us." He spat at my feet. "Because of you. Because of what you did. You thought of yourself and your people only. And we have paid with our lives and the lives of our children."

I released my grip on my Malice and read his memories. I picked through eons of freedom to the moment the Gate fell, and all Elphame realized what had happened. The Satyr, on an island away from the wars, did not think it would matter. For the briefest of moments, they were grateful the mortals would no longer suffer. Their happiness was short-lived when bodies began to show up on their shores. Their people were dying. They had become the hunted. They had become the new Crows of Elphame, the Crows of the Golden Court. And when they'd sent out a call for help, no one had heard, and no one came, except our enemies. The Mages who had come for my life were forced to ward the island, to help the Satyr exact revenge. The Mages ran once they realized they would die on the island the moment I arrived. But the Satyr didn't need the Mages any longer. They had their rage and desperation, and it was more than enough for them to take from me what I had taken from them—family, safety, peace, a future.

"I didn't know." I gasped and pulled back.

"It does not matter to us if you knew or not. You are still responsible, and now you'll suffer as we did." He smiled. "Go ahead, kill me, but it won't bring back your people. Just as killing you won't bring back ours, but it'll still feel good. Come sunset, your people will die."

"If they die, you all die with them," I answered.

"Whether we live or die matters not, because you'll be dead just the same. And once you're dead, your court will fall, just as ours did."

"No, it won't. I'm sorry for what has happened to your people. I truly am. But like you, I will do horrible things to survive and even worse things for my people." I looked him in his eyes, and I delivered his fate. "You brought doom to your land when you put your hands on my people. And you will die tonight for what I know you did to Nix. You bear the wounds of a gnome, and now, you'll bear the wounds of a Crow."

I walked away from him and left him to a group of men who now knew he was the one who had beaten their friend nearly to death. I didn't hear him scream when he died, but my soul felt it. Finn sat beside me on a rock, far enough away from the others that I didn't hear what they did to the Satyr, but not so far from them that they couldn't grab me if another came around the corner.

"Are you okay?" he asked.

"No…are you?"

"Not even a little. But for Nix, I'd do so much worse. All I could see were the scratch marks on his face and chest, and I knew Nix had fought for his life. I wanted to do worse for Nix but knew he wouldn't have approved." He sighed a long and tired breath into the night.

"I wanted the same thing. But every death adds up, changes who you are and what you're willing to do," I replied.

"It should change you, even the ones you know are for some greater good. When it stops getting to you, it's your turn to die. I hope that day doesn't ever come for you because it'll be us, your friends, who come for you."

I nodded slowly, agreeing, accepting a fate I'd have earned if I became one of the monsters. "You all made it look easy. None of you flinched when I said the man would die."

"Killing someone *is* easy. That's the truth of it. The act of taking a life is as simple as eating lunch. I've struggled with peeling apples more than taking a life. Feeling it and knowing you were part of it is a different story, and that pain comes later, when the war is over. I have killed thousands upon thousands, and each one hurts my soul like the first. I don't ever want it to be easy for my soul."

"Why do you do it, then?" I asked.

"Same reason you have and will continue to. And we both will pay the same price, regardless of why we do it," he replied.

I'd do it for love, for family, for justice, for peace, for war—all good reasons to leave chunks of yourself scattered around. "Can you tell the others we leave in the next hour? It's time to go scrub off the rest of our souls."

"It'll get worse the closer we get to our people. When we get home, the memories eat you up and your soul is too raw to take another step, we won't leave you. We suffer together." Finn stood and held out his hand. "Let's go tarnish that shiny new crown of yours."

Chapter Nine

Before dawn had stretched her dreadful wings, we were in the tunnels, racing against time. Each tick of the clock thumped against my soul, and with each passing minute, I couldn't shake the feeling that I'd fail and wouldn't find them in time. I shook the fear from my mind and pushed it down to save for another day. Now that we all had tasted the energy of the Satyr, tracking them wasn't hard. Hiding from a Soul-Eater, backed by the Aos Si, was a near impossible task. But the Satyr didn't want to stay hidden. They, like my family, were counting on us to find them.

We moved through the underground world, covered in darkness and secrecy, and plowed through all those who tried to stand in our way. With the Aos Si clearing the path, we pursued our enemies with little resistance. We didn't stop for anyone. Bodies that had never deserved to fall at our hands, I stepped over. Fates I had unknowingly handed them hadn't stopped me as I knew they should have. I had told myself the moment my family was taken, my enemies had sealed their fates. But each new body chiseled away at my reasons.

Zephyr's words played over and over in my mind. I wouldn't like who I would have to become to save him. And as I bled the tunnels dry of life and drank down every drop of power, I knew he was right. Tomorrow, if I was graced another day, I wouldn't feel like I deserved to have it. Tomorrow, I'd wish I had died in the tunnels I painted red. I didn't need Zephyr to warn me. My soul already felt bloodied and torn beyond repair. Every push forward felt like salt on a raw wound.

The back of my mind felt the webs of magick that flowed in the air, like strings caught in the wind, and tickled my face. Little by little, the magick gripped my chest in a warning, and I stopped running toward the unknown. I pressed my hand against the wall and used my Malice to see what I could not. I closed my eyes, my heart hammering in my ears, as the Aos Si stood guard around me like a forest of trees you'd never brave climbing. Beneath the stone ran line after line of spells and markings. I opened my eyes and tracked the power. I pointed out symbols on the walls up ahead. It was the end of the line for Fae magick. I knew, if we went any farther, I wouldn't be walking in as a Soul-Eater. That magick would be left in the tunnels.

"Wards." I turned to Aeden. "I hope you can still fight without magick."

Aeden leaned down. "We do not use Fae magick when we fight, Perdi. Where's the fun in that?"

"I don't need this to be fun," I countered. "Ready?"

"Lead the way." He motioned.

We walked the rest of the way, fifty feet forward, each step feeling like trying to run full speed through hip-deep mud. The Aos Si looked unfazed while my feet dragged on the floor. Unlike me, they were solid muscle and likely trained to fight in slop to their ears. The shadows tucked themselves behind me and pushed me from there. In any other case, I'd have been angry about the manhandling. Today, I appreciated the help. My legs would have worn out had I kept trying to force my way through the energy that pushed back with more force than I had.

The tunnel stopped at a stone doorway. On the other side, a room I had only seen in dreams stood our fate. Solas and Zephyr knelt in the middle of the room, their arms twisted behind their backs. Behind them was one Satyr, as big and hateful as the first one I had met. I didn't need magick to know he was not alone. The energy that poured out of the room told me a small army awaited our arrival. I glanced at the walls, symbols of protection, wards against magick and spells over spells. The power that rolled from the room made me take a step back at how full it really was. I couldn't see them, but dozens of men stood in that room. They'd never let us all come in as one. No one was stupid enough to see us all and invite us in. And once I stepped in alone, they'd have me at a disadvantage.

"We will release your two men in exchange for you." The man with all the cards spoke from behind my people.

I pushed my Malice against the glass wall of wards. I could barely feel Solas or Zephyr. Without having to touch them, their fading energy told me they were close to death. I doubted a pearl could save them. Death was already in the room with them, shaking their hands in an introduction. I thought of every option I had, every tool at my disposal, every sneaky way of winning—and came up empty each time. Every end result, if we fought, told me one or both of them would die before we could win.

"If you remain, your men can take these two freely. If you choose not to, they will both die," the man said.

I glanced around the room again and finally nodded. I couldn't break the spell and fight them off before Solas and Zephyr were safe. I couldn't do both. "I agree."

"Perdi." Aeden grabbed my arm.

"Get Solas and Zephyr out of here." I pulled away and motioned to the shadows. "Take them to Elda."

The wards holding us out of the room dropped away. They fell like flower petals in the breeze. All the power and hate in the room rolled out and twisted my stomach into a ball of nervous tension. My throat clenched as my stomach threatened to vacate. Two Aos Si stepped into the room, with me in the middle. They picked up Zephyr and Solas and left the room with the shadows.

"Return to the Dark Courts," I commanded my men. At first, they didn't move a muscle. "Please," I added, and they moved from the doorway.

"I'll be staying," Aeden said as he moved into the room behind me. "I am your Royal Guard. They'd have to kill me to get me to leave."

"What about Jayde? You're risking being lost to him."

Aeden leaned in. "You'll make sure I get home, or you'll take my body home for burial. A soldier cannot hope for anything greater than that."

"You will be sentenced to death, along with the one who remains." The Satyr's words cut through the room. His voice grated along my spine like nails on a chalkboard.

I opened my stance and dropped my arms to my side in preparation. I forced my body to relax. I had no intention of dying in this slice of hell. But I also didn't want to do what they would force me to do…fight my way out. There were never any easy ways out in Elphame. It was pain or suffering or death.

"I have come to understand what has happened to your people," I spoke calmly, although I had a raging river of fear in my stomach. I didn't want to do this. I didn't want their people to hurt more than they already had. And I certainly didn't want to be the one who offered more of it. "Because of this, because of the suffering you've already endured, I give you a chance, only one, to never come against me or mine again. If you agree, I will leave here and ensure no one steps on this island again. I give you my word."

"We refuse. And you have no army to make bargains. You are alone, save one who was foolish to remain."

"And I'm telling you, we are more than enough," I replied. "Please. I'm asking you, don't make me do this. I do not want to kill you. I would be happy with just leaving and never coming back. Please don't make me fight to leave, because me and my guard will be the only ones leaving this room alive."

"It is war."

"No. It is only death," I whispered. The only war that would happen would be in my soul, knowing what I would do. "If you force me to defend myself, I will leave no soul alive. Do you understand me? You will all die. I'll mourn your passing at my hands, but you will still die. All your people will be dead. Your kind will die on this island, and no one will have known you were even here. There will be no one who remembers your name."

"We will have your death, or we will gladly accept our own," he answered.

"Sir, we were born for war and death," Aeden spoke. "Let us leave, and you'll taste neither. You stand between choices for you and your people. Force us to stay, and you'll have chosen death for you all."

His eyes focused solely on me. "You are nothing within these walls."

"You're wrong. You invited a witch into your home, and she brought with her a wicked little creature," I answered and whispered to Aeden. "This is going to hurt, Aeden. Don't let go of me. If you let go, you die with them. I can't control it like Zeph can."

"I won't let go," he answered.

"No matter what," I said. "And when you think this is over, it isn't. Save your energy. This isn't the last fight of the day."

"They are fools," he whispered.

"They are broken," I answered.

The room was spelled against Finis and Fae. But I was born a witch. I called on my Malice and pulled the energy from the air, which I would pay for later. But I'd live long enough to regret the debt owed to fate. I didn't call on magick to break the wards or to end lives. I asked for the simplest of tasks to be done, bring one stone down from the wall. The spell, missing a piece, would fall on its own. I focused my attention on the stone, where the lines of magick overlapped.

I watched the rock come loose and felt the energy dance, like opening a curtain and letting the light into a room never once touched by the sun. The Satyr watched as the spell came down with one rock. He rushed to my front with his sword drawn. Aeden, with his hand gripped on my collar, spun us. With one slice, the Satyr's head rolled against my feet. The room erupted in screams as the other Satyr were now in the open. I unleashed my darkness as Aeden unleashed his own.

My Malice, wild and free, ate the souls who weren't smart enough to run. She was greedy, she was hungry, and so she ate heartily. I twisted my enemies and their fears, bringing them to their knees and finally to their deaths. I pulled everything they were and splashed the walls with their anger and blood, like paint. Even as I did it, feeling backed into a corner and having no choice, I hated myself for it. Knowing the reasons for their actions and hateful motivations, didn't help their cause. It wasn't enough for me to pause or stop. Guilt and pity wouldn't be enough for me to willingly die.

"Don't let go!" I screamed to Aeden as a familiar warmth tickled the back of my mind.

The shadows exploded through the room and ate the light, while my Malice ate everyone who was not touching me. I drank down their grief and anger and need for revenge. My heart broke for them, but I still killed them—or they would have killed me. I screamed as they died. I cried as I pulled their pearls from them. I felt each and every one of them wish for my death—death they prayed to the Gods for. But their Gods left them long ago, just as mine had.

I burned their world, and Aeden didn't leave my side. Flames, the very fire of my rage, burned the walls and everything that stood between me and tasting absolute freedom. Those who tried to come for me, Aeden brought them to the ground with his sword. I ate pieces of their souls and wrapped them with Malice. I would be taking a parting gift with me. I'd use their very lives to save the lives of my family. Given that they were responsible, I felt it only fair to use them to help me.

We cleared the room and ran through the rear tunnels. Aeden followed me and my Malice to the top. Before I even stepped out of the cave, on the backside of the island, I knew an army waited for us. Aeden squeezed my shoulder when the energy rolled in to greet us. He knew right then, just as I did, what Fae had helped the Satyr. Autumn was a very distinct smell, moss and forest and cowards. Zephyr had searched for the Autumn Court for months, but they had been here, on the island, waiting for him, waiting for this moment.

"Hello, Parrish. I would have thought you'd had enough of me by now," I said as I walked out of the tunnel, shadows of those I had just killed slagging behind, forced by the many souls from wars Zephyr had won. I brushed the dirt from my arms and smiled as the sun finally touched my face again. I used the sleeve of my shirt to clean the blood from my face, feeling it smear down my cheeks.

Parrish, king of the Autumn Court, was one of the few survivors from his court, from the war. He stood with a scraggly group of soldiers. "You've sent all your men home. How foolish of you."

I smiled. "Not quite."

Aeden stepped out behind me and stretched his shoulders, coming to a stand with his sword up and a grin on his bloodied face. "Say the word, my lady."

"If they run, do your worst." I drew two blades from my thigh holsters and rotated my neck. "They don't get off this island alive."

"One? You bring only one with you?" Parrish laughed.

"You know, that's the same thing the Satyr said before they fell." I shrugged. "What can I say? Good help is hard to find. You keep ones like this," I replied, and Parrish shook his head. A look of disgust rolled across his face. Had I been in his shoes, I'd have been just as disgusted by what I had just done. "So, how shall we do this? Do you want to run away and have us chase you down, or just line up, and we'll kill you one at a time?"

"If you line up, please do so in an orderly fashion, and we'll be in and out as fast as can be," Aeden added, and Parrish stared at him. "What? I'm only trying to help. If the line is a mess, it'll take us longer. I, for one, have other plans this evening and would like to move this along. Unless, Perdi, we could use this as a training exercise? Zephyr is a stickler for training, and it's been many days for us both. If we train today, maybe he'll let us skip tomorrow? Either way, it's your party. Just tell me where you want me to stand."

"No, no, I have places to be as well. You're right. A clean line. Time is money, and Parrish doesn't look like he can afford to spend another minute with us. You take the right, and I'll take the left." I told him. Hopefully, he'd handle everyone on his side, and I'd only have to worry about mine.

"You offer only games? You don't want to bargain for your life?" Parrish asked as if he had expected my groveling. "I was looking forward to turning you down and killing you as you begged."

"You won't get to do either, Parrish. I don't make deals with people like you," I replied.

"People like me?" he asked.

"Yes. The dead don't deal," I answered. "You can't pay your debts without a pulse."

"You and your one do not scare me." Parrish laughed.

"What about a few dozen of us?" Finn stepped around the cave from behind, and he didn't come alone. He looked over with a grin. "Oh, now you want us to follow your orders? We were picking up trash along the beach."

"That was considerate." I smiled.

Finn tossed a man to the ground beside me. I could smell a hint of magick lingering on his dead body. "Parrish, you left your Mages unprotected. Worry not. We found them all for you. The Sluagh hunted them through Elphame. A wee one dumped this on the shores, a message from the Court of Shadows. Nothing is free in Elphame. And now, you pay like these men did." Finn nudged the man with his boot. "This one was the only Mage the Sluagh didn't swallow whole. Unfortunately, he didn't have much to say after they were done with him."

"Dear God." Parrish stared at the body of a bloodied man and back up at what now stood behind me. He paled and took a step back.

"Your God doesn't live here, little king." Finn glared at him and winked at me. He'd play games with Parrish until the man took his own life out of fear, if I had let him. "Leave no one alive this time, little Crow. We don't have time to hunt them down later, and the Sluagh are busy right now."

I was eaten by the shadows, who grabbed both Aeden and me and pushed us through the air, landing and slicing, drifting and moving as one. We blasted through the little corner of the island. I was dropped to the ground for one kill shot, then to another location. We moved over the land and left death in our wake. We worked together and killed the last of the Autumn Court. Those who fell from my hand, I pulled their pearls from their screaming mouths. I focused on only those I killed, or I'd have eaten my people as well. With the shadows pulling me in and out, I understood why Zephyr was so deadly. In a matter of minutes, even if I had been alone, I'd have wiped the Autumn Court off the map. This was why we were drowned at birth. We held the balance of Elphame in the palms of our hands. It was unsettling and calming to know that if I was pushed hard enough, I could save myself, with or without an army at my back. But having them there made me feel like I could have walked straight into hell without flinching.

"You Soul-Eaters always hog all the glory," Finn complained from the rocks behind me.

"Get off your ass next time, and you can have as much glory as you want." I swallowed my laugh and stood over Parrish, Aeden's sword in my hand. Parrish struggled at first, then resorted to cursing my name.

"The next time someone comes for me, they had better bring more than one army." I spat the words. "You should have known that by now. I am Queen of the Dark. You should have brought all Elphame with you."

"You can't kill a king," he countered.

"Who said I can't kill a king? You wouldn't be my first, and you won't be my last." I shoved the blade into his neck until it came out the other side. "Huh, would you look at that? He's still alive."

"It's not iron. I'm still in training, Perdi. We don't leave with iron unless it is war or I'm promoted. Only the highest rank carry iron at all times," Aeden said. We both leaned over Parrish. I stared back at Aeden in question. He blushed. "I forgot to change my sword, okay? I was in a rush, and it's not like we need iron to kill."

I looked to Finn, who shrugged. "Sorry, no iron here. I keep burning myself with it, so I don't bother."

I glanced back at Parrish. "If we take his head, would he die, or would I be carrying around a blinking head?"

Aeden laughed until he realized I was asking a real question. "Sorry… I thought you were joking. Yes, he would die, just like everyone else does without a head. Even the Fae need their heads. Allow me, my lady." Aeden offered to take his head.

"All I have is a small dagger of iron." I pulled out my king-killing blade. "It would take me hours to cut off his head with this."

"It won't take me but seconds," he answered.

Parrish grabbed my foot. "I curse you."

"Get in line." I stepped back as Aeden took the head of a king.

* * * *

I landed on the lip of the caves of Sluagh and ran through tunnels, screaming for Solas and Zephyr. I got to the mouth of Elda's room to find it filled with Aos Si. All at once, I felt Zephyr's and Solas' pearls, and I staggered. In the middle, Solas and Zephyr were placed upon a stone rock and covered in white garb. Between them, a healer, Jare, tried to help. He looked up, his eyes glittering, and shook his head. At the front of the room, Elda stood with Nix cradled in her arms and tears streaming down her flushed cheeks. With one nod, I knew Nix would make it. We had gotten him to the caves in time. I sent up a silent thank you to the Gods. For once, they had heard my cries. But it was the tangible sadness pouring from Elda's soul that forced my feet forward and told me that not all my prayers had been answered. I pushed my way through the room, shoving those who were in my way. Everyone stared at me. Their eyes held pity and sadness, as if fate had already come and gone with her decision. The room was hot, and the walls were wet from body heat. The moment I stepped in, I felt like I was standing close enough to a fire to burn.

"No!" I screamed as I stood in the middle of them. There was so little left of their souls. It felt like dying stars inside. I couldn't feel them. "Don't go. Please, don't go."

I tried to push what little power I had left into both of them, but it wasn't enough. I knew it would never be enough. When the trainees finally got to the cave and stepped through the others, I screamed and tried to block them from Solas and Zephyr. I pushed, but it was like trying to shove a stone wall to the other side of Elphame. I held one blade but was willing to do as much damage with it as I could.

"You'll have to remove my dead body before you touch either of them! They're not gone yet." I screamed and backed up again. They would not take them from me. I would die before I let either of them go. "Back up!

I swear to whatever God is listening, I will kill whoever tries to take them."

A screech rippled through the cave from the halls and bounced off the walls, adding to the blazing heat. My leg tingled as a small Sluagh, the one I had leashed, pushed his way in and belly crawled on the floor. He moved to my side and screamed at the others, forcing them to take a step back. He drew his wings wide, blocking any who dared take Zephyr or Solas from me. His mouth snapped the air in a warning.

"Don't let anyone take them," I whispered. I touched his leathery shoulder. "Please, not yet. I'm not ready to let them go."

"We're not here to take them," Finn called out over the Sluagh's growls.

In unison, the Aos Si turned their backs to me and faced the room, protecting my two men. In a shoulder-to-shoulder circle, they guarded me. Instead of taking Solas and Zephyr, or removing me, they would stand against anyone else who tried to.

"My queen, tell us what you need." Aeden was the only one who could step around the beast, who had inched to the foot of the stones but didn't relax. He filled my nose with hot leather and a spicy scent that poured into the room as soon as he landed on the lip of the caves.

"Energy," I whispered. "Enough to bring them back. And I'm empty. I used it up already. I have nothing. Not even fate would allow a spell this big. I'd die trying to twist it."

Aeden knelt. "Take what you need."

"You don't have enough. I'd kill you, and it still wouldn't be enough," I answered. "Solas and Zephyr are too powerful. They'd need more than what you have."

"I would willingly give my life to answer the call of my queen," Aeden said. "My life is truly yours, a gift from me, free of will."

"I can't take your life, Aeden," I whispered, my words hitching in my throat. "But I won't forget this offer."

The guards all knelt in unison. Aeden looked up. "If you take from all of us, no one should die. We've done it before. We can do it again. Jare can make sure it's taken evenly."

"And if you do?" I asked.

"We trust you not to screw this up." Finn smiled. His face softened. "Take it all, Perdi, if that is what you need. In a world like this, it is rare to find something worth dying for."

"I'll try not to kill you," I answered. I smiled in return and tried to focus on Finn's face through tear-filled eyes. "I will never forget this, Finn."

"I'm not worried, Perdi. You've failed every time you've tried to kill me so far. I doubt you'll succeed today." He winked. "Not a day will go by that I don't remind Zephyr of when his trainees saved his ass."

I stood between my men and opened my Malice to the room. I let her drink down the power given freely by the very men who'd helped me save my family. I pressed it into Solas and Zephyr, but it still wasn't enough. It barely moved their pearls. I'd have to bleed Zephyr's men to ash, and still, I doubted it would help. I screamed my frustration into the hot room. I stared at the ceiling and shouted to the Gods and Goddesses. "For once, help me, please. Damn it, help me!"

The small Sluagh's scream answered my prayer. My body jerked as the very rock under my feet trembled. The room filled with Sluagh, and I drank from them.

The room churned with bodies, each coming with power and leaving, empty of Elphame magick. Jare stood at my side, draining the energy in the air and pouring it into my men. I held my hands over both Zephyr and Solas and pushed the power offered by their people into them and, with it, pieces of myself. I tore the scabs off my soul and bled my own will to live into them. I broke myself in half and gave them everything I had. The shadows hovered over me, giving me the souls I had taken on the island. I broke apart those who had stood against me and shoved their pieces inside Solas and Zephyr. I ate all who they were and saved nothing. Everything I was, I gave to them freely. I felt both of them climb back up from their darkness. I finally breathed, staggering into the stone. Those who I had bled of power trembled with me.

"Foolish little Crow," Zephyr sighed from the stone.

"A Soul-Eater, saved by a Crow, again." I crumpled to my knees.

"Perdi…" Solas whispered as if he were still far away and taking his time to come back.

"I win," I mumbled to Solas and felt his laughter dance across my skin.

"Perdi." Aeden reached for me. "You smell… different."

"Nothing is free. I took from fate a few too many times, and now she will take from me. Oh, this one is going to fucking hurt," I answered. I felt the payment seeking, the cost of my Malice stealing energy was due. I had spelled and taken power not mine to freely have, and now, I'd pay the price hanging over me. It rolled in my stomach, and I felt the fire start. It had been a long while since I had to pay a debt this grand. I had almost forgotten how awful it was. I was surprised she had waited this long to collect but was grateful, regardless of how much it would hurt.

"What do we do?" Aeden asked.

"There's nothing you can do." I reached out to the shadows. "Bring me somewhere safe, before I burn us all."

The shadows picked me off the floor and wrapped me tight inside, where I couldn't burn the world. The first few licks of flame came and stole my breath like a thief in the night. I curled into a ball and fought against the pain. Everything came with a cost, and this was mine to bear. It felt like being pulled apart and jammed into a small box, all at the same time—both hot and cold, heavy and light, cramped and stringy. I twisted against each wave of pain, unable to scream or breathe more than a gasp. But the tears came—they always did—and they were blistering.

I landed on the ground, hard and fast, knocking the very little wind I had out of my chest. My vision filled with little stars that wouldn't stop moving. I reached toward the stars, hoping I'd finally pass out. This was always much easier when I wasn't awake for it. It was the only solace to be found in payment, when it finally ate the world, and I sank into a deep sleep.

"Perdi!" The shadows swirled around me, and it was too much for me to focus on. It was like hearing a voice while my head was underwater. "Get up! You have to run!"

"What?" I groaned, sprawled on the ground with a belly full of fire. "Can't…run."

"Something is wrong. Magick that does not belong is pushing into the Gate. The magick we felt before, it is here. We can't carry you. You're being pulled toward it. You must move away," they replied. "Get up!"

I rolled to my front and onto my knees, only to fall forward. My arms wouldn't work. The cost that rolled through my body didn't care if I needed to run. The time to pay was now, regardless of what went on around me. At my side, the ground was littered with bodies. Mortals were in heaps. I felt the first pull of magick in my stomach. Something was calling me home, back to Whitwick.

"What's happened?" I groaned through gritted teeth. My stomach cramped, and another wave of darkness ate at the edges of my sight. Just moments ago, I welcomed the thought of passing out. Now, I fought against it.

"The mortals, they're doing something to the Gate. They're coming for you," they replied. "Open your mouth. This is the only way, and it is going to hurt."

"What are you…" I asked and choked on the shadows pushing their way in. I screamed around them slithering down my throat. It felt like a person was climbing inside—too big, too hot, too much.

The world swam, and I struggled desperately to stay awake. As the shadows coiled inside of me, I burst with energy, not of my own. I crawled across the grass. Each time I fell, the shadows pushed me from inside to get back up. I whispered for help, barely audible, but enough for those who listened for me to hear. My eyes opened to the feeling of being carried. I curled my Malice and pulled on the soul of whoever was stupid enough to pick me up off the ground.

"I'll drop you on your bloody head if you pull another drop from me." Finn's voice filled my ears. "Let's see you heal your fragile brain after it's bounced off the rocks, little queen of mine."

"Something is happening to the Gate." I stirred in his arms. "Don't let them get in."

"They won't, Perdi," Finn replied.

"Pin a note to anyone foolish enough to step through and send him back, our only warning. Any other person who is sent through will be killed on the spot. We will *not* be invaded."

"You've done enough, little Crow. We'll do the rest," he answered.

"Little Crow," I whispered.

My stomach rolled, and I turned my head. I heaved the shadows back up. The moment they left me, the pain returned. I'd make a note to talk to them about them helping me with the cost later. Right now, my words and willingness faded as the edges of the world darkened, and I was out cold. I didn't fight it. I knew whoever was trying to come through the Gate had to get through dozens of Aos Si and Sluagh, as well as the rest of these cursed lands, before they could get to me. If they still got me, nothing I could do awake would matter, and I'd probably be thankful that I wasn't conscious.

Chapter Ten

My three men had survived Satyr Island, but it had come with a cost I would now pay. I did as Elda had said I would. I broke my soul in half and bled on the world to save them, to save myself. I had ripped myself in half for them. I felt shattered once again. When I had first closed the Gate, I didn't think of how far those consequences could reach. And when I couldn't stop the destruction of it, it caused a ripple that ruined the peaceful existence of the Satyr. They, like me, had done what they had to do to survive, but it had boiled down to who could be more ruthless. For a Crow who wasn't born for greatness, was rebirthed in war, ate worlds to survive, ruthless didn't cover how dark I'd allow myself to venture. But that didn't help me afterward, when I had to face what I had done to those who did not deserve to be pulled into a war that was not of their own making. They died for a Crow who ate souls. I'd remember them, even if no one else did.

What was left of my soul had been dragged over the coals. And now the payment for my brokenness was due. I'd scuffed the last bit of soul from my body, trying to save my family, and replaced it with death and screaming and a war fought by a desperate Crow. No amount of healing would take that memory from me. And as each moment I had spent trying to find my family came into focus, I suffered all over again. But that was the only way to heal, not by pretending it never happened but by looking it dead in the eyes and letting it hurt. Soul scabs only formed once you admitted, 'yes, I did that'. And they would only heal fully once you said, 'I'm sorry'.

What had happened hadn't entirely been my fault, but it still hurt like it was. My shattered pieces remembered each face, each soul I'd taken and every cry I'd heard. I wouldn't change what I had done to save my family or myself, but I wouldn't have been so foolish to begin with. Every choice has a consequence well beyond that which we can see, and my decisions would always come full circle. The pain I felt, I earned, whether I put the ball in motion or not. Taking a life, irrespective of the reasons, should bring pain. It should mean something. It *should* hurt. And Zephyr had tried, almost to his death, for me not to have learned another brilliantly painful lesson.

But one day, not even eating the world would keep me from the pain fated to my soul. Sooner or later, I'd learn that suffering was a path I willingly walked, and those around me would suffer all the more for it. At each turn, fate stood with those I love tucked under her arm and dared me to best her. And I fought her tooth and nail to keep them. Eventually, I was going to lose. No one would win against fate. All we could do was distract her with shiny things, and right now, my bleeding soul was distraction enough.

Tucked into the shadows, I rested, remembered and understood why Zephyr was so willing to give his life for me. It was better than watching me be taken from him. I'd have sooner died than be without him. Like me, it was his fate to suffer. He saw me walk the same path he foolishly thought he could stop me from. And as raw as I was, as close to a final death as I had neared, I didn't regret it. To live is to suffer. But to love is to suffer gloriously. And nothing in this bloody world, on either side of the Gate, came without a price to pay.

Solas hadn't told me to tuck myself away, to save myself. But I felt it each time I went to his dreams. He didn't want me to come and was willing to die to save me. He knew I would burn for it, but I'd never scorch the Dark Courts. I'd eat my fire to protect them. All he had ever wanted in life was to find someone to love and to love him back—to find someone who would stand between his people and the gates of hell. With me, he found love for him and his people...*our* people. The moment I'd stepped into the room to save him, he'd fallen in love with me for different reasons. When he saw me, he saw a reflection of himself. He was no longer the only terror that roamed his lands and ate those who came for stragglers. He loved my inner monster more than I did.

I had given everything to save my family, to save myself, and now that it was over, I had nothing left for myself to live off of. I had cleaved myself in half, drained my very will to live, into Solas and Zephyr. The shadows rolled around me and pushed the world away. No one, not even Zephyr, could get to me, because they were mine now. They listened to the arguments around me but didn't let anyone touch my raw soul. Just breathing felt like pouring salt on a wound. Although I knew I was slowly fading, I wasn't scared this time. To die for those you love wasn't scary and wasn't nearly as painful as a pointless death. I knew I wouldn't stay in the shadows until I died, but I'd wait it out as long as I could. I needed a thin skin over my soul before I could come out of my dark cocoon.

Aeden had stayed in my bedroom, and not even Solas could command him from my side. Orrian fluttered in and out of the shadows, healing the wounds on my body with salve. Nix? No one dared tell him to leave. He'd have laughed as he had many times before. And whenever it began to feel like I couldn't take another breath, the shadows would loosen their grip just enough for me to hear Aeden and Nix. They would take turns telling me of their dreams, the reasons they still clung to life and faced their worst fears. And they guarded me and my pain, allowing me to remember and mourn. The trainees hadn't left, either. I could feel them in the distance, roaming the halls, walking through my bedroom and reading out loud to me. But it was the moments when I hated my memories that I would sense Solas or Zephyr. They'd feel my pain, and I'd hear their voices, sometimes just a whisper carried on the wind. But it was enough.

"Respectfully, sir, I am *her* personal guard, not yours. I cannot leave. I will *not* leave her side while she is like this, as is my duty. But I'd be happy to take a note and let my lady know you believe this is bullshit when she wakes," Aeden explained, on more than one occasion, to Solas, and each time Solas thought he knew better.

"But I am the king." Solas had rebutted several times.

"I'm glad you remember, sir, for it was the king who ruled that Perdi would be put before him in any great time of danger or need. As you can see, she is in need," Aeden replied, and I heard Solas' slew of curses before he slammed the door. "Good evening to you, too, sir." Aeden sat back on the bed with his book. "Does no one here have manners?"

"Perdi, you can't close it all out forever. You're fading, and the others can feel it," the shadows whispered.

"Just a little while longer. It doesn't hurt as much in here."

"It would, if we allowed you to feel it. Oberon is here, eating your fear and sadness, but even a Bodach gets full. His people are getting sick, consuming more than their little bodies can handle, trying to keep it from you. Perdi. What is left of your spark of soul is withering."

I pushed out their whispers. It hurt too much to think I'd have to leave the shadows. I'd have to face the world again, with all my smashed pieces far too fragile to feel the truth of Elphame. I had done it before, stood in this cruel world with a broken soul, and it hurt more than what got me to that place to begin with. But I knew it was time. Time to feel it all. It was only through that pain that I would come out to the other side.

"Do you want us to let you die?" they asked.

"No. I did, at the start, but not anymore," I answered and felt the shadows shift around me, letting the world in little by little. And inch by inch, I cried out in pain. It felt like standing in the middle of a storm made of fire, and the flames held shards of hot glass.

"Perdi." Nix's voice whispered through.

"Nix." I smiled at the sound of him. I always have.

"I gift you my pearl to rebuild what you have given," he replied. "I'm ready for you to see."

I watched the first spark of life flow through the shadows. *A pearl. A tiny star in a sea of darkness.* I reached out my hand and held it. Nix…all of who he was and would be. And I cried for the bravery it would have taken for him to give me his memories and his truths and fears. As the smallest drop of Nix rested in my chest, the burning emptiness cooled just enough for me to finally take a cleansing breath. I sighed as his memories breezed through me. He was beautiful inside. The sheer loyalty and love was almost too much to feel at once. I saw the moments he never wanted me to see or know. But who he had become, to overcome who he had been, made me weep for the nights I knew he couldn't look himself in the eyes.

"Little Crow." I could feel his warmth as he called out to me.

Another pearl came on the heels of Nix's. It was Solas'. I knew it was him. If the night had a smell, it was Solas. And the moment I touched it, it felt like he was wrapped around me. His memories felt as raw as I was, each twisted around the other to make a knot of memories he wished he never had. But before the sadness could drag me down, another pearl dropped into the shadows—Aeden's and all his dreams, wishes and hopes. I knew he'd reach for his dream for no other reason than love. But it was Faolan's and Oisin's pearls that surprised me. I didn't know they had returned and didn't think they cared enough to save me. Faolan's was familiar. Oisin's felt like eating ice cream too fast, leaving my head pounding from his frosted power. On their heels, one after the other, the Aos Si gave me their memories. They gave me what I needed to build parts of a soul that I no longer had. And although their souls tasted of days worse than this, they also tasted of reasons they fought to come home from battle—love, loyalty, forgiveness. And someone, in all those pearls, had learned to love potatoes because of me. I was their home now.

The shadows set me back onto my bed, into the arms of Solas, and I slept, really slept, for the first time since we had been home together. I stretched out, as only one does when they feel safe, and he twisted around me as he always had before. He whispered in my ear and ran his hands over my skin. Whenever I stirred, he'd send me back to sleep with whispers of everything right in the world. He stayed with me until the broken pieces were solid once again—days in bed, eating, loving each other, being together, remembering the reasons why it had been worth it. And not too far away, I felt Zephyr. Each night, before I slept, I felt him kiss my forehead and whisper to Solas. It was as if the world hadn't just handed us our souls on a platter. The wheels of the courts never stopped turning, scheming continued and war was back to being a breath away.

On my first day out of bed, I stood on my balcony and watched as the Sluagh left the yard and the forest behind my bedroom. One by one, after seeing me with their own eyes, they dipped their heads and returned home. The little one was the last to leave. But somehow, I knew he wouldn't be too far away.

"Why were they here? Has something happened again?" I asked.

"They didn't leave, Perdi." Solas wrapped a blanket around me from behind and hugged me into his warmth. There was no safer place in the world than tucked inside the arms of the man I loved more than my own soul. "They saw your cost, and when you were brought here, they followed from the caves. They stayed close by in case you needed pearls—and a great many were needed."

"Did someone ask them to do this, or did you order them?" I asked.

"Neither. The young one, who follows you around, brought only the strongest pearls of honor with him, for you are the only other they've followed. They came for you, Perdi, the Crow who bled for their king. All the Unseelie court is here. Faolan brought his strongest, and Oberon finally returned home with his people. Orrian came with a dozen from her army. Every Aos Si came, but it was the trainees who stepped forward for you. They're a little protective now. And they'll all likely linger around until they see you are okay. And are you okay?"

I turned to face him and shrugged. "Yes and no. I feel better than I was, but I'm still pretty raw. I don't regret it. I only wish I could have found a way that didn't leave my soul patched up again. Elda and Zephyr said I'd rip myself in half, but I wish I didn't have to, when things go south."

"Tearing your soul in half is part of learning how to be Finis and survive. Hell, it's how everyone in Elphame learns. But there are better ways. When Zephyr comes to you, to teach you how to be more than this, how to walk this path, don't balk. He can guide you in ways the rest of us can't. You are him, and he is you. You both are bound. You're Finis. Take his guidance, but don't take his shit. You're also the last Crow. You aren't made to take anything lying down."

I smiled. "Warmonger."

"Soul-Eater," he teased, and we both turned to my bedroom door.

Zephyr strolled in with Aeden close at his back, chastising him. "Sir, you can't just walk in here."

"Fuck off, Aeden," Zephyr barked back. "If you want to be helpful, push that breakfast cart onto the deck, so we can eat. We always have breakfast together. Get used to it or go away."

Aeden looked around Zephyr to me, and I nodded. He stopped trying to force the immovable object that was Zephyr and turned back to the door. He pulled a cart in and hurried it to the balcony.

"He has no manners," Aeden grumbled and gave me a wink. He was enjoying the leeway he had within his new position and would probably hang himself with that extra rope. Until then, it would be entertaining. "Good morning, Perdi."

Zephyr turned to face him. Anger mixed with insult played over his face and iced his blue eyes. Little bits of shadow leaked from his fingertips. "What did you call her?"

"Perdi," I answered. "Let it go, Zeph. I've asked them not to call me by title, and if you force them to call me 'ma'am' or 'my lady,' I'll burn you alive while you sleep."

"I'm not comfortable with that. It's too informal, too personal," Zephyr replied.

"Zeph, anything else makes me feel…not real, not me, not loved. Here, in my home, at least let me pretend." I answered and watched him release a breath of hot air. When he finally nodded, begrudgingly, I smiled. "Thank you."

"Only during informal meetings, sir," Aeden added, then yelped as Nix whizzed by him. "Christ, I didn't even hear you."

"And you wonder how we kill so many of you giant ones? No one ever looks down. Hardly surprising that your life expectancy is half of a gnomes." Nix jumped onto one of the chairs. "Good morning, Perdi."

"Good morning, Nix." I grinned ear to ear to see him. Not a single bruise was left on his little body.

"Call if you need me." Aeden left us on the balcony.

"Who put a table and chairs out here?" I finally noticed and took a seat.

Zephyr thumbed toward the door. "Aeden and Finn. All the trainees had their meals here, while you were healing. They refused to leave, and each took shifts guarding your room. They're a cocky bunch."

"They're a good lot." I smiled at the thought of them. I could almost picture them playing their games, deciding who they'd fight.

It hadn't gone unnoticed by any of us how we fell into our rhythm once again. Each moved around the other, passing favored foods and drinks, making jokes and small talk. Breakfast together was exactly what my soul needed, and it was why they each had come. We always had at least one meal together each day. And dinner was usually reserved for Solas and me, unless a war was brewing. Given the brink of world's end we frequently teetered on, Zephyr and Nix would find their way to our table for dessert.

"So, what have I missed?" I finally asked as I nibbled on my muffin.

"Your father has been moved to the Dark Courts," Solas replied. He wouldn't bother telling me to focus on myself. It hadn't worked the last time he uttered those words, and it wouldn't work now. "Lily informed me he came right after you had been there last, when you felt the magick was off."

I nodded. "There's no reason to go to the mortal realm now."

"Eventually, they'll come to us," Solas replied.

"They already have. Most of the Mages were mortal, not Fae. I may have been out of it when I left the caves, but I saw the bodies at the Gate. They tried to come again. And I don't think that will be the last we see of them," I answered, and a collective groan filled the air. "I hope you all got some rest on your little island vacation. I don't think we'll be kicking back for much longer."

Solas winked. "There will always be war, and we will always be ready for it."

Chapter Eleven

I spent a week with my mind on anything other than what had happened on the island, and no one brought it up. I needed to fill myself with happiness before I dipped my soul into a pool of horrible sadness. I wasn't ignoring it, but I was finding a comfortable pace to process it. I spent that time with my dad, helping him build his new life in Elphame. When my father had come, he'd told Lily he would not be returning to Whitwick. Elphame was my home, so it would become his home as well. Wherever I was was where he wanted to be. On Lily's command, Fae entered Whitwick, and in a matter of hours, they had moved my father's house to Elphame. It had caused a big enough stir that Lily had sent several dozen through just to keep the peace. Although no one was killed, Whitwick had tried to stop them. And as selfish as it was, I was thankful my childhood home was close enough that I didn't need to risk being burned as a witch just to see my father.

The home I had grown up in was exactly as it had always been, right down to the front gate. When I touched the latch, it gave me the same feeling of returning home as it always had. Guarded by Aos Si, my father's entire house was moved across the Gate, including the garden, which Nix had promptly moved back into and scowled at the brutality used against his tomatoes. He always had a home with me, but having a garden of his own was what gnomes lived for. And the first time I watched him sink his hands into the dirt, his entire body filled with calmness. His home would only be found among his herbs and fruits. He'd follow me into hell, but he needed his garden to heal from whatever we endured with the monsters.

My father's house was on a small piece of land near the manor. He was given the position of Mortal Emissary. It was nothing more than a title, since the mortal realm was off-limits, but it gave my father something to do each day. So far, he'd done nothing more than explore Elphame, something he had always wanted to do. With Nix on his shoulder and the Aos Si keeping a close eye, he mapped a world he had wanted to see since he was a little boy, back before he understood the fog. Some days Zephyr would go with my father, other days, Solas. Morrow allowed my father access to his lands, and the Golden Court couldn't do much about it since we had their king, and he wasn't in a position to stop us from the bowels of a dungeon.

The week of respite ended, as I knew it would. I stood with Solas at my side, on the beach of Satyr Island. I didn't want to take another step forward. The pain of what I had done still bled like a fresh nosebleed. I closed my eyes and huffed a long and hot breath of dread. I grabbed onto his hand and led him to the caves, into the belly of the island. He followed me down into the tunnels we had taken during our hunt and rescue.

"Are you sure you want to do this?" Solas asked.

I shook my head. "Not particularly, but I need to. If I don't, I'll never be able to heal from this place."

Solas followed me through twists and turns until we came to a room with a door. I pushed it open to the surprised faces of those I had let live. Women and children, and several men who hadn't stood against me, were clustered together. Their wide eyes and fear charged the air with a stickiness that coated my skin instantly. The men quickly moved in front of the others, blocking me from reaching the weak. But I wasn't there for war or harm or anger. I was there to make reparations. I came to the island out of duty, responsibility and humility.

I lifted my hands to show I wasn't armed. "I am not here to harm anyone."

A man, a little older than the rest, stepped forward, a small knife in his shaking hand. He held it out as though it would be enough to stop me. It wouldn't. But I stepped back just the same. "Why are you here, witch?"

"I have come to answer for the crimes against your people. Those who had acted against you are either in prison or dead," I answered. "I didn't know what was happening here in my name. I didn't know you were being hunted or that your people were being killed for sport. And by the time I found out, it was too late to do anything to help you. But I am here today to help. I am here to repair what has been done."

"We don't need your help," he spat. "You've done more than enough for us."

"I understand." I nodded and felt the first tingle of tears begin to form. I hadn't hunted them for sport. I did it for war, for my family. But broken souls didn't care much for the details or the reasons. As someone who had been hunted, I understood his pain. And like him, I hated those who hadn't earned it all, simply because it felt good to put a face to my pain. I understood the man better than most others ever could. "I will leave if that is what you wish. But, if you will not accept my assistance, would you take the help of someone else who isn't me or of my court? I do not have to be involved, but the offer for aid is still there."

"Yew, enough war, enough death," a female's voice called out.

"Yin, it is not your place," Yew replied to her voice but didn't turn to look at her.

"These are the last of our people. It is my place to wish for life over death." She stepped forward and put her hand on his. "We've lost too much. There is no reason to lose more. Pride and revenge are no longer reasons to bury more of our people. We should not have taken her family to replace our own. It has cost us, and I'm not paying for any more losses." She stepped in front of him. "My pride is not bigger than my wish for life. We are in need of food and medical supplies. We no longer have our tools to make more medicines, and our food sources above are damaged. We would starve long before we could regrow what is needed."

"Of course. I can have medicines and food delivered until you're able to regrow your crops. If you need any specific plants or roots, I can have those replaced, if needed," I answered. "Do you want me to ward your island again? It will take me some time, but I can try."

"No, we've hidden long enough. If we continue to remain in the past, we will die there. This island was a refuge, but that is no longer the case. It is nothing more than a graveyard, a reminder of what we've all lost."

Solas stepped up with his hands loose at his sides to show he had no ill intentions. "You do not have to stay here. You have safe passage into my lands or back to Blood and Bones."

"We would sooner die out than face another day with Solene," Yin answered. "It was not a place we fared any better than here."

"She's dead, and those left behind are not like her," Solas replied. "But if you do not want to go there, I would grant you safe passage through the Dark Courts and would be willing to speak on your behalf to any court you'd prefer."

She thought about it for a moment. "Winter. We chose this land because the Winter King, Amphion, refused us sanctuary. Winter was the only other territory with lands far from court. We would be grateful if you could find us a way into their mountains, where the rest of our people went."

"The old King of Winter is dead, and we don't speak his name. His son, Faolan, is now the king," I replied.

"I am sure he is as missed as Solene," Yin replied. "I will lose no sleep for his death."

"I don't think many did," I replied. "You mentioned the rest of your people?"

Yin nodded. "Those who left with us. They are not Satyr, but we were one people in the belly of Blood and Bones. If you could find us safe passage back to them, I would consider any debts between us paid on our end. How can we make amends for our acts against you and your people? We have little to give, but over time we would be able to pay."

"I want you to live, nothing more. Let us leave here today without hate and with no more suffering. There is so little room in Elphame for kindness and forgiveness. Let us use this space for only that," I replied, and she nodded. "I'm going to call on the shadows and request they bring the Winter King here, Faolan. He will not harm you, but I cannot grant safe passage through a land that is not mine."

"Very well," she answered and stepped back to her people. She looked hopeful, and I prayed Faolan would be as understanding as I was. I'd bribe him if I had to.

I stepped out of the room and asked the shadows to request Faolan and Oisin join us on the island. "Tell him of what has happened here and what I need. Ask him if he would be willing to help."

I waited in the hall and paced. I rolled my shoulders and neck, feeling the tension in my muscles with each passing second. I didn't like being down in the tunnels on an island I had conquered. Memories of me running by this very room rocketed my pulse. I closed my eyes and tried to breathe through the horror of that day—the screaming, the sounds of hooves on the rock, babies crying. I had watched the last of them creep into the room where I found them today, praying to the Gods that I hadn't seen them...but I had. My Malice had tried to steer me in their direction. She wanted them all. Instead, I led the Aos Si away from them. When Aeden had hesitated, I glanced back once and shook my head. With one nod, we decided to do what Zephyr had taught us not to do. We left them alive. It would either come back to burn us or give us a chance to do what was right. I was okay with either option. If they came back with more vengeance on their fingertips, I'd take their lives and wouldn't feel guilty for it. But if, by some twist of fate, they choose life. I'd help them, and I'd sleep better for it.

The shadows returned with Oisin and not Faolan.

"Where is he?" I asked Oisin. "Why didn't Faolan come?"

"He is busy, so he sent me," he replied.

"What the hell do you mean, he's busy?" I asked, my arms now crossed and my temper rising enough for Oisin to grin.

"The court doesn't stop because you want it to. If what you had to say was so important, you should have come with your shadows instead of sending them to fetch us," he replied, and I dropped my arms. He was right. "Faolan sent me. Deal with it, or let me get back to caving. The shadows already told us what you're looking for."

"And?"

"And I need to speak to them before I make a decision."

"Faolan will hold it up if you agree?" I asked.

"He will. He trusts my judgment. It's why he sent me."

Oisin followed me back into the room. "This is Oisin, the Commander of the Winter Court. He speaks for his king, Faolan."

"My king has agreed to allow you sanctuary within our lands. However, you must agree to a few things first," Oisin said.

"Such as?" Yin stepped back to the front.

"Before you are permitted sanctuary, you must agree to honor the treaty we have with the Dark Courts at all times. That is the only treaty he has, which he will protect fiercely and without mercy. You will not come against the throne or its people, family and friends. Of course, you can protect yourself from all, but our court is neighbored by family and friends, and our king does not permit acts against those he cares for. The Hallows, where you'll be going, where the others who left Blood and Bones have gone, neighbors only Winter Court. From the mountains, you can see the Court of Shadows, a Dark Court. The caves along the backside are off-limits. We cannot stop what will happen to you should you venture into the caves of the Sluagh."

Yin nodded. "Respectfully, Commander Sir, what would be the expectation of us, should your throne war against another court?"

"War leaves no one untouched. That is the unfortunate truth of Elphame. But, our expectations of you will be no different than the rest of our people. If there is war, we expect you to run and hide and save who you can along the way. You will *never* be asked to fight. We have an army for that. But you will be asked to save those you can. The Unseelie courts stand together, both Winter and Dark. All our people band together and all are saved, regardless of court or bloodlines. That is absolute. We help each other, *always*."

"That is fair," Yin replied. "We do not wish to fight, but we would save those unable to save themselves."

"If you can agree to those terms, we will help you get to those who left Blood and Bones and will help you get settled. There are several cave systems you're free to use. After which, you will be expected to work, trade or barter for whatever else you need. There's lots of work, so there'll never be a shortage of opportunity for you to prosper."

She turned back to her people and whispered. She glanced back once, finally nodding. "We agree."

"An oath between our people will be cast the moment your feet touch our soil," Oisin added.

"And an oath you shall have," Yin replied.

"The Dark Court will give supplies and gold to help you until you're on your feet," Solas added. "If you uphold our treaties, bring no acts of war against us or our people and friends, you will have freedom within our lands."

"We would wish to remain a secret in the hills of Winter, if this is possible?" she asked. "We very much wish to live our lives away from courts and wars."

Solas nodded. "Then that is what you will have, a peaceful existence away from court."

"When would you like to leave?" I asked.

"Now," she answered. "We suffer greatly, remaining here. The sooner we move, the sooner we can rebuild."

I nodded and motioned to the shadows. "Can you help Oisin take these people to the mountains of Winter?"

"It will take time, but we can help, if Oisin shows us where to take them," they replied.

I stepped toward the door and turned once, facing the woman who had spoken for her people. "I'm so utterly and completely heartbroken for what was done to you and your people and for what I did when I came. I'm so very sorry for what I've done and for what I've taken from you. If ever you need an ally or a friend, know I will be there. I will never miss your call for help again."

She nodded. "As am I, Perdita Darkmore. My heart breaks for the sadness we all feel. I hope if our paths cross again, they cross as friends and not as enemies. And I thank you for coming back, for making sure we fared well. Go with peace."

We waited until the Satyr collected what they could and watched as the shadows pulled them all from the island in three trips. On the last trip, they took Solas and me and left us in the forest by the manor.

"I'm proud of you, Perdi." Solas kissed my forehead. "That wasn't easy. Most wouldn't have gone back for fear of facing what they had done."

"There's blame to be shared with many, but my guilt wouldn't allow me to walk away. I took enough from them. I had to give back what I could."

"I love you." He pulled away and looked at the position of the sun. "I'm running late. Orrian wants to negotiate for more land. She says she needs four feet on either side for hedges."

"Hedges?" I laughed. "Are you going to give it to her?"

"I'd give her our very house and property if it made her happy. A few feet is nothing," he replied. "I owe her my life and yours, many times over. But, as she is a queen and I am a king, she is pushing for us to do this the old-fashioned way."

"Fight to first blood?"

"God, no... She'd peel the skin from my face. She is coming to bargain before the throne. She would like to trade fruits for the sale of the land."

"Tell her I send my love," I called out as he dashed back toward the house.

I wandered through the trees to my favorite spot and took a seat. It was the only place in all the Dark Courts where I could see for miles and not be interrupted by houses or hills. It had just the right amount of sun and shade, and the wind always blew in just the right direction to catch hints of lavender and mint.

I looked up to a familiar pull on my stomach. "Hello, Zeph."

"Little Crow." Zephyr sat beside me. He passed over a small white bag. "I packed a picnic."

I smiled. "Aeden sent this, didn't he?"

"Yes." Zephyr laughed. "Why him? Of every Aos Si, you picked the lowest member. Hell, Finn would have been a better choice, and I can't even stand that guy. Why would you pick the least likely to win?"

"Obviously, I didn't, given we are all still alive." I playfully elbowed his shoulder. "Zeph, when I first came to Elphame, I was the lowest, beneath the dignity and courtesy of all others. There literally was no one lower than a Crow in all Elphame. When I met Aeden, I knew he wouldn't just help me save you. He would help me save myself. He knew what it was like to walk a path you'd sooner die on than take another step forward. With Aeden, I saw pieces of you in him, pieces of me. There was a fight in him that I could relate to. Once, I was the least likely to win in this entire realm. But here I am because I chose those who I knew would fight for me, not just win for me. And you can't find that in ranks or titles."

"Well, it's gone to his bloody head," Zephyr joked. "He's ordering people about, making demands in your name. He moved my bedroom at the manor because he says I snore and it's too close to your bedroom. Apparently, your sleep is a concern of his. He says you work too hard, and it's his job to ensure you rest, better than the rest of us. What is it that you actually work hard at doing, besides wars and creating a soul garden out back? Now that I've mentioned it, I've never seen you work a single day here. What job do you have that's so bloody important?"

I laughed and leaned into his shoulder. "Do you want your bedroom back?"

"Do I look like I want to fist-fight your personal guard?" he asked. "I think he'd do it, Perdi, just to prove a point. And it's not like I can fight him and win. He's a Royal Guard. I might as well be punching you in the face. It comes with the same penalty."

"First, like anyone could possibly penalize you to any great extent and live. Second, you *have* punched me in the face—many times, in fact," I countered. "Two days before you were taken, you broke my nose."

"Training doesn't count," he answered and grinned mischievously. "I think it's time Aeden reports for training."

"Let him find his way, his place in the world. I think he just wants to make a good impression, prove something we both know he doesn't have to prove. But we all need to make our point in the world." I picked through my lunch bag and smiled. Nix had sent fruit and vegetables from his garden. I passed Zephyr an apple. "You know, Aeden is not proving anything to me, Zeph. He's proving himself to you. He wants *you* to see that he was worth not giving up on, that he became something more because you kept him alive when he wanted to die. You gave him hope. Let him show you what he's done with it. Aeden wants you to be proud of him. He looks to you as the sun and the moon. The entire time we were on the island, Aeden spoke of you and what he thought you would do in that situation. He is driven by your faith in him. He's determined to be more than just a soldier. He wants to be someone you're proud to have trained, someone you'd mention as a worthy example to others. They all feel that way. You kept them alive when they wanted to give up. Let them show you that they were worth it."

"He's a good lad. They all are." Zephyr bit into his apple and moaned at the sweetness that poured from apples Nix had once tended to for a decade. "I felt them coming…all of you. The moment the wards went down on the island, I knew every single soul who was with you and knew you'd burn the world and they'd help you light the fires. There was no doubt in my mind, once I knew who you had selected, you would find me, and they'd die to clear your path."

"Solas made fun of my choices," I added.

"Both he and I would have done the same thing. We'd leave the full-ranks to guard our people and take the others to find our family. But you are not us, little Crow. I'd have surrounded you with the absolute best, not trainees. Though, I am proud of what they did and who they've become."

"Lucky for me, you weren't there to make those decisions," I replied, but I couldn't hold on to my cheerfulness. "You tried to stop me. You sent me away. Why? And don't give me that crap about trying to save me from myself."

"I did. It was a strange feeling. I wanted you to help me. I didn't want to die any more than you'd want to. But I also didn't want to ask you to do what needed to be done. I didn't want to be responsible for your pain. I felt this overwhelming need to still protect you, even while chained to a wall—and I still do. Nothing will ever change that. It's partly because I love you and partly because we are Finis. We are driven to protect each other, even to our deaths. I'm glad to be alive, but I still think you risked far too much."

"I told you I would. I oathed myself to you."

"I released that oath when I released my shadows."

"You're not getting your shadows back."

He kissed my forehead. "I'll fight you for them."

"Do you want to risk death again so soon?" I asked and winked. "How the hell did they even take you? You're a Soul-Eater. Why didn't you just eat them?"

"They waited until we were in the Wildlands. We do not war there—or so I thought. They took Nix first, and I had a split second to choose. Do I save myself or save you? For me, that has always been more than enough time to decide. But I couldn't just save myself. At that moment, all I could think of was, how could I save you? If they succeeded and killed me, how would you protect yourself? I knew they'd eventually take Solas, as well, and you'd be on your own. So, I did the only thing I knew would work. I sent you my shadows and hoped it would be enough. I hoped they would keep you safe, and you'd keep our people safe. Then I woke up in that stone prison. Once they told me of their plans to get to you, I decided I'd rather die than allow you to kill yourself to get to me. You rescued me once, and it ripped your soul apart. How could I ask you to do it again? I couldn't watch you suffer like that again."

"This is why Soul-Eaters are always alone, so they're never faced with having to choose," I asked, and he nodded. "But we're not alone, Zeph. We are bound. You can't leave me, and you can't save me from everything. I love you for trying, but I will always come for you. There will never be a time I won't. It's best you decide the least painful route for me, or I'll drag myself through glass every time."

He nodded. "You are as loyal as you are ruthless, but I didn't think you would come. Nix kept telling me you would, but I thought he was just hopeful."

"Why would you think that?" I asked. "How could you think I'd leave you there?"

"I have your pearl, little Crow. I've felt every anguish you have. I didn't think you'd risk going back to that dark place for anyone. But when Solas showed up in the same boat as me, I knew you'd come for him. You'd burn the fucking world for him."

"It wasn't just Solas. Yes, I would kill anyone to get to him. But, Zeph, I'll cook off my soul to bring you home and wait for you to put me back together once we are safe. Solas is my oathed partner, and I'd do things for him that I don't even want to admit out loud. And Nix? I'd have to get in line behind a list of others. But you? You're something else entirely. You're a part of me."

"I've never had someone who would always come, Perdi. I've always been the one doing the saving, the one suffering, the one who has been alone. I thought I was saving you."

"You're not alone. Not anymore." I hugged his arm. "I'll always come."

"While dragging my ragtag army with you." He smiled and shook his head. "This is a first for them, to cross a border for war with only a five-minute warning, led by a little Crow and a trainee. I've heard the stories, and it's probably the craziest thing any of them have ever done. And I'll never get over them calling you by your first name. It's too personal."

"You are their family, and someone took you. It was very personal for all of us," I countered, and he scowled. "I was queen for a week. It's not like I knew what I was doing. I was winging it."

"No king and no queen command the Aos Si. We do not follow a throne or a crown. We refer to Solas as our king out of respect because he deserves it, which terrifies the other courts into submission. But they followed *you*, Perdi—a little Crow, not the queen. There will never be a time they don't answer your call. They see you as their family now," he replied, then laughed. "I'll never hear the end of it, the trainees who saved the scary Soul-Eater. You've cursed me until I die."

"Zeph, you must know in your heart how very deep you live in mine. You're not alone anymore." I curled into his side. "When you showed me your darkest memories, I felt that day you brought the bird back to life, that you feared from that day on you'd be alone."

"Then I saw you and knew I wouldn't be. I have seen you throughout all my life. As you've railed against your own fate, I, too, have fought mine. To have someone means you can lose someone. I don't want to be here if you're not."

"One day, one of us will be standing here alone," I whispered. "I don't want it to be me, either."

"Bound Soul-Eaters usually died together. The longer we're together, Perdi, the less likely the other will survive our deaths. It has always been that way. It is why we remain alone, away from the rest of Elphame. It is for no other reason than to protect Elphame from the sorrow that follows us."

"Sounds about right. Fate seems to be really keen on the suffering part of my life. Why not throw in going down in a fiery blaze with another Soul-Eater?"

"Solas will end the world at the loss."

"I'll be dead, so I won't care who burns under his touch," I answered.

"When you left the caves, I felt the Gate pull on you. Solas rolled off the stone and was crawling to get to you. He sent out a call to the Sluagh, who were led by the little guy you've favored. But it was the trainees who were first out of the caves as soon as your voice whispered through the room. I remember thinking, the world will never be the same now. You had saved us only to die, and I regretted not being able to die with you."

"I don't think we've seen the last of the mortal world," I replied. "This is only the beginning. I can feel it, like a storm taking its sweet time arriving. I can smell the rain in the air, and now I'm just waiting for it to pour."

"So do I."

I spent the rest of my afternoon with Zephyr, healing parts I didn't want to poke at and shedding light on the mortal world and the risks they could present, should they be foolish enough to come. We knew they would. It was the nature of all creatures to either run from danger or toward it. In this case, the mortals weren't running away anymore. Zephyr's people were patrolling the area and had wards placed around the perimeter, just in case. We weren't the trusting bunch. Whatever could happen has happened and will continue. Until I knew there would never be a chance, I'd keep my eye on the courtless lands and the Gate until my dying breath. To do anything less would be to invite the monsters out of the closet.

"I'll see you tonight." Zephyr stood and offered me his hand. "Happy birthday, little Crow."

"It's not my birthday yet," I replied. "I don't need a party."

"Tell that to Nix and Aeden. It's all they can talk about—the little Crow and her needs. They're running Solas ragged with party demands," he replied. "They want to host the party now, before you're eating cake in the middle of a mortal war."

I rolled my eyes. "I hate banquets."

"As do I, and that is exactly why they're doing this. Eventually, they'll stop meaning the horror you remember them to be and will become a time to celebrate, as they should be," he replied and walked me back to the manor. Along the way, four Aos Si were walking to the forest, each carrying a small fruit tree from the island. My gift to Orrian.

"Shouldn't you be preparing for your party... Perdi?" Finn asked, and Zephyr growled at the informality. Finn grinned ear to ear. He knew it irritated Zephyr and chose to do it out of spite.

"If you purposely piss him off, you can't hide behind me." I shook my head at his stupid bravery. "I'm heading there now. Will you be there?"

"If Zephyr doesn't break my legs between now and then." He hefted his tree a little higher onto his shoulder. "I have to run. Solas gave Orrian more land. We'll be moving trees around until she eats up the entire Dark Court."

"See you tonight," I called out.

"I told you to stay away from one person, and he's your new best friend," Zephyr grumbled.

"If it helps, I tried to kill him a few times," I replied.

"He looks mighty healthy for someone who was hunted by a Finis," Zephyr replied.

"He grows on you, you know?" I grinned. "Zeph, if it weren't for Finn, Cal would have killed me the first chance he got, and he would have succeeded. With you and Solas gone, I stood very little chance of defending myself against a power as great as Cal's. Finn was the only one who could play the cat and mouse game and have it be believable to everyone else. Finn never once left me, and he did it for you. His love for you is deeper than his will to live."

"He does have a way about him that makes you want to kill him in his sleep," Zephyr replied but smiled. "He's been looking for his home, a family of his own since I met him. I think he's finally found it with you."

"With us, Zeph. He sees you as his family as much as he looks to the rest of us. Go easy on him, and maybe he'll go easy on himself for once."

We left the trees and headed back toward the manor, with Zephyr muttering about training, broken bones and teaching hard lessons. A week with me, and apparently, I'd ruined his trainees. Zephyr and I headed in different directions—me to the shower, him to yell at Aeden.

I dressed with the scent of flowers in my bedroom and didn't recoil from the smell—a gift from Zephyr to help take away memories I didn't want. I stood in front of my mirror, and for the first time in a long time, even after sloughing off most of my soul, I could look myself in the eyes and didn't feel ashamed of who I saw staring back at me. I still felt the deep ache of sadness, but I wasn't filled with sharp regret. I would mourn for what I had done but wouldn't let it pull me into the wound. I spun in the mirror and grinned. I didn't *need* the party, but I wanted one to feel normal, like it had all been worth it, to show the others that the pain they'd carry was worth it, and I'd show up for them. This banquet wasn't just for me. It was for us all to come back together for reasons that had nothing to do with planning a war and everything to do with why we went into battle in the first place.

"Perdi," Solas called from my door with a knock.

I opened my door with a smile and stepped out. "Good evening."

"Happy birthday." He pulled me into his arms. "You look radiant."

"And you look… Do you not own any other color than black?" I asked.

Solas wore his usual black dress pants and white dress shirt, untucked. His hair, always wild and free, hung to his shoulders. "Shall we?"

I linked my arm in his and smiled. "I feel like we've done this many times before."

"If you play your cards right, you'll end the night screaming again."

I felt my face flush. "You say the sweetest things."

Solas led us through the manor into the banquet room. I wasn't flooded with thoughts of death and war. The usual dark colors of the court had been replaced with bright purples, pinks and greens. It was decorated for a birthday and not a show of strength and power. The looks from the others were smiles and the lifting of glasses. We walked the ballroom, as we had many times before, only this time, the very first time, I wasn't looking for an escape plan.

"Wine?" Solas slid into position beside me and passed me a glass. It reminded me of the nights he and Elswyth had kept me sane at the Golden Court.

"Thank you." I smiled at the memories. They weren't all bad. When I stopped long enough to look for the moments that weren't tarnished by war and hate, I saw the calm touch of love and family.

"Little Crow, I think this is the first time you've come to a banquet and not plotted someone's death," Solas whispered as he kissed my cheek.

"The night is young," I replied with a wink. "I'm sure someone will do something to tick me off."

"And I'm the warmonger? Dance with me?" Solas held out his hand. He gripped me around the waist and spun me through the hall. "I don't even remember what I was doing at your age."

"Probably stabbing someone, Solas." I laughed as he spun me a little quicker. "You didn't become the nightmare of Elphame with your dance moves."

"If nothing else, you keep me humble, wicked little creature." He pulled me tighter and spun until I screamed. "I have moves you haven't seen."

"I'm pretty sure I've seen them all."

He pressed his hips against mine and wiggled his eyebrows. "We shall see, won't we?"

We danced until my legs wobbled and my feet wanted no more. Eventually, I moved to the edge of the room, where I had always felt more comfortable. I stood and watched with a glass of wine and was content with where I stood. Gone was my need to seek revenge, and I didn't miss it in the least. The party was all the things I needed and wanted. My family, all of them, were safe under one roof. My friends from far and wide joined for one night. Morrow and his wife, Elda and an older fellow no one knew about, Faolan's court, and those I knew from our court, graced the dance floor. Sluagh filled the yard, creatures and critters gorged on food. Orrian danced with her people, far above the feet of others. It was all I could have wanted and everything my soul needed.

"Happy birthday, Perdi." Nix jumped onto the table beside me and passed me a little red box.

"You didn't have to get me anything, Nix. Thank you." I opened the box and smiled.

"I made it for you," he answered. Nix had given me a necklace with a small pearl pendant, a symbol of the pearl he had given me. "I traded grape jelly with a water nymph for a clam."

"I will treasure this and your pearl," I replied, putting it on right away. "Thank you for everything."

"Always," he answered and tipped his head.

"Happy birthday." Zephyr cleared his throat, and Nix took his leave.

"I got your flowers, thank you." I turned to him, and he shoved a box into my hands.

"It is a key," he answered. "Nix said I should put it in a box as a surprise."

"Yes, what a surprise." I laughed and opened the box. Inside, a small worn key. It looked as if it had been rubbed down over years of touch. "If it's for the island, it's a little late, no?"

"It is to no door still standing," he answered. "My mother gave it to me when I left home. She said it would help me always find my way back. You, little Crow, can use it to find your way home whenever you're lost. And through it, I'll always find my way to you."

"Thank you, Zeph." I strung it onto my pearl pendant necklace and would hold it over my heart as I did my love for my family and friends.

Faolan, to my surprise, gave me a small snowflake carved from a Winter Court stone. A token that I was welcome in his court and would be protected. Oisin presented me with a new iron blade because he recognized my soul's deadly force and said I went to war more than he did. He was ever-practical, that man.

"Good evening, little Crow." Finn passed me a glass of wine. Hearing the crow comment was endearing. It made me feel included, valued and cared for. And in a place like Elphame, you couldn't buy that or bribe your way to it.

"Good evening, Finn," I replied.

"Happy birthday." He passed me a small envelope. "A small token to show you how deeply your soul has touched mine. No one takes from you, Perdi, without paying for it."

I opened his card and found eleven names crossed off. "What is this?"

"You said you'd settle for them dying horribly, those who killed your blooded mother. I assure you that it was quite horrifying for them, when I knocked on their doors." He was blank-faced. "It was…horrific, every drawn-out hour. I promise you that. I would have spent more time with them, but alas, Aeden had planned this party for you, and I didn't want to be late."

My eyes grew wider. "What? Who are they? How do you know for sure?"

"You are not the only one with talents. It took a little digging, but there isn't much you can hide from an Aos Si, such as myself, and a Seer." He smiled. "Lily came along for a hunt. You cannot hide from me *and* a Seer. To be honest, I think Lily enjoyed it a lot more than I did. She's one scary lady."

"I don't know if I should be happy or uncomfortable," I answered.

He leaned into my ear. "We both know how you feel about it. You don't need to hide that part of yourself from me. I would have done the same for my own mother."

"Thank you," I finally answered. "I didn't tell you about my mother as an ask that you would do this."

"Little queen, if we'd cut out our own souls for you, what do you think we'd do to someone who has harmed you?" He bowed in an over-the-top embellishment and left me with a list of people who'd died in my name. I wanted to be sorry but wasn't, and I knew I never would be.

He walked across the room to Lily. I waved the card and mouthed my many uncomfortable thanks. I tucked my card in my bag and found my dad. I saved my last dance for my father, who said my gift would be given to me later. Solas had it. It was private and not for the display of the court. Aeden had chosen my outfit to match my father's, black with deep purple.

Dancing with my dad in Elphame had never once crossed my mind as a possibility. And it was the best gift I could have been given. Before I kissed him good night, I told him what Finn had done. I had always known my mother's death had changed him. But until that moment, I hadn't known how badly he had wanted to avenge her death, even after so many years. I knew he was angry and hurt, but the moment I gave him the card with names crossed off, the satisfied look on his face told me he would keep it in a special place. It wouldn't surprise me if he framed it and put it on display in his living room. On seeing his relief at each name crossed off, I was no longer uncomfortable with what Finn had done. I should have been, but Elphame rubbed that part of my soul off, hours after I had been named a Crow.

I finally yawned from the edge of the room.

"Drink. It'll help." Elswyth tapped my shoulder from behind.

I spun to find her and a very swollen belly. "Els, my God, you look fantastic."

She patted her stomach and beamed. "I feel like I'm carrying a house of gnomes around on my bladder. He's so spirited."

I awkwardly hugged her over her bump. "When did you get here?"

"Yesterday," she replied. "Faolan sent an invite to my oathed partner and me, asking to make amends."

I cringed a little. "How did that go? That must have been really hard for you."

"It was awful but healing. Stepping into Tylwyth felt like willingly walking through my nightmares. Old wounds have a way of opening long after you think they're healed," she replied and squeezed my arm. We both had an understanding of old wounds. "He offered me Animus, my right to revenge."

"I just saw him, so you didn't kill him," I replied. "Or is that the entertainment for the night?"

"No, although it wouldn't be too late," she answered with a wink. "But I wanted to, so badly. I know it wasn't Faolan, it was his father, and there wasn't a thing he could do to help me. Had he answered my call for aid, his father would have killed me for it and likely anyone else he showed mercy to. But my soul doesn't understand or care much for his situation or station. It hurts just the same. It hurts because he didn't act sooner, if that makes sense. By the time he ended his father's reign, I was already broken."

"What stopped you from taking his life?"

"Helio, my oathed mate. He didn't really stop me as much as remind me of who I am today. I do not want to bring my firstborn into a world with more blood on my hands. Faolan is trying to repair that which is broken, not just by himself but by his father. That takes courage and care. I have accepted what has happened and his wish to make amends in the old ways of our people."

"Do I even want to know what that would entail?" I asked. "Jesus, you're not going to lash him, are you?"

"Most certainly not. These are the ways before the wars," she replied. "I will return tomorrow. Faolan will announce the wrongdoings of the Winter Court against me, will offer me land and remove his crown and offer me a sword. I will choose which I will take, some of his territory or his life. It is purely for show, as I've accepted a piece of land that borders the Court of Less and Autumn Court. The land will then be gifted to bridge Autumn and Dark. I heard from Nix that Solas has gifted Aeden land for his home in Autumn. This will shorten the road back home."

"Why not keep it?" I asked.

She smiled a very Elswyth grin, lighting up her entire face. "I do not need more land, Perdi. I have what I need, and I'm grateful for what I've been blessed with. Greed risks all, and I've too much to lose now."

Helio found his way through the room, his eyes only on Elswyth. Seeing her light up by his very presence and how his body molded into hers, told me I could let go of my worry for her. Solas had helped her choose a fine man, one who loved all of her, including her broken pieces. We chatted as though I had known Helio for as long as I've known Elswyth. We laughed, and I cried when she left. I'd see her again upon the birth of their son. Her gift to me couldn't be held in my hands, only in my heart. She was hope. She, like me, had once been delivered into hell and clawed her way out on her knees. Every time I thought of her, I thought of courage and determination. She never gave up, and finally, the Gods and Goddesses had taken notice and blessed her with the future she deserved.

The evening had worn me down into something pleasantly tired. I wanted to sleep but didn't want to leave. My soul stretched her lazy bones and breathed a sigh of relief. She, like me, felt utterly relaxed for once. Aeden stepped to my side. His outfit had changed from white to black leather, like a full-ranking Aos Si.

"Did you get a promotion?" I asked.

"I look damn good, don't I?" he answered. "Zephyr thought I should look the part if I am to be your private guard. I even have a shiny new iron-tipped sword."

"My, my, I bet Jayde is impressed."

Aeden moved to the side and extended his hand, pulling his partner to my front. "Perdi, I'd like to introduce you to my oathed mate, Jayde."

Jayde was built a little softer than Aeden but just as muscular. His hair was light, and his eyes were a deeper shade of blue. He held out his hand to shake mine with a smile that made me see why Aeden loved the very thought of him. "It is an honor to meet you, ma'am."

"Don't call her that," Aeden whispered.

I smiled ear to ear. "I've heard so much about you, Jayde. I feel like I already know you. I hope you've received my gift, as a thank you for sending Aeden to help me."

"Indeed, the sun will feel nice from those hills. Aeden has already begun to till the land." He winked. I'm sure he had heard a play-by-play of Aeden's victory. "Thank you for the home. It's as ridiculous as Aeden has always wanted. We already have several young ones who are on their way and have many others who will be volunteering their time with us."

"It's not the Summer Court, but the Autumn Court is just as lovely." I smiled.

"The Summer Court, no matter how hard they try, will never be Unseelie. And nothing short of a massive fire could cleanse that land of the stench," Jayde teased. "It is an honor to meet you, Perdita, Perdi?"

"Perdi is fine." I smiled. "And the honor is mine."

"It's been a fun run." Aeden looked out over the crowd. "I'll miss this."

"I don't think you will, not once you leave. Does Zephyr know yet?" I asked.

He shook his head. "Solas knows, but not Zephyr, not yet. I think he knows something is off. My mind is elsewhere. But he rarely pries and waits for us to come to him. I think, though, he'll be happy for us."

"I'll miss you." I smiled. "But when I wake up tomorrow, I'll be happy you're gone."

"I'm going to go tell Zephyr I need to remove his bedframe, that it squeaks when he moves, and I feel it'll disturb you at night." Aeden grinned. "I'll tell him he needs to put his mattress on the floor. I can't wait to see his face."

"Good luck with that." I laughed.

"It'll be my parting gift to him. When I leave, it'll make him smile every time his bed makes a peep," Aeden replied. "You know where I am if you need me."

"I'll come and visit," I answered. "Please stay. Enjoy the evening."

Jayde linked his arm through Aeden's, and I felt blessed to know Aeden had made it home, and Jayde wasn't faced with an empty home and heart. I glanced around the room and felt full. The Aos Si, who were always stiff as boards, were dressed casually, with partners and loved ones and shared laughs. Each time I met their eyes, those who came to the island, we shared a smile that said more than words could ever say. We'd all given there, to our very souls, and we all came home a little more broken than before. But we'd patch and repair the pieces together, as only a family could.

With the night ending, I stood on the balcony off my bedroom and motioned to the shadows. "Thank you for all you did for me. But you don't belong with me. I release you back to Zephyr. I bind you to his soul as he once did with me."

"We are happy to go back, Perdi. Trust you are loved, but you are erratic and uncomfortable. It feels like the eve of war, every minute, with you," they answered. "But we will always come to your call."

I watched them climb over the rail and land on Zephyr, "Perdi! What the hell…? Oh, hello again. What has she done to you all? You're a mess. God, you feel like her anxiety."

"You're welcome, Zeph," I called down to him.

"Good night, little Crow," Zephyr replied. "I'm off to take apart my damn bedframe because your sensitive ears cannot handle the sound of me moving. I'm going to strangle Aeden during training with the sheets he says I can't sleep with because they lint too much and may bother your nose."

I laughed and watched him leave in a blast of shadows. "I have delicate ears!" I screamed after him.

"Little Crow." Solas' voice pulled my attention to the door. He held two glasses of wine. "Are you done tormenting Zephyr?"

I turned with a soft smile. "No. Probably not ever. With Aeden leaving, someone has to pick up the slack around here."

"I've heard many dark and terrible things about you picking up the slack during your week on the throne." He set down the wine and walked to my front. He knelt and glanced up at me.

"Such as?" I leaned against the railing.

"You smoked out a Solene supporter, a traitor, a hunter of Crows—and with him, several others who stood against our court," he said.

I nodded. "They deserved their fate."

"You were kinder to them than I'd have been," he replied. "I also heard you killed a king while deciding whether he would live without his head." He took off my shoes. "What an uncomfortable thought."

"He was still blinking. It was an honest question," I replied. His heavy look made me smile. "Yes, I did that."

He kissed my calf, and I shivered. "And killed the rest of the Autumn Court, who hide for months from the Commander of the Aos Si?"

I blew out a chest of air. The heat in my body began to slowly rise as I looked Solas in the eyes. "Yes, that was me."

"Threatened to burn down the home of another because he wouldn't allow you to cross his territory?" His fingers danced along my lower leg.

"Technically..." I started, and Solas raised his eyebrows. "Yes, I did do that, as well."

"And the bribery you offered?" he asked.

"Yes," I answered.

"You waged a full-on war against a king while trying to enter a territory with not just one army but the entire Aos Si and Sluagh, the Dark Court, accompanied by the Winter King and his Commander and held him at knifepoint?"

"Yes."

"You bound souls to you?" He stood.

"Yes…many."

"Then brought a king and an Aos Si Commander back from the dead?" He stood, lifted my wrist to his lips and placed a light kiss.

"Yes."

"And, for the first time, since the history of *ever*, you promoted the lowest member of the Aos Si, not even a full rank, a trainee, as your personal Royal Guard?"

"That, too."

"So, to test my understanding of your reign, little Crow," he whispered into my mouth, "in under a week, you threatened to war against the mortal world if they stepped foot inside Elphame, and we lost treaties with the Seelie courts."

"Yes," I whispered back.

"And entered into a new treaty with your once-sworn enemy." Solas continued with a grin. He helped me to the lounger and passed me a glass of wine. "You invaded a Seelie territory, launched every Unseelie Army into enemy lands, held a king at knifepoint and forced your way into his lands against his will, killed a king *and* his remaining people *and* ate their souls, sent another to a dungeon not of our own and likely to his death, and killed everyone else who stood in your way?

All aided by Aos Si trainees, leaving the actual guard here?"

"It was a Reign of Ruin," I answered. "Queen for a week, and I damn near burned your territory to the ground."

"Rest assured, little Crow, we Unseelie like the heat." He sat beside me and pulled me under his arm.

"However short-lived it was, I never want to do it again. The stress was unbearable. I don't know how you juggle that many problems at once. It doesn't end, does it?"

"This is why I never want to get out of bed in the morning."

I snuggled into his chest. "I can think of a few other reasons you don't want to get out of bed."

He lifted me from his side and placed me on his lap, facing him. "As can I."

"You're lazy, that's why," I teased. His laughter set everything right in the world. "Solas, our enemies, they may be many, but I'll always come for you and those who get in my way..."

"Will burn."

"Do you understand the life you will have because of me?" I asked.

"Yes," he answered. "Do you understand the hell you will have with me?"

I smiled. "Yes."

"We've chosen to walk a path made of glass shards," he answered.

I nodded. "This is going to hurt."

"Everything in Elphame hurts, little Crow. But I'm willing to bleed. Are you?"

"As your queen, no one will bleed harder than our enemies," I replied. "I hope there are more perks than this last week or I'll be giving notice, and you can shove that crown."

"I debated on telling you but ran out of time. I thought I'd wait and try your customs first. I had planned to court you, as you would say, and ask your father for permission. That is the way, no?"

"I would suggest you ask me first. No one makes my choices but me," I countered.

"Perdi, would you oath yourself to me?"

From below, under my balcony, Aeden called up to us. "Sir, the ring, and you should be on your knees. It is the custom of her people. I enclosed a brief overview on your desk, which you clearly didn't read. Perdi refers to this as a 'cheat sheet'."

"Thanks, Aeden," I called out and blushed. "Go spend your evening with Jayde."

"Umm, I'm here, ma'…Perdi," Jayde answered from below.

"He's like your bloody shadow. He's worse than Zephyr." Solas picked me up and carried me inside.

I screamed as he tossed me to the bed. He rushed toward me in a blur and pulled me to the edge, kneeling in front of me. I braced myself for what would come next, but he pulled away. I reached for him as he drew a small velvet box from his pocket and opened it. Inside, my mother's wedding set. My breath came out at once, and I couldn't see through the tears.

"My mother's…" I whispered.

"Your father gave them to me," Solas answered.

This was the gift my father had referred to, and I smiled. "You asked him?"

"I'd already asked him before tonight, as that is *my* custom. He has agreed, but the choice is yours. Perdi, this world is terrifying and even worse when you're alone. It's so much harder on your own. But with you, the world doesn't feel so big. I don't feel so powerless. With you, I feel like anyone could come to our door, and I wouldn't fear opening it. I know, whatever happens, you will protect our people, and only then will you burn the world to find me. I can't do this without you. I can't go a single day without knowing you're mine."

"Yes." I smiled.

"Yes, you will oath yourself to me, or you'll burn the world?" he asked.

"Both." I laughed and pulled him into my arms.

"She said yes!" Aeden screamed from below my deck. The cheers from the grounds rose up, and the party I thought had ended, filled the night.

"It's my turn to hog your attention." Solas pushed his darkness to the door and closed us in. "I love you, my wicked little queen."

"I love you, *Soulless*," I teased, as I had since the day I first saw who he really was.

"I'll never tire of this," he whispered into my mouth. "Are you ready, little Crow?"

"Ready for what?" I asked.

"This," he replied. "You have my pearl. Get ready to feel it all."

His darkness swirled through me, not just around me. I couldn't breathe, I couldn't think, I couldn't do much more than hold on to him. He curled around me, and with his energy pouring through the room, I felt like hell could knock on the door, and neither of us would so much as flinch. I felt every emotion as if they were my own, pleasure, happiness, rage, his need to protect and his need to be loved. I could smell every inch of the Dark Courts and taste every power as if I had known them my entire life. The energy started soft and graceful, then I could hear the Sluagh and their wings as they glided through the sky, free and wild. I could feel the wind on my face and smell their spice. It ended with the sound of waves crashing down against the cliffs during a storm. As I floated back down, having touched heaven, I smiled lazily.

"What was that?" I asked.

"Me," he answered. "All of me, without holding back."

"Solas, don't ever hold back." I rolled to face him, curled in his arm.

He lifted my lips to meet his. "If we weren't tied together, bonded, it would have been a very different experience for you."

"How could that ever be bad?" I asked.

"The same way you walking through my soul can feel either amazing or like death dragging me into the cold earth."

I nodded. "I could do that until I die."

He ran his hand over my skin lightly until I felt like I was floating in bliss. "Close your eyes, little Crow. Happy Birthday."

"I love you," I whispered and felt my body grow heavier. "I can still feel you."

He kissed my shoulder. "And I can still feel you."

"You feel…happy."

"I am. And you feel tired," Solas laughed.

"I love you," I replied.

"And I love you," he answered. He pulled me tighter against him. "Close your eyes and *sleep*."

His magick rolled me over, and I slinked to sleep in the arms of the man I'd tear my soul apart for. I'd do many horrible things for those I love, but there was no end to what I'd do for him. And in the moment before sleep gripped me, I knew he would eat the world for me in return. There was no safer place for a little Crow than in the arms of a man who loved as fiercely as he fought on the battlefield.

Chapter Twelve

Walking into the Winter Court made me grin like a child waiting for Christmas morning. At the caves, I dropped a package into the darkness, a gift of baked goods and a few quilts I had made for Oberon and his people for what they had done for me while I was healing. Fear is a good meal for a Bodach, but they had eaten so much many had gotten sick and needed their own healer. When he poked his head out to wave his thanks, Finn screamed like a little girl and jumped behind me. It made the feeling of dread thick enough to chew on, worth it to see an Aos Si shake in his boots. We all knew dread lived down there, but having it pop up with a smile and a wave was an entirely different experience.

As the fear fell away like a snake shedding its skin, Tylwyth stood and was all I had remembered it to be. It smelled of every good memory I had as a child, my mother and father, sledding in the hills and hot chocolate on cold nights. There was a softness to its appearance, a kind of warmth you wouldn't expect in a place found in the middle of Winter Court that made you want to stay awhile. The honesty that rested within its beauty made you feel welcome and like your worries didn't matter as much within the city's walls. The sparkling hints of blue and white and the faintest gray painted this world in Winter. Those who called Tylwyth home smiled once they saw me, then backed up several paces when Solas and Zephyr strolled in behind us. Although they tried to recover quick enough to appear friendly, their shyness and fear were noticeable. Part of me felt sad for Solas and Zephyr, because all they had ever wanted was to be loved, but they settled for being feared.

I watched Faolan and Oisin walk toward us. Oisin was, as he always is, a mirror image of Zephyr in all the rough edges and soft middles. Faolan smiled as he approached us. He always tried for kindness first. I think he pushed the best parts of himself to the surface, refusing to be who Elphame forced us all to be, brutal and untrusting. I wondered about him and who he was when no one was looking, where all that anger went that the rest of us didn't see. As long as it wasn't directed at my people or me, I suppose I didn't really care. I ate worlds when I got angry. Throwing stones would be ridiculous at this point. And after he'd come when I'd needed him, I didn't want to throw rocks at him anyway.

I hugged Faolan as soon as he was within reach. It caught him off guard and made him nervous, likely because Solas and Zephyr stood at my back, clearing their throats. It wasn't often I had a reason to hug Faolan, nor were there many reasons he had deserved it. Today, however, he both deserved it and needed it.

His soul was as dirty as my own, and I knew just how bad it felt to tarnish myself to protect my people.

"I didn't have a chance to say thank you, Fao, for what you did for me—for you honoring not just our treaty, but your word."

"You're welcome, Perdi." He finally relaxed into the hug and hugged me back. "I trust your father is settled?"

I finally pulled away. "He's getting there, but he's happy to be back in Elphame. His childhood dream has come alive, and he loves every moment he ventures out into the forests of Elphame. Thank you for keeping him alive for me."

"You're very welcome," he answered. "Those we will never mention again are settled in the hills with their people. That was an incredibly brave and humble act. You'll never be the monster you think you are."

I smiled at the thought of the Satyr starting new. I stepped back to Solas. "Thank you."

"I hear congratulations are in order," Faolan motioned to the rings on my finger. "I wish you both long life, deep love and a warm home."

"This isn't awkward at all," Oisin muttered. "I feel like we've done this dance one too many times, with a wee Crow in the middle."

I smiled and shook my head. "It's nice to see you, too, Oisin."

"I hate to break up the reunion, but I hate the cold," Solas interrupted with perfect timing.

"Welcome to the Winter Court." Faolan grinned at Solas, who was dressed in more layers than the rest of us. "This is your first time here, Solas, not as my enemy. It's a strange feeling."

"The day is still young, little king." Zephyr moved up to my other side, and I fought not to laugh.

"Welcome back, Zephyr." Faolan's face didn't lose the smile, but his eyes remained on Zephyr for a few seconds longer than was comfortable. "I trust you know your way around better than the rest of us. You've spent more time in my court these last months than I have."

"It's been weeks since I've been here, for the record," Zephyr answered.

"Because you've been in prison, then trying to put your soul back together. That doesn't count," Oisin added.

Zephyr shrugged. "Do not think I haven't seen you poking around the border, Oisin."

"But unlike you, I've not stepped over," Oisin countered. "So, that, my friend, doesn't count."

"Friend?" Zephyr turned a heavy stare at Oisin.

"Do you like caving?" Oisin asked. "I bet I could last longer in our caves than you could."

"I doubt that very much," Zephyr countered. "The Bodach doesn't scare me."

"We've better things in our caves than boogeymen."

I stepped away from them and walked the streets of Tylwyth with Finn at my side. Now that Aeden was gone, Finn volunteered to come along. Zephyr had warned me that the trainees would remain a little closer for a while. It was their way of healing parts of themselves they had scrubbed off on the island. Being near me was part of that way, and I wouldn't complain. It felt a little better, having them close. And coming to the Winter Court excited Finn more than the others. But everything excited Finn if I was involved. I think he thought war followed me, which it usually did, and the closer he remained to me, the likelier he'd be to get called on to fight. Today, however, the thought of seeing Tylwyth, the unconquered land of the Winter Court, made him giddy. He was both nosey as hell and curious. He and I shared many similarities, all of which were reasons we were both always in the middle of chaos.

As we walked, I pointed out the little shops and the school and told him about the people. Although Finn was impressed, I couldn't help but notice him plot a way in and out, around every corner. "Finn, are you memorizing the city?" I asked.

He nodded. "Faolan is *your* friend, not mine."

"Things would not go well for you if you harmed anyone here."

He grinned. "It is not much of a threat when my own queen issues it on behalf of Faolan."

I linked my arm in his and pulled him snug against my body. "But you will be dead just the same, so does it matter who is threatening you?"

His smile never faltered, and he didn't pull away. He was perfectly comfortable in the most uncomfortable situations. "Little queen, you will hunt me again, I have no doubt, but it will take you many years to stomach what it will take to end my life. That is a long fucking time for me to do my worst."

"Deadly games…"

"Come with deadly prizes." He finished my sentence, unbothered by the prospect of having his life drained out of him by me. "You do not have what it takes to make me scream even once."

My smile got wider. "I'll take that bet. You best pray I don't cash it in."

"And we wonder why the Gods have kept us apart? I look forward to burning the world with you. May the better monster win." His grin slipped into a friendly smile. It was uncomfortable how quickly he could morph from enemy to friend. "If it'll help you sleep at night, we haven't taken this court because Solas and Zephyr will not allow it, not because we can't."

"Why not?" I asked.

Finn wiggled his eyebrows as though he had a secret I didn't know. "That is the question, isn't it? The Winter Court is the largest court in all Elphame. It has the most resources, land others covet and unmatched beauty from any mountain top. But Zephyr has never allowed it, nor has Solas. Sure, they trust him a little more today than a month ago, but for someone who isn't trusted by the deadliest court in Elphame, Faolan certainly has a strong pulse and a hearty court."

"That *is* the question. Do you have the answer, or are you going to speak in riddles until I guess it?" I asked.

"I can only comment on what I've heard, not what I know to be fact," Finn answered.

"Now is the time for the gossip, Finn." I nudged him. "I'm all ears. No one ever tells me gossip."

"I heard you walked in Zephyr's dreams as a child?"

"Sort of. More like Zeph showed me his entire life," I answered.

"That is why this court stands. He could smell the Winter Court on you when you told him you were trying to find him. He smelled both Solas *and* Faolan. Zephyr told Solas that you'd need this court standing and all who call it home—that, for some reason, you needed Tylwyth and the friends you'd find here during your most desperate hours. When your greatest gran came and shared your fate with Solas and Faolan, it cemented Faolan's future. He's only breathing because Zephyr and Solas knew you'd need him. Solas has never invaded for that reason alone. Hell, in the war to close the Gate, Solas kept Faolan locked up to protect him. During the second war, he commanded us all to leave Faolan and Oisin alone, to protect him. At every turn, both Solas and Zephyr have kept the little king alive, because you'd need him as much as you'd need everyone else you have in your life."

"Are you two done gossiping?" Zephyr twisted around my side to stand in front of us. His shadows lingered at his feet. "You're going the wrong way."

I looked back at the others, waiting for us, then to Zephyr. "Zeph, when we step into the Hallows, and if it doesn't go as planned, what do we do?"

"Do you feel like it won't go as planned?" he asked and gave me a stern look.

"I don't know, Zeph. For weeks, something has felt off, and I'm not sure what it is. I think I'd just feel better if I knew what to do. Like the rest of you, I'm trying to have a backup plan."

"I've had the same feeling, but it doesn't stem from Tylwyth. I'm not sure what I'm feeling, but I know we'll find out soon enough. Good things come to those who wait, but bad things come like a bat out of hell, regardless of if we're ready." Zephyr proceeded to detail the entire Hallows dungeons, escape routes, rooms I could get out of, how many guards would be there and the weapons they have. "Should things not go to plan, the shadows have already been instructed to get you out first and take you back to the Dark Courts, to the manor. Once you're safe at home, half the Sluagh will come, while the other half remain to protect you. The Aos Si will come if either myself or Solas is at risk. If the Dark Court is at risk, Finn has been instructed to take you to the caves of the Sluagh. From there, you'll command the rest of the army."

"Why the caves?" I asked.

"Lily. She said it was the only place in this entire realm where you're safe from everyone, and the Sluagh can better protect you if you're there with them. The magick of the Sluagh is different than that of Elphame, as you can attest. They're the only ones you can't burn or drain, should things go wrong. You can't eat their souls, little Crow, unless they will it so."

"Huh, I didn't know that," I answered. Good information to have if I ever lost control. "And what do I do if the shadows can't reach me in the Hallows?"

He looked at me as if I had said something foolish. "Depending on who is closest, either Solas or I will grab you. There is no power in Tylwyth who could stop all of us from getting you to safety."

"You really do think of everything, don't you?" I asked with a smile. "Plans over plans over plans."

"As a general rule, yes," he answered. "But you never ask what the plan is. You simply trust we have one. Is your gut telling you not to go?"

"No, I'm fine." I smiled. "I'm glad your planning is better than mine. I don't think I can crawl over glass today."

He turned my shoulders to face the others and nudged me forward. "I hope, little Crow, one day your plans won't include peeling off your soul to win."

I shrugged. "I wouldn't count on it."

We followed Faolan as he moved down through tunnels. We were leaving Tylwyth to the Hallows. "Why are we leaving your courts?" I asked him.

"We, like you, do not have dungeons," Faolan answered.

"Never?"

"My father did. They were well known and feared by all," he answered, and for a split second, I saw a memory he hated ripple across his face. "They were filled with earth after his…untimely death. Those deserving of prison are not kept within my lands. They're sent to the Hallows until their sentencing can be carried out."

"You're better than your father," I whispered, and I knew Faolan would hear me.

I walked between Zephyr and Solas. Although they moved with ease, almost casually, they were on high alert, watching, waiting, ready. I, on the other hand, was far from calm. I could feel magick in the air. It felt like walking through webs, each string licking my flesh, tasting who I was and what I was. It was uncomfortable and edged the line toward gut-wrenching terror. Had I been alone, I'd have turned around instantly. If I were a prisoner, I'd be kicking and screaming and begging.

Through the stone halls, Faolan stopped at a wooden door and pushed it open. I had expected it to squeal, aged from years of abuse, but nothing came. It had been oiled and well-used. That, on its own, made the place all the scratchier against my bravery. I stopped at the doorway and glanced inside before stepping in like the others. The room was made of stone bricks, with no windows, one table and half a dozen chairs. One light hung in the middle over the table, and there was a drain in the floor, under the table. I shivered as I walked into the room. Everything, from the door to the chairs, looked washable. It was built for interrogation. The room was made for people to die in it.

"It feels like death in here," I whispered.

Solas grabbed my hand. "It's not your death, so it doesn't matter."

"Shouldn't it?" I asked.

"No" was all I got back from everyone.

We took a seat and waited as Theo was brought into the room, chained and looking like life in the Winter Court was not to his standards. He looked duller, in some way, like the cold didn't agree with him. His father, Aelfdene, had been like that, the glamor melting away with each day. The more I got used to him, the less his magick worked on me. Here, in the dungeons of the Hallows, he still wasted his energy on appearances, even though we all saw him for who he was. I think I would have been more concerned with keeping my heart beating and not what I looked like. But appearances were everything, especially in this cursed land.

Theo's eyes grew wider at the sight of his audience. "What is the meaning of this?"

"It's nice to see you again, Theofanis," Solas spoke first. "Imagine my surprise to learn you've been imprisoned and for the reasons. Hunting our people… That's a new low, even for Fae."

"You have no right to hold me," Theo barked as if we would follow orders.

"I'm not holding you." Solas held up his hands. "As you can see, I'm not the one with the key to your freedom."

"Your Crow is."

Zephyr growled from behind me but stayed put. He offered his warning, but I doubted Theo would listen.

My chair screeched across the floor as I pulled it to the table. "Hello, Theo. I hope your reception here at the Winter Court was as gracious as ours."

"Why am I being held here?" he demanded.

"Straight to the point. I do love that about you all. Do you know what I had to do to get my people off that island?" I asked. "I had to kill those you hunted for sport. You killed them through me. When the Gate closed, you turned your attention to the only other people who were weaker than you. You hunted and killed hundreds of Satyr for sport. You butchered them for pleasure. And now, you will pay for your crimes."

"You are not my judge," he countered.

"From where I'm sitting, I am," I replied. "When I had to kill an island of people because of you, that put you on that side of the table and me on this side."

"I did no such thing."

"If I were you," Solas added, "I'd speak the truth before you are put to death for lies."

"That's rich coming from you, Solas." Theo's face reddened, torn between lies he thought would save him and truths he knew would end him.

Faolan pushed away from the wall. "This can be quick or it can be drawn out over many years. I'm fine with however long you'd like to rot in here. But the truth always comes out, no matter how hard you fight it." He leaned against the table casually, his face pleasant. It made us all uncomfortable. His energy felt wrong, far too calm for a situation like this. While the rest of us were on edge, Faolan felt peaceful. "You will face punishment for what you've done, Theo. We all pay for our crimes in the end, regardless of our reasons for them. Nothing in Elphame is free, and no one escapes payment, not even the crown."

"You have no right to hold me here. There will be war for this, Faolan," Theo replied.

"There will always be war," Solas replied. "If any come, they come for the entire Unseelie court. I truly don't think you matter enough to anyone to cross over the river."

Faolan's smile didn't falter. The room held the slightest scent of candy canes. It made my stomach flop. "Theo, you are in control of your fate, no one else. You choose how you want to live out the rest of your days and if you'd like your people to be fated the same."

Theo's shoulders hunched as if he hoped he could shrivel up and disappear. "It is true. We hunted the Satyr. But my people are not responsible. I am."

"Your people *are* responsible!" I yelled at him. I didn't bother trying to calm my anger. Theo forced me to kill to save my family. I hated him with every fiber of my being for who he helped me become. "They hunted with you, Theofanis, and now they will suffer with you."

"Are you taking me to the Dark Court prison?" Theo asked as I stood from the table.

"No," I answered.

Finn inched up to the table and smiled. "You were told once how nice it would be to feel the sun from your hills, as your gardens were tilled as our own. The smell of the flowers was cleared from your land this morning when I lit the first fire."

"What the hell does that mean?" Theo asked.

I leaned forward. "I never lied to you when I told you we didn't have enemies. It's the same reason we don't have prisons, little king."

"We kill all our enemies. We don't house and feed them," Solas answered. "Only those who fear their enemies keep them alive for secrets they're too scared to find on their own."

"You burned my lands?" Theo whispered.

Finn nodded. His smile made me squirm. "I hunted your people like the animals they are. Those with Satyr blood on their hands begged for their lives, as the Satyr did. And I made it last a lot longer than I normally would have. I left them in ditches as you had done to those you had hunted, stacked four deep and broken beyond repair. That is the cost they paid when they decided to follow a dead king."

Theo glared, but his anger was directed at me. "I curse you."

"So did the Gods…but here I am." I had to force myself to smile. I wasn't happy to be sitting across a table from a dead man. "I warn you to be honest when answering my next question. I would hate to need to ask this question of your people. Why were you working with human Mages?"

His eyes grew a little wider. "They came to us. We did not take them from the mortal realm. I swear this to you."

I knew how they had gotten into Elphame but didn't know why Theo would have them. "Why would they come to you?"

"Parrish brought them to us to heal Fae sickness. They came here to kill you. They knew you had been held in our court. They knew everything about you, including your time here in Elphame. They asked for our help."

"Who told them about me?" I asked.

"I don't know, and they didn't say. I swear, I didn't think to even ask. They said someone powerful had invited them here as retribution for you killing Solene," he answered.

"That's an awfully long time to wait it out in your court."

"It was many months," he answered.

I nodded. "And so, you agreed to help them kill me?"

"We told them they were not nearly strong enough to kill you. They didn't believe us. They said they were told how to kill you. That if they could trap you, they could kill you. They said they would use iron to bind you, then drain you of your magick. They were told how to kill Fae by someone more powerful than I. They knew how to steal the magick from Fae and use it against them…ways not even I knew of," he answered. "When things started to turn sour in the mortal realm, we told them to leave and not come back. We didn't want to draw your attention back to our court. Parrish found them when they left. His hate for you is deeper than mine. Parrish has spoken about killing you many times. The island vanished a few days after they left, and we couldn't return."

"Why did you come to the island with us, if you knew we would see what you had done?"

"To hide what we did—but did not get the chance. You wouldn't allow us to split up."

"There were two Fae Mages caught. Which court were they from?" I asked.

He swallowed hard. "They were mine. They went with the mortals to the island to show them how to use Elphame energy to build their wards."

I closed my eyes and released a long and angry breath. I weighed Theo's truth and knew that if I didn't look for myself, I'd always wonder if we had killed every enemy still on Elphame soil or if I had to look over my shoulder. I looked Theo dead in the eyes and opened the door to my Malice. Her hunger burst throughout my body, heat, energy and thirst. Her need to splay him for the birds made me clench my fists and dig my nails into my palms. She, like me, hated him for what he had done. But unlike me, my Malice had ideas on how to make him pay for it. She tempted me to let her do her worst, but I held on to her with an invisible leash and crawled through Theo's soul with ease. His mind was much weaker than I had thought it would be. Digging in a bowl of jelly would have given me more resistance than the mind of Theo. I could see his mouth open, the veins in his neck and forehead plump, but I tuned out his screams as I read his twisted mind.

"Soul-Eater," Theo whispered.

"Dead man walking," I whispered back. "You should have kept that to yourself."

Theo's hands jerked as if wanting to wrap around my neck. I whispered that it would be his last mistake to touch me. I wasn't the only one to notice. My Malice saw his movement and pushed her weight down onto his arms, forcing him to pull back. I tilted my head. I hadn't seen her physically force another. She twisted around and looked back at me, both of us realizing that we could bend Theo's mind, making him do as we wished, without having to take his pearl. I was horrified. She was elated. I was reminded of what Aeden had said back on the island. The more I used the muscle of Malice, the stronger she'd become. I pulled back as fast as I could and shoved her back into the cage where I kept her.

"Ten Mages came from Whitwick through the Gate," I recalled what I found in his head. "All ten were granted safe passage through your territory. They were housed and fed for months at the Golden Court," I whispered. "Only eight were found within your territory and killed by the Sluagh. Where, oh, where did the other two go? Do you want to answer, or do you want me to reach back in there and rip the truth out?"

"The two weakest died in the Golden Court," Theo sputtered. "They had spoken about returning to Whitwick. They were scared. But the others thought they would go to the Dark Court and tell you of the mortal's plans. They killed them."

"How did you know Parrish would find them when they left?" I asked.

"We allowed him to stay within our territory. He had nowhere left to go," he answered.

"Because you wanted my death as much as he did." I shook my head, disappointed but not surprised.

"The mortal realm wants your death more than any other," Theo replied. "I overheard the Mages discuss plans to end your life. They're not going to stop until you're dead. You need allies, not more enemies."

"Odd news," I replied. "Goodbye, Theo."

"But I told you the truth!" He screamed and tried in vain to stand. Faolan pushed him back down and towered over him in a warning.

"You were already warned," I replied. "We do not have enemies. They're either dead or being hunted. And you, Theo, are very much our enemy."

"Until my very last breath, I will pray to the Gods that the mortal world gets what they want from your very soul," Theo yelled across the table.

"Your Gods can't hear you from here any better than they could from the hills we burned," I countered. I walked out and left him to the same fate as his people and the graves they'd dug the moment they'd hunted innocents.

"You make me uncomfortable, sometimes." Oisin walked Nix and me from the dungeon.

"Why?" I asked.

"You're a prettier version of Solas," he answered.

"Why, thank you." I batted my eyelashes in jest. "Why are you out here and not in there?"

"I've seen the song and dance before. I have dinner plans later. If I stay, I won't eat for days," he answered.

"Why?" I asked, but Solas' face gave me all the answers I needed.

Solas stepped out of the room as the screaming started. His skin was a few shades paler, and his eyes were wide with whatever he had seen in the room. "I now know what Faolan looks like when he's angry. Bloody hell, I'm not going back in there."

"And that is why." Oisin shuddered. "You should go, Perdi. You will not like what you see when he steps out of that room."

"I'm oddly curious," I answered. "I've never actually seen Faolan angry."

Oisin leaned in for a hug. "Don't be. Don't ever be curious about that. It would hurt him to know you saw his rage. If you saw it, he wouldn't be able to pretend anymore. It's hard enough being a king. Don't take away his carefully won friendship with you. It gives him hope."

When Finn came out of the room and vomited on the floor, I grabbed on to Solas. "Where is Zephyr?"

"Don't worry about him. Nothing Faolan can show him will be any worse than what he's seen and done himself," Solas answered. "He's in there with Faolan. He won't leave until it's over. He won't risk one of the men living. But we are not staying for it. I don't need this memory."

"Neither do I. I have enough memories to last a lifetime," I answered.

Solas wrapped us in his darkness and carried us home, where I paced until Zephyr returned. Nix took his leave, a little shaken from our journey and the power he had felt roll out of the dungeon. He wanted to stick his hands in his garden and remember all the good things left in the world. When Zephyr returned, he didn't speak of what happened, and I wasn't curious enough to ask. He looked as he always did, in control. But in the places where I knew to look, he wasn't in control. His eyes held a new haunt, his smile was a little flatter and his shoulders carried a new weight. One day, he'd see too much and be crushed under the weight of it all. For now, all I could do was offer him a hug. Later, I'd probably offer him a can of fuel and help him burn it all down, because that's what Soul-Eaters do. We burn worlds and eat whatever managed to escape the flames.

Curled into the warmth of the monster who ate my nightmares, I wrapped myself tightly around Solas. He was what stalked the halls and haunted our forests, and I loved him all the more for loving the monster who looked back when our eyes met. Never once has he flinched when I've walked into the room or cowered when others did. He stood at my side, ready to put out my fires, and dared fate to take another shot each time she couldn't knock us down.

In a world where there was no room for greatness, those in my life came pretty damn close to it. But I wasn't made to shine like the others. I was made for dark and terrible things and would do just that for those I love. I'd eaten the world to get here, and now I waited for the world to bite back. Fate never left a door halfway open. Nothing was free in Elphame. But I was ready for her.

My reign will always be ruin to any who stands against me or mine.

Damn the consequences.

Want to see more from this author? Here's a taster for you to enjoy!

A Cursed Crow: Broken Wings and Wicked Things

Lanne Garrett

Excerpt

Hell can be found between two moments. Entire lifetimes are lived, destinies are decided, worlds are built and destroyed, life is given and taken just as quickly. Between these points, no matter how short or long they may be, the fates decide what the next will bring. Nothing stops fate or her cruel touch. And she walked today through the fields of Elphame, just as she had down the streets of Whitwick, looking for me. Like the last time she reminded me of her incredible power, I would crumple under her weight again. She walked slowly while I enjoyed little slivers of peace in a world made for war. She was like that, slapping her surprise across your face just as you got comfortable. Her claws would dig at my insides like choices not yet made—and regret for those yet to come. That's what happened when you ignored the inevitable. It needled you until you bled to death from the holes of ignorance.

It was not bliss—ignorance. It was a punishing and cruel death. It was suffering and looking back, seeing where it all went wrong and knowing you could have prevented it from happening had you acted sooner. It was foolish hope that the inevitable would spare you. Win or lose, there was nothing blissful about willful blindness.

There were few cast-iron certainties in Elphame. But one thing I knew for sure was that nothing lasted forever—not war and not peace, not life—and for some of us, not even death. Nevertheless, we still tried to hold on to the good bits for as long as we could. We each held a death grip on the moments that brought us a brief respite from the calamity that is Elphame, however fleeting they may be. It was worth the struggle to hold on. In those instances, between heaven and hell, we found reasons to get back up, to keep pushing forward, to look death in the eyes and hold on for dear life. We found the courage to stand on the frontlines, shoulder to shoulder with those we love, and motion for our enemies to take their best shot.

And that's what fate brought our way again—enemies to face and trials to overcome. It would not be Elphame if we weren't preparing for another war. We had not heard the last from the mortal world. With each passing day, we risked more to a realm we knew would make a final stand against us. Although I was born in Whitwick Gates, it was no longer my home. Where I'd once felt conflicted and tried to protect my people to my death, I was no longer torn between realms. I wouldn't risk my life for those who cared nothing for me, who treated me like I was just another one of the monsters. I'd tried to save them and had been chased away with the rest of the Fae. I would not willingly bleed for them again.

The oath between man and Fae was gone, thrown away by the mortals, and I feared the results would be devastating for us all. The cost would be felt across both realms, because no one escapes the price we pay. No one is free from the suffering of war, no matter which side of the field you stand on. Like fate, war was a bitch and spared no one the grief of his touch. The graves would be dug by us all. Some would die, and some would only wish for the sweet mercy of death. Memories had that way about them, when it was all said and done, to make you regret not dying with the others rather than live with what you did to survive. I was walking proof of that.

This time, though, we'd be prepared. We wouldn't leave it to chance or to fate. It would be a blood bath if we waited on Whitwick to make their first move. If the mortal world stepped through the Gate, those who didn't wither away from Fae sickness would be slaughtered. There would be no more warnings. Whatever man decided to do, we'd be ready for it. Solas wasn't one to gamble, especially not where I was concerned. I had been the target too many times for him to sit idly by and wait on others to decide on war. He wanted plans over plans, because he didn't win every war by waiting for the other side to choose whether standing toe to toe with him was a risk worth taking. Swift and merciless decisions won wars, not hesitation or clemency.

Blood and Bones stood before me, and it took my breath away. It didn't matter how many times I had seen the wall surrounding the original court of Elphame. I was still taken aback by the clotted and macabre appearance of it. Centuries of spilled blood stained the walls, darkening over the years to something almost black and utterly revolting. As far as the eye could see, a dark obsidian wall flanked the border. The sight of it was enough of a warning to make all who came here rethink their life choices and turn around. It looked like it had been carved from a mountain, encircling the court from all sides. Not many had been inside the original court, and most who had attempted it under the rule of a dead woman, Solene, were what created the walkway into the once-upon-a-time hell of Elphame.

The first time I had stepped beyond the wall in search of answers, the dried blood had flaked off under my touch. I could hear the sound of it peeling away like a crusted leaf underfoot. It had made my skin crawl and my mind conjure images of my death. The memory of it had the same effect.

We walked up the crushed bone path, through the skeletons and long-rotted parts, to the notorious wall. The bones crunched under my boots, and it took everything I had not to vomit. Like the last time, the sound reminded me of my first day in Elphame and the pathway into the Golden Court. I'd never liked this place when I'd first come—but I liked it even less now. I had almost died when I had been in the basement of Blood and Bones, the day I'd come for a knife to kill the Caller of Crows. I had been stabbed, saved three Aos Si prisoners and waged a war I wasn't ready for. Here's hoping this visit wouldn't be like my last. I wasn't holding my breath, however. Nothing surprised me in Elphame.

For Solas and Zephyr, coming to Blood and Bones was like going home to their childhood. Neither looked bothered by the sights. Their boots crunched the bones to dust and fazed them none. But they *were* war and nightmares. Walking on the backs of the dead was not unusual for the two men who were the very reason people were afraid of the dark. Seeing them banter back and forth was unnerving. Their laughter rolling over the bone graveyard was an uncomfortable combination of horror and revelry. It was no different than hearing them laugh on the battlefield. They could ignore the bodies a lot longer than I could have. I was still too new to the world of war. It still bothered me to see it. For me, coming to Blood and Bones was nothing more than memories I didn't want, of being desperate enough to kill. And each step I took brought fresh emotions of my last trip into the basement of this awful place. But that was what it meant to lead, to win, to protect those weaker. We tainted our souls. We faced our horrors and gave ourselves new nightmares. We were always ready to look into the dark corners of the world, stepping over those in our way and planning the exits before our enemies swallowed us whole.

Within the breeze that swirled the bone dust into little funnels, I could almost hear Seth's wings in the background, the Gargoyle's last flight. Seth had died the last time I had come to Blood and Bones. He'd given his life for me to end the Taking of the Crows. The tingling in my thigh grew, and I glanced back once, hoping I'd see the Gargoyles, but they had been gone since the day we'd killed Solas' sister, Solene. The Gargoyles had taken Seth's stone body home, wherever that was. It was their custom to place his rocky statue at the gates to their home as a reminder of who died to protect their realm. Every now and again, when my nightmares became too much, I could feel a faint draft from wings I couldn't see and knew it was him. There had been so many deaths since my arrival in Elphame, but his was one of my greatest regrets. I had been told he'd died a glorious death, but he hadn't. There was no beauty to be found when a life as great as his was taken. War is ugly. Death is hideous. Everything else is a lie we tell when it hurts too bad to be honest with ourselves.

"Your little pet is following us." Nix stood on my shoulder, looking behind us. His feet danced side to side as I navigated a path I didn't want to fall on. The day Seth had died, I had skinned my hands and knees as I was thrown onto the ground. I'd needed to pick shards of bones from my skin for days. The thought of doing it again made my stomach flop and reminded me to be careful of my footing.

"I know. My thigh is tingling. Every time the Sluagh are near, my scar acts up," I replied. I looked back and watched a small Sluagh making his way over the bone path toward me. "Why is he following me?"

"Because you claimed him," Solas answered from a few yards ahead of us, his ear always tuned to my voice. "He hasn't left since you leashed him. The other day, I found him in the library in front of the fireplace."

"I let him in. It was raining," I replied.

"He's not your pet," Solas called back to me.

"I told him to stay at home." I flushed. I turned to the creature and motioned for him to pick up his pace. "If you're coming, hurry up. I don't like standing around out here. It makes my skin crawl."

"So eager to be bitten again?" Solas asked and laughed. "Your landing will be worse on these rocks than at home on the grass."

I winced at the memory and held my ribs. I chanced a look around, and although I couldn't see the other Sluagh, they'd be wherever Solas was. I could feel them watching me from the shadows of the forest. Their eyes felt like prickly needles along my spine. The small one made his way to me and walked at my side in an awkward shuffle and drag. He walked on his two back legs and used the crook of his wings as his hands. He looked like a bat trying to walk instead of fly. It was both awkward to watch and terrifying to see.

Somehow, he looked scarier without the grace found in the sky.

"What's your name?" I asked, patting the top of his head. His head came up to my ribcage. "I can't just call you 'the smaller Sluagh'."

"Sluagh do not speak, Perdi," Solas called back and shook his head.

"How do they communicate if they can't speak?" I asked.

"They follow Solas and communicate in their own ways," Nix replied. "They aren't of Elphame, so the rest of us don't understand them."

"I shall call you...Milo." I finally said and smiled. "Yes, that's a good name."

"If he were a mortal dog, which he's not," Solas called out. "Again, he's not your pet."

"But he's still mine," I answered.

"Up until you lose your hand," Solas countered. "And so that you're aware, you can't regrow limbs if a Sluagh decides to bite them off. Their wounds can't be fixed by Elphame magick. Just look at your thigh. Don't say I didn't warn you."

I leaned in closer to Milo. His spicy scent filled my chest and calmed me in ways only monsters could. "You're mine."

He looked up, and for a moment, I swore he understood me. Or, he was hungry and was sizing me up for how much he could get down before they made him spit me out. I was willing to bet on the latter.

"If you're going to eat me, make it quick," I whispered to him. "But trust me when I tell you, hell spit me back out. No one likes the taste of Crow once they've had a bite. I'm too bitter to swallow."

Nix muttered from my shoulder that he wouldn't climb into Milo's mouth to rescue me, should I be eaten for my stupidity. I ignored his warnings, as I often did. We followed Solas and Zephyr through the wall, and I froze. I didn't like being there. I didn't like how it felt against my skin or soul and hated the smell even more. The heat pressed against me, and the sweat that had started before I had even stepped into the wall now trickled down my spine, leaving a cold trail on my skin. Milo chittered from behind me and nudged my back, forcing me forward with his head. I wanted to scold him. I didn't like to be rushed toward doom any quicker than the next sane person, but I swallowed my anger. Milo chittered again, and I stopped in my tracks.

Small rocks fell from above, and I told myself not to look to see what I could hear scratching at the stone wall. Whatever haunted the walls of Blood and Bones wasn't something I needed to view today. Milo looked up, his chittering finally stopping. I followed his stare and froze. Holding onto the walls were small and colorful winged creatures, some no bigger than a potato. For a moment, I thought they were Sluagh and relaxed. But once their wings shimmered, changing their colors, I knew they weren't. They reminded me of fairytale dragons told to children as bedtime stories. A bright orange one snapped his teeth in the air, and I flinched at the sound of whatever it had eaten. They may have been no bigger than two feet long, on the larger end, but I wasn't foolish enough to think that size mattered in any way, not in Elphame. Slowly, dozens of them began their climb down the wall, and a small scream escaped my lips.

"What the fuck are those?" I squeezed out. My words were barely audible.

"Dragons," Nix answered as if that would be enough. "Don't worry. They eat bugs and grubs and fruit. They're harmless and pretty friendly, if you give them a chance."

"Where the hell did they come from?" I asked. "I've never seen one before."

"They've always been in Elphame. Many creatures are coming out of hiding now that Solene is dead. She used to kill the smaller Fae for no other reason than being able to do it. Many of the smaller, defenseless Fae hid from her sight," Nix replied. "Now that Blood and Bones is a refuge, the dragons have returned."

"Because the place isn't scary enough?" I muttered.

"Most would say the Court of Shadows is worse," he said with a laugh. "And you don't have a problem strolling around in there."

"I don't stroll through the Court of Shadows. I run," I answered. "I'm not that stupid."

Nix cleared his throat. "This coming from the Crow with a pet Sluagh?"

"Point made," I replied.

Nix moved to my other shoulder and reached his hand to one of the dragons. Before I could pull back, the dragon scurried toward Nix's hand for attention. I waited for it to latch onto a few digits but heard a soft purr as Nix scratched the tiny beast's head.

"Not everything here is meant for war, Perdi," Nix said. "You see the worst in all creatures because it's all you've been shown since coming here. If you stop long enough, you'll find that most of us want to live in peace and are only forced to become monsters. Many of us haven't had the chance to live as we'd like." Nix patted the dragon and left them be. "If you're lucky enough to bond with a thunder of dragons, you'll have friends for life. They're more likely to be found in gardens, eating insects, rather than fighting for territory or titles. I'd give my arm to have a few of these guys protecting our gardens from pesky slugs or beetles. Plus, it would irritate Zephyr and Solas to see we had invited dragons to live in the backyard. Solas is already attacked daily by the pixie clan. Could you imagine dragons going after him every time he stepped into the backyard?"

"The stories we were told as children said dragons breathed fire," I replied. "I'm starting to wonder if our fables were based on the creatures of Elphame more than our imaginations."

"Oh yeah, these little guys can roast a marshmallow or two," Nix replied. "Or singe a few of Solas' hairs." Nix pointed at the wall. "When we first walked in, their colors were vibrant and rotating, in a warning to the others. Now, they're calm and no longer shifting. And all it took was a moment of kindness. Sometimes, that's all we ever need, a break from what Elphame throws our way. One act of kindness can mean the difference between life and death."

I laughed at the imagery of Solas putting out small fires in the backyard. The break we had taken, to look beyond first impressions, to see life over death, was enough to settle the urge to run. Blood and Bones wasn't my favorite place, but our shared moment was a good start at building new memories. In all his war talk and willingness to eat his way through a battlefield, Nix tried first for compassion and understanding. It was something I was trying to relearn since coming to Elphame—how to be more than the nightmare Elphame had forced me to become.

"Thank you, Nix, for always making sure I see things through the eyes of love rather than war."

"Elphame is scary enough. We shouldn't create fear where it not ought to be," he replied. "I'm getting myself a dragon. If you can have a Sluagh, I can have a dragon."

"It's only fair," I answered and laughed.

"You're not here alone, Perdi. We're all in this together," Nix replied. "It's not as scary when you remember that you're not alone."

I inched my way through the halls of Blood and Bones, with a small beast pushing me from behind, eventually guiding me into a large room where a massive stone table sat with chairs. I scanned the room for an alternate exit and found none. If all hell broke loose, there was only one way in or out. I didn't like those odds. I hated being in a room with one door. How Zephyr was so calm was beyond me. He either knew of a different way out of the room or knew he could kill them all and not need any other escape plan.

"They'll never be able to hold you," Nix whispered from my shoulder. "Don't worry. I've got your back. On my own, I can buy you enough time to get out of here."

I smiled. Nix was a good gnome to have on my side. I'd seen firsthand what gnomes could do to an army of warriors. Standing between a gnome and their family was suicide.

"Thanks, Nix."

About the Author

Lanne Garrett writes books. Considering where you're reading this, it makes perfect sense. She lives in Vancouver, here she spends her days getting lost in the beauty of reading and writing and can be found behind a mountain of books on any given Sunday.

Lanne loves to hear from readers. You can find her contact information, website details and author profile page at https://www.finch-books.com

FINCH
BOOKS

www.ingramcontent.com/pod-product-compliance
Lightning Source LLC
Chambersburg PA
CBHW020821260626
47169CB00003B/775

* 9 7 8 1 8 0 2 5 0 5 9 6 2 *